## Chemo

ALSO BY BISHOP & FULLER

Tapdancer (novel)
Blind Walls (novel)
Akedah: the Binding (novel)
Galahad's Fool (novel)
Realists (novel)
Tapdancer (novel)
Co-Creation: Fifty Years in the Making (memoir)
Seven Fabulist Comedies
Mythic Plays: from Inanna to Frankenstein
Rash Acts: 35 Snapshots for the Stage


Available at
www.DamnedFool.com

Conrad Bishop & Elizabeth Fuller

# Chemo
— a fantasy —

WordWorkers Press
Sebastopol, CA

Chemo

© 2024 Conrad Bishop & Elizabeth Fuller

All rights reserved.

This work is fully protected under the copyright laws of the United States of America and all other countries of the Copyright Union.

No part of this publication may be reproduced in any form without prior permission of the copyright owners.

For information:
Bishop & Fuller
indepeye@gmail.com

For purchase:
www.DamnedFool.com

ISBN 979-8-9856835-6-1

*Contents*

1 — The Warm-up Pitches — 1
2 — Which Is Judith? — 10
3 — Back in the Game — 21
4 — Moshe — 29
5 — Project Chemo — 38
6 — A Goddamned Moving Day — 43
7 — The Shrink — 51
8 — Puzzling — 57
9 — Caffeine — 64
10 — Lights! Camera! — 72
11 — Jared Aroused — 82
12 — Digression: Apologies — 90
13 — Death — 94
14 — A Dog's Breakfast — 102
15 — Appointment at Four — 110
16 — Getting in Gear — 117
17 — When People Disappear — 125
18 — Into Hiding — 134
19 — Stumbling toward the Light — 142
20 — Breath, Waves, Gulls, Finger — 149
21 — Pruneface Unmasked — 158
22 — Negotiations — 168
23 — Goodbyes — 174
24 — Flight — 183
25 — The Deeper Meaning — 192

—*To Our Friends*—

## —1—
## *The Warm-up Pitches*

I might be who I say I am. I might even be who I think I am. We of the 21st godforsaken century specialize in multiple realities. In the offices, the factories, the schools, gas stations, chicken farms, the floor of the Senate, it's all one big costume party. That was the view of my dog Turk, who kept his nose close to reality. He was a fat mangy mutt, the sole purebred of a nameless breed. He could sniff a dapper poodle's butt and detect the brutal truth. His moist reddish eyes saw the world for what it was.

As for me: if you'd seen me in my years as Victor Otis, you'd assume the obvious. Here's this stringy old fart sitting on a park bench in your dusty backwater town or your murderous metropolis, strumming his banjo badly. Long white hair, bushy eyebrows, a beard like weeds bristling up through gravel. He's wearing a limp-brimmed leather hat, and beside him a battered briefcase splotched with anti-war stickers. You might see him pushing his overloaded bike—crap strapped onto the seat, rear carrier, handlebars, with the dog straggling behind—down a random street to nowhere. Homeless old hippie, you'd say. And indeed those guys are scattered over the homeland like peanut shells in the monkey house, so that would be a logical supposition. But you'd be dead wrong.

Every little kid gets asked, "What do you want to be when you grow up?" and the kid thinks fireman or football star or terrorist. Later you get asked, "What do you do?" But once you retire from being an exploitable commodity, it becomes, "What do you do with your time?" meaning, "When will you have the good grace to die?"

Of course they never ask, "*Who* do you want to be?" I doubt I ever asked myself that, until those fleeting months when I became an ex-hippie without ever having been a hippie. I became Victor Otis for a year, but Victor was somebody else and Judith was five different souls and Moshe just grabbed a name from the toxic debris of Planet Earth and Josh was fifteen, meaning he didn't have a clue, and the whole human race was hurtling down the freeway to Hell. It was unusually complicated.

My saga began fifteen months ago when I was put out to pasture. Top officials at the Shop, however senile, could carry on forever, but for veteran grunts like myself the cut-off age was sixty-five. We were getting that old-folks smell: musty, acrid, and urinary. And so, with a little late-afternoon party of wine, cheap cheddar, balloons and zip-whistles, they retired me. I was toasted, presented a tin service medal and a gift certificate to Starbucks. We stood around drinking until all the wine—of a classic Nebraska vintage—was gone.

Jared Van Mullen, my one true friend at the Shop, was dubbed by the wags "Van Muffin," in reference to his quiet tentative voice, his soft dumpling face, and his ambivalent sexuality—a quirk allowed by the brass, who prized data they could blackmail you with. The only contrasting element in his creamy demeanor was his necktie. However bland his shirt and suit, his neckties spoke rage. Today's sported placid ducks with rabid sinewy grins.

Our nostalgic party conversation was constrained by the knowledge that each wine glass held a nano-bug chip to monitor staff chat, but Jared's tie clasp contained a jammer that overrode the bug with a country-western station. He tapped it, and whoever was monitoring our talk was drenched with poignant howls for faithless floozies.

"Well, Edward, congratulations," he said. (I was an Edward then—Eddie Funston at your service.) "I trust they've provided pension, etcetera, and assistance in relocating you, changing identity, safeguards, so on?" That's how he talked. I nodded. "I would only suggest that you be apprised of the number of agents, to my knowledge, who have had, sadly, very brief retirements."

"How so?"

"Fallen out windows. Mistaken their prescriptions. Stuck their fingers into sockets. Rashly hanged themselves. Remarkable carelessness." Jared was head of the Shop's so-called legal department, so he was hip to our ghastliest crimes, charged with making them legal.

"So you're saying...?"

"Only suggesting that the Shop has an ongoing concern about former agents speaking indiscreetly, in ways that the media might misconstrue?" He always de-balled an assertion with a question mark.

Jared was telling me that my identity might soon be changed to *Defunct*. With that, he flashed a sweet grin, tapped his tie clasp again, and burbled congratulations.

From this little chat it might be assumed that I worked in a covert agency, perhaps the CIA. Yes and no: I worked for ERP. For those who don't know—and if you knew you'd be dead—ERP is what the CIA is a front for. Don't ever tell that to the CIA: they think they're the ultimate hot tiger shit, but we did the heavy lifting. ERP, of course, is an acronym, but even veterans of ERP didn't know what it was an acronym for. We kidded around with it and we all had our favorite jokes, but normally we called it the Shop. In any case, we all took pride in being the best killers on the planet.

If I sound like a creep, well yes, I was a card-carrying creep for most of my adult life. I have processed eighty-seven individuals over the course of forty-one years. Those were the ones who were countable. Others weren't in a countable condition. I'm not proud of that but I don't feel any guilt. Some of those folks deserved to be defunct, others were happier that way considering the alternatives, and some just had the rotten luck to be named Mohammed.

Over the years I was part of covert operations in Iran, Afghanistan, Nicaragua, Niger, Canada, Israel, Omaha, a shopping center in West Des Moines, and two or three countries where the cover was so deep we didn't know where we were. There, we did stuff late at night in huge luxury hotels. Got stoned and walked down the hall and did it and went back and called Room Service.

Many things impelled the agents of ERP: patriotism, salary, team spirit, and perhaps a touch of gleeful savagery among some of the newer recruits who were galled at the decline of America to the status of cornered rat. We agents would have made superlative cleaning ladies, embodying a virulent urge toward good housekeeping, driving ourselves to expunge every mote of filth from the kitchen, to scrub the crud off the counters, to mop the feculent floor, to pick the scabs till Miss Liberty's complexion was baby soft in the crinkles between the scars. Most of the stuff I did was evil to the core, but if I hadn't done it somebody else would have. That's the lie we all live by, and it tends to be true.

I was the cold fish who liked wine and women, but hold the song. The career gave me equal measures of pride at a job well done, lots of great free meals, gourmet hookers on my expense account, and nightmares that might inspire blockbuster horror flicks. Like Jesus we took the sins of the world upon us, and unlike Him we were very well paid. We pulled stuff that every new President was too chickenshit to admit, though in the old days we were careful not to let the world know our vile deeds. Today, obviously, the strategy has changed. The sociopaths dangle their wigglies in your face: no shame. They leak to the press what they did and that tells the world what mean motherfuckers we are. In the long run, I guess, it saves wear and tear.

I do respect my former colleagues despite fantasies that they die with their mouths stuffed full with shit. I still dream in their language: lots of acronyms. Suffice it to say that I spent forty-one years in service to ERP, and yet for a golden time, a matter of months, I sat on a park bench in a cute little town, strummed my banjo and enjoyed all the hard-won, God-given human freedoms that I had worked so hard to subvert.

∽

With Jared's tip ruffling my sleep, my immediate concern was to save my ass. Fortunately, upon retirement, I kept the codes to the Shop databases and the codes for changing the codes (which I helped write), and the codes for foreign agencies that tapped into our unbreakable codes. I checked our files for towns with a nice climate and a reasonable diversity where I might fit without much notice. So I came up with Gravenstein, California: population seven thousand, an hour north from San Francisco, twenty minutes to the ocean, lots of lefties and old Deadheads and nouveau riche and placid rednecks who seemed to live and let live without a lot of fuss, except when somebody wanted to put in a Burger King, and then all hell broke loose. They had a good thing going with Gravenstein and wanted to keep it. And an added plus: lots of conspiracy theorists thereabouts, with their suspicions of chemtrails, fluoride, the Trilateral Commission, the Deep State, the Illuminati, and so on. No question: the best place for conspirators to hide was among conspiracy theorists.

A month into my jitters, I booked a black helicopter from Langley AFB to Fresno CA. Long hike for a chopper, but George owed me a favor. I'd had a fling with his wife, for which he was grateful as an excuse to file for divorce. From there I took a bus to Santa Rosa, hot-wired a pickup to Gravenstein, abandoned it and spent the day roaming. Pleasant vibe: tourists shambling from boutique to boutique, a first-rate ice cream parlor, coffee shops galore, a town square sprinkled with old guys on their morning outings, ladies with small dogs, a Mexican crew emptying trash bins, a beer-bellied fortyish jogger in a hoodie, and a couple of serene pot-heads. A sweet place to hide my depravity.

And I spotted Victor.

When I saw this individual—the original, unimproved Victor—I knew that's who I wanted to be. Gangly, not much of a butt, at least what you'd surmise under his raggedy harem pants. A bony Giacometti face with lively eyes. Short choppy beard. Over a couple of days, I saw his repertoire of costumes from second-hand pagan fests—long robes, homespun capes, glittery dragon shoulder pads—but always the hair in dreadlocks, turbaned in motley fabrics to match the fashion of his pudgy mutt with a braided rag collar and blue cummerbund, whom I first mistook for a pig.

"How's it going?" I said.

"With any luck it's gone." His voice was a swazzle rasp.

This was October. I calculated that I'd still have a month or so before the Shop felt it appropriate to spare me the pangs of old age, but I couldn't waste time. I exchanged my slate gray suit for casual tourist garb and scouted Victor a week. He'd be sitting on a bench in the plaza, twanging his banjo with lots of flair and no tune, or pushing his heavily-laden bike along the sidewalk or down 116

South, with his pork-sausage dog hobbling after. Tassels and a spray of dried blossoms on the handlebars, but otherwise the derelict's vehicle, unrideable but a home away from home. Except that he wasn't homeless. Fourth day there, I spoke with him again.

"So it looks like you're pretty well set for camping out?"

"No, I got a room up over the rock shop there."

"Isn't the rent pretty steep around here?"

"Well, I got my veteran's benefits, alimony from my second wife. And dividends from what started with one share of stock in Apple, going way back. I manage. What are you, FBI?"

He would have assumed that from my neat hair trim and the suit I'd worn the first day. I assured him I had been much worse but that I was now retired. And I pointed out that if I were FBI I wouldn't be dressed like FBI. He allowed that made sense. We talked sports for a while.

Here was a guy I could trust, but he had no reason to trust me. This guy was no nut case. He was just a survivor, open to all options. After a few days of chat, I sat beside him on his park bench and made my proposal. I don't recall what I said. Some conversations are no great lyrics, but you fall into a common tune. I followed the fibrillations of his eyebrows and wiggled my words in sidewise. His life passed before me on his face, the doubts, dilemmas, delights. Intriguing flick. A blue jay screeched. He glanced up. "Like who am I? Who are you? And whatta we mean by *who*?"

"You could look at it that way," I replied, "or like I'm just trying to find a way to cover my ass, whatever name you call it."

"I'd call it Life."

"You have a point."

I offered him a quarter million dollars, plus I'd ship him to Idaho. No big bucks in my own bank account, but I could access the security codes to a Saudi princeling whose wallet I'd lifted as he frisked with the forty-nine virgins I'd supplied him. His accountants would never catch the few hundred thousand I'd skim off as needed. My princeling wasn't great at keeping receipts.

Victor's aspirations were modest. If I'd offered him ten million, he'd have yelled, "Sic'im, Turk!" (Not that Turk would have sicced'im.) But I was lucky in hitting him right at this point in time. He felt Gravenstein was becoming too touristy—some asshole from San Diego had asked him to pose for a selfie—and the yappy-chihuahua factor was a bit stressful for Turk. The notion of starting over—a new soul born while the old was still strumming on Gravenstein Square—struck a harmonic convergence of gravitas and frivolity.

He said yes. A quarter million bucks, given that Idaho was now hip to good coffee, meant sixteen-ounce lattes every morning of his life and blended mochas on Sundays. He succumbed to benign caffeination.

"So, only question, Eddie, if I take this gig, who am I? Like, what's my name? Like, I don't see myself as an Edward. There's kind of a stature to Victor."

"Marcus Gunderson." It came to me like that. His eyes told me he liked it.

"Would I need to shave?"

"I think a Gunderson would shave."

"I guess you're right."

My Shop experience served me well in my transmutation into Victor. It was harder than I thought to learn to play banjo badly, but I persevered and wound up pretty bad. I let my beard grow, he chopped his whiskers back to a length I could match in the short span of time, and I found some on-line dreadlocks to extend my tresses till I could grow hair. At last my scalp flowered out like ragweed, and I acquired a floppy leather hat to wear in rotation with his turbans. I insisted on custody of Turk: Victor agreed reluctantly, and Turk got used to my smell.

It was more of a challenge with Rosella. I hadn't anticipated a girlfriend, but God moves in mysterious ways. She was a nice lady in her early fifties who spoke broken English, and my Shop Spanish was more suited to making deals with dictators' secret police than pillow talk with a roly-poly nympho—*nympho* meaning any chick who'd put up with me. It would have been simpler to bring her into the plot, but I couldn't risk simplicity. Fortunately her relationship with Victor was only once every couple of weeks and rarely the face-to-face kind of thing—more of a rooting around each other and grabbing whatever got found. Rosella had a sweet

Barbie-doll face, but the rest of her didn't follow suit: to put it bluntly, Rosella was fat. Still, after a time, I came to enjoy rambling around the acreage. And as with my many past relationships, our lack of communication proved to be an advantage.

For about a month I crashed on Victor's couch, practicing his voice and his ramrod slouch, making friends with Turk by dint of feeding him Gummy Bears, and peeking from the closet as my namesake went a couple of amorous rounds with Rosella, just to pick up his style. At last I risked the ultimate test. Fortunately Rosella liked the lights low, so we sat on the couch, one shaft of light, drank a couple of Coronas while she chattered away, something about her brothers and digestive disorders and the Holy Virgin, and then she squinted at me and whispered, "Quien eres?" That much I understood and I thought the jig was up, but I said, "Soy Victor." Whereupon she grabs me, drags me over to the daybed and we're off on the muskrat ramble. We did fine.

Afterwards, I lay there congratulating myself on my capacities of deception, when Rosella said, "Eres similar a mi otro Victor. Excepto el pene." I worked on this: similar to my other Victor? El pene? It took a moment till her fingers gave me a hint.

"Mi pene esta alegre," I said.

"Y yo." We generated sweat but no great poetry.

Victor watched from the closet and gave me notes afterward. He explained that she'd asked who I was because she had a couple of other boyfriends and couldn't always remember. To her it was a point of honor to know whom she was actually fucking. I could tell that he felt a mite chagrined in seeing her knowingly accept a substitute, but as long as she was happy, no big deal. He wasn't the jealous type, so it was one of those win-wins that top executives write best-sellers about.

At last, my namesake and I said farewell. The night before he left, I helped him trim his hair to businessman length and try on a navy blue slim-fit suit. He liked the suit: "Hey, I dig weird costumes." He was a new man, as was I.

"Hey, I never asked," I said, "what's my last name?"

"I forgot. Make one up. How about Otis? Johnny Otis, I knew him when he lived around here. R&B, rock'n'roll, cool dude."

"Otis does it. And where was I born?"

"Denver."

"Other stuff I should know?" I tied his conservative salmon necktie for him.

"Lessee, my kindergarten teacher was Miss Little. Sweet lady, I loved her. Kind of Rosella-shaped. Never thought of that." For a moment the Freudian implications gave him pause.

We stood face to face, two guys who'd become each other. I got the better of the deal, I felt, though I had a hunch that once he got to Idaho the suit and tie would hit the dumpster. We gave each other a silly good-luck salute.

Next morning, as the Former Victor—now Marcus—caught a bus to Pocatello, I walked out onto Main Street, Gravenstein, California, with my faithful canine companion. Of course I knew that allowing the newly-minted Marcus to stay alive was amateurish, that a real pro would have gentled him into the wetlands, but I was no longer the pro. Long ago I'd felt better suited to another line of work, if I'd known what it was and if it paid as well.

## —2—
## *Which Is Judith?*

Hard to answer. Imagine this wiry lass in her late thirties, early forties, blonde, slim, medium height, breasts and hips pretty much like any gal's breasts and hips, and yet I could sense sweet curvatures and succulent textures to die for. One moment, the last week I ever saw her, she was looking out to the sea with a naiad's eyes—the river sprite's first whiff of salt.

Her farm girl's face was simple, scrubbed, bleak, but always with a flickery waver of faces shimmering through. A photo could never catch it. The face of an Alice, astonished, plunging down the rabbit hole, but not an Alice out on a stroll with her English nanny: a hard-scrabble Alice, a working-class Alice, an Alice who knew the smell of asphalt and baby shit. I was in love with this woman instantly and always, unrequited though it ever was or ever shall be. I still am.

Chrissake, I still am.

∼

I was retired from all traces of Eddie Funston, or so I thought. I settled into what I felt would be placid retirement in my golden years. I only regretted my metamorphosis to Victor when I hadn't washed my beard for a couple of days and it started to itch. No reason that Victor couldn't shave, but if you're established as the village weirdo, you don't want to start raising eyebrows by abnormal normality.

Rosella was a nice distraction from the balmy weather. She seemed to run through boyfriends pretty fast, but she was always happy to fit me in. Various local characters acted as if I should know them, and I managed a convincing "Oh, hi!" as needed. And there was Turk. I could never rev up a great fondness for that scroungy digestive tract, but he grew on me. A brown and white mutt the shape of a boar, he spent most of his day lying flat on the sidewalk, rolling his watery eyes up at the human tide—one of the few creatures on Mother Earth who adhered to that core physicians' ethic, *First, do no harm*. When his ratty red bandanna got totally threadbare, I replaced it with a motley kerchief and a little string of collar bells that he was too butt-lazy to tinkle. A poor thing, the saying goes, but mine own.

Contentment at last, for about a month, and then the tedium of retirement slammed me. There was a sameness to my days, some itch that even Rosella couldn't scratch, no matter where her fingers probed. The old-time galley slaves had a tough life, but at least they must have felt some pride in the forward surge of the ship. Had I saved my ass only as a fertile field for mushrooms? My synapses demanded some function beyond feeding the sparrows or twanging the banjo or strolling the wetland paths at the edge of town. I was trapped in my own micro-Ponzi scheme: the more energy I invested in staying alive, the less the pay-off. Time was a grifter with a great gift of gab. What would I do with the rest of my piddly life?

∼

Second month into my sentence—twenty years to life—I was seized by a lust for revenge. Maybe I'd stared too long at Victor's briefcase stickers. I was stricken with deep loathing for my former fellow fiends, and I took a sally toward being a whistleblower. I knew what I risked from the evidence of colleagues who had succumbed to a similar urge. One was serving life in solitary, two had hanged themselves, three contracted a rare flesh-eating microbe. Still, sheer boredom impelled me toward going out in a great blaze of stink.

I tried to give my story to the *New York Times*. The criminal deeds of Uncle Sam would be worldwide headlines, rocking Planet Earth like one big jiggling buttock. They might drone-strike me, but I envisioned my puffy-white soul floating up, chuckling into the cumulonimbus. I scribbled a note, sent it off. No response. I phoned, got a kid named Jeremy. Every big outfit has a pimply kid named Jeremy to deal with the crackpots. Jeremy said he'd check and call back. No call-back, so I tried threats: Print this or die, asshole. I've got your address, your credit history, your ex-wife's bra size, and a file of your sixth grade book reports. In fact I didn't mean any harm, just trying to top the decibel level of the squawk that infests their heads.

It didn't work. Clearly those editors considered Covert Action and the Death of the Planet as just the last squeezings out of the toothpaste tube. I thought I might get a literary agent to storm the barricades. At the library I looked up a bunch of addresses and sent a swarm of emails. Besides my years at ERP, which of course no one had heard of, I outlined my interactions with the FBI, CIA, NSA, DHS, and the undercover wing of the National Endowment for the Arts. I argued there'd be a market for a bombshell book that'd spill the beans and all subsequent gastric results. I got some replies, but they wanted to know what "genre" I'd be writing. "Truth," I said. That emptied my in-box fast.

～

There followed, for me, a frantic upsurge of lechery, perhaps the denial of death that drives men in their late sixties, myself anyway, to cling by our nails to the crumbling cliff. Of course I was grateful for Rosella. Not a soulmate, just a sweet pneumatic stranger along on the same scenic tour. She liked to muss my hair down over my eyes and giggle. I liked it.

Still, coming into the bucolic California landscape, I felt a Napoleonic urge for universal conquest. I was in a Santa Rosa coffee shop, and a skinny college girl came up saying she was doing interviews for her class and could she talk to me? She had a peculiar ocular off-focus connoting a feline ardor, a promise of arousal. I said okay. She was supposed to be surveying "homeless," she said. I replied that since I had an apartment and a pension I wasn't really homeless, but I didn't mind lying if that would help. That threw her for a loop, and then I asked her, "Hon, why don't we go up to my room and you can make an old man very happy?"

At first I didn't think she heard me because she had her ear plugs in, listening to her iPod. "No, I gotta study for mid-terms," she responded at last, "plus, I think I'm gay."

"You realize as we speak," I asked her, "that we're facing the extinction of the human race?" I'd had some startling updates from Jared just the night before.

"Awesome," she said.

But a few days later, with the promise of designer drugs, I did get into the skinny college girl's pants. It was mildly enjoyable even though she was listening to her iPod and didn't pay much attention. In a way I felt like a louse, but I got the impression she was chalking it up to experience and would write a tell-it-all best-seller some day. She might have an interesting life if she ever decides to live it. Maybe after mid-terms.

When does human need expire? We start with the urge to find the nipple and creep methodically toward the rest of it. Why God or Darwin adopted this design puzzled me. Philosophers have noted the design flaw of putting the reproductive and excretory systems right next door, but it's not that the sex is too close to the ass, it's that it's too far away from the brain. For a start, the whole two-sex thing is kludgy. Why not just have the lady split down the middle, and the two of her go trotting off? Or simplify the algorithm: she lays an egg, the guy comes along and pisses on it, that's it. That's the relationship. You can glim a lot of my marital history from that.

The only reason I mention the college girl is to be honest that in some respects I'm just one notch above a goat-fucker. And to inject a bit of cheap eros to last through my spasms of yearning for Judith, Judith, Judith. There is a love story to be found here among the rubble, and some sex along the way, though I never get detailed about who puts what into where. If you need specifics, check your owner's manual.

One afternoon I was sitting at a coffee shop just south of Gravenstein—Hard Core Espresso, good coffee, cool name—contemplating my macchiato. Another girl about twenty came up to the table and handed me a leaflet about some political protest, squeaking truth to power. Pointing to my briefcase, she said, "I like your bumper stickers."

Tears clogged me up. She had freckles, kind of Irish maybe, and a tattoo peeking above her neckline. She was so sweet and stupid I might have tried the "You could make an old man very happy" routine, but instead I started to wheeze. I get asthma pretty bad whenever I start to think. "You okay?" she asked. I wanted to put my hand to her heart and speak whatever phonemes might bring two souls together and seed this derelict planet with nameless flowers. But I took a leaflet, waved her away, with fears that she'd crack her skull on the icebergs of life.

My costumes were having their effect. I felt a seepage. Edward Funston was ebbing. My Victor was elbowing out my Eddie.

~

About every other week I would catch Golden Gate Transit down to San Francisco, just to walk around and drink coffee and have my photo taken by Iowans from the upper deck of a tour bus. I took perverse pleasure in watching clerks or security guards deciding whether or not to kick me out: I looked like a bum but a highly decorative bum. Maybe they saw me as performance art. Maybe I was.

This time I was down to the city for the Symphony. I'd always been fascinated with the notion of some demented musical crank at a piano, dotting flyspecks on sheet after sheet of foolscap, and suddenly here were fifty musicians arrayed like Marines set to storm Hamburger Hill, and at the sweep of a baton they launched the barrage, sawing and twitting and blatting right up to the end of the flyspecks. They were scheduled for Mahler's Seventh and I couldn't miss that. What Mahler couldn't do with an orchestra couldn't be done by the Strategic Air Command. He raided the fridge, tossed it all in the pot, and served up an orgasmic pottage.

So that morning I got a lift from Rosella, who had a hot afternoon date with an ex-con who lived in the Tenderloin. Rosella had her obsessions and the talent to make them manifest.

"I him make go straight," Rosella said.

"No question he'll straighten, hon. Just watch out for bedbugs."

She didn't get the joke, but she could tell I was saying something cute enough to deserve a giggle, so she giggled. She let me off at Civic Center.

I had lots of time to kill, so I was walking down through the Mission in April's warm chill, enjoying the sidewalk trees and window vines that were getting a running start on summer. And this was strange. I'd come here five months ago, and all last week we'd had rain. We were into December, not April. It felt as if Time were shuffling events out of that neat single-file line that Miss Little had taught us to stand in. But Miss Little was Victor's kindergarten teacher, not mine. More seepage.

I had better things to think about. I found myself over on Folsom and 23rd shambling after this foxy wench, light jacket, tight skirt, walking fast as if late to work. I lagged five yards behind her, indulging my helpless fancy for staring at women's bottoms. No further intentions: I just liked the scenery. I couldn't get sidetracked from my hot date with Gustav Mahler.

My briefcase with the stickers held some bugging gizmos with which the Shop had gifted me upon my departure without their knowing it. Of course they had rigid procedures to prevent such shenanigans, but I had helped design both the procedures and the shenanigans. The neat thing about state-of-the-art surveillance technology was that it could catch not only what got said but even what got thought—at least at the point where thoughts induce contraction of musculature in lips, tongue, and larynx to form phonemes. Gurgle and we grab it.

Tapping this lady was a breeze. The technology had limitations: for a subject whose thoughts were dim or whose epiglottis was unresponsive. We might have to set the acuity so high it would pick up static from the lower digestive tract. But this gal actually mumbled to herself. That made it easy. The oddity was in deciphering all the minds inside her.

"I'm not late, Marge. Just shut up."

"Not much." The second voice—Marge?—was low and croaky.

"Just get off my back. Leave me alone."

"I might just do that."

Weird: was I picking up another passer-by? a radio station? this lady talking to herself? Well, people did talk to themselves. I talked to Turk, same thing, though he rarely talked back.

"Just let your freaky boyfriend take care of you till he's sick of you." The voice of a disapproving mom. "That guy's scary. You know it yourself. I don't have to tell you."

"Then stop telling me."

A young guy in a faded hoodie was passing. "Say something, babe?"

"Shut up!" the mom voice shouted.

"Dyke!" the guy muttered. Ah, the Voice of America.

"Stop doing that! I can't stand it!" the daughter voice hissed. She was talking to her own insides, which didn't sound like pleasant company.

"Sure, let the bastards walk right over you," said Marge, dragging claws down the inside of the face. "If you took care of yourself I wouldn't have to be on you like a big sister changing your diaper—"

"We're at Bryant," said the daughter. "You said you'd go when we crossed Bryant."

"You say he loves you. Love! You don't know how to love, you're incapable of love, you're so fake!" The voice had been subvocal, but the final "fake" came out loud and clear.

I didn't want to lose her. I rushed across as the light turned red, and a delivery truck honked a curse. She stopped a moment to scrape her shoe, and I halted, pretending to wait to cross 23rd. She looked as if some huge guy's fist was squeezing her jaw. Then the fist relented, and I saw her face for the first time: plain, unmemorable, stunning. Something about the eyes and the wry twist of the mouth—

She sobbed and kept walking. I followed, further back than before. Whatever she'd had to say to herself, she'd said it. Dead air now. In surveillance you get used to the fact that for long spans of time nothing happens. You're hearing your terrorist sit an hour on the toilet reading *The New Yorker*. Most of the Earth's chronicle is just traffic mumble. Those are the deadly boring epochs of history—the only times when it's halfway safe to be on the planet.

Then I was hearing someone else: the voice of a vampy slut played by a third-rate actress, a kind of sultry moo like a cow in heat. Later I found that she normally bobbed to the top of the babble only when in bed.

"Would you look at the cute ass on that Mexican dude? Stick out your boobies, girl!"

"My God, Drucie, it's ten o'clock in the morning."

"I could get us laid inside of five minutes." Drucie, it seemed, had a one-track mind.

Then a thin little girlie voice piped up. "Are we going to the zoo?"

"No, we're not going to the zoo. I'm going to work. Play with your dolls or something, Sweetie."

Ten a.m. What kind of work shift started at ten a.m.? Later I understood it was one of those part-time jobs where they call you in at any hour to slam you with a full day's work at a half day's pay.

A long gap. We crossed Folsom heading east. A kid passed with a boom box blaring out heavy metal mariachi. I hadn't seen a boom box for years, but some kids were precocious: they went senile long before their time. A bus belched, and the woman took a deep breath.

"Gonna be a long day."

And a mellow baritone voice: "You will survive it, sugar."

"Help me, Ray."

"As always, Judith. My goodness, we're actually on time. Aren't we special?"

Her name was Judith.

She turned into a doorway with a small brass plate on the brickwork announcing Blecher & Huddle Assoc. An Assoc could be any damned thing: investments, canned mackerel, waste disposal, a string of topless car washes, art thefts. It was a huge building, once a factory or warehouse—one of those lockups, likely, with two-story ceilings and a labyrinth of cubicles bathed by a sixty-cycle hum exuding a baleful calm of manicured morbidity. She checked at the reception desk, was told to report to Section G. "That's Accounts Receivable."

On my bugging device I could hear her subvocal impulse: "Oh shit!" But the mellow baritone overrode her with an audible "No problem-o!" Faintly she mumbled a mix of thank-you and fuck-you, and her male persona started whistling some idiot tune from *The Sound of Music*. She walked on, and I realized that I'd followed her into the Assoc and the receptionist was about to call Security. I waved vaguely, said something about mixing up the date of my appointment, and shambled my ass to the sidewalk.

For about ten minutes I stood outside Blecher & Huddle Assoc., groping for a clue. I realized that somehow I'd known her name was Judith before it was ever spoken. Extremely screwed-up individuals, such as she, have a special allure to other screwed-up dolts, such as me. She exuded a magnetic aura that transcended the stirrings of my genito-urinary system and drew me to her like a moth to flame—with nearly the same results, as things transpired. At the time I never sensed that Judith would become a major life issue and spur me to heroic deeds. As happened often during subsequent exploits, with the fate of Planet Earth in the balance, I just stood there.

～

Judith was a multiple. I had been eavesdropping on a conversation between Judith and Judith and Judith and Judith. The voices were all Judith, all Judith all the time. Most of her words were subvocal, but they came through loud and clear.

For a couple of years at the Shop, my work had involved experiments with DID, Dissociative Identity Disorder, which used to be called multiple personalities, which used to be called being nuts. The popular image was the woman with three names, but in fact there's a wide range. Sometimes there's total amnesia between the alter egos, but on occasion they know each other, have little meetings, divvy up the chores. There are claims that their blood pressures differ, their faces, even their contact lens prescriptions. In a sense they're like anyone else in this rat-race, where you'd better have multiple personalities just to survive. This minute you're dead honest, then you go with the flow; now you declare undying love, now you hedge your bets; now he's your blood brother, now you throw him under the bus. Take it another step, it's the guy who by day is the CEO, at suppertime the loving daddy, by night the serial rapist, but in all these roles he's perfectly functional. My mom always said look on the positive side: even the serial rapist is cordial two-thirds of the time.

Among shrinks, DID was the subject of fierce debate, maybe still is. Skeptics argued it was induced by suggestive therapy. To the believers, it was a survival response to trauma, possibly the sudden loss of a loved one or Daddy's penis somewhere in the tropics. But no question that, except for a few documented charlatans, the folks who had it believed it.

At the Shop, we ran experiments to produce the same results. It wasn't practical to rely solely on agents who had come by their schisms within the clutches of a loving family; we needed operatives who could split off parts of themselves guilt-free to do what had to be done. And in fact we made progress, even secured a couple of patents. Of course if you put new stuff out into the world, you expect glitches. One guy who left the Shop, a very hard-ass conservative, made a run for Congress and found out that his opponent, a far-left Democrat, was himself. The Democrat won.

After a while it got to me. I'd wake in the morning with a vague sugary salty taste in my mouth, so I asked for a transfer to the Tourist Bureau. Many field cases of DID had come from encounters with Tourists, so I felt my expertise would be well employed without my being directly culpable for felonies. My request was approved, I think because my supervisor Fred coveted my big oak desk.

~

I had most of the day to kill before being mauled by Mahler. Turk had been left back in Gravenstein with Roscoe, a little rat-faced alcoholic who had a room two doors down from mine. The beast seemed to like him: they both had a similar odor. Turk was picky: if I left him in the apartment alone, even with half a rack of pork ribs, I'd come home to find he'd shat in the bed—no mean feat for a fat dog with stubby legs. So I'd bring Roscoe a fifth of Scotch along with this red-eyed lard-assed mutt, and all parties were content. Somehow I had an urge to be loved, however inconvenient it might be, and I hoped that Turk would miss me, though I didn't place any bets. I thought to call Roscoe to see how the dog was faring but decided against it. It was past ten in the morning, so Roscoe would be halfway through the Scotch.

I had an inexplicable urge. I took the bus crosstown to SFMOMA, the museum for modern art and other assorted debris. In my student days, we were deeply into Postmodernism, which supposedly, instead of just being art, was defined as art-about-art, sort of like a cat chasing its tail and having the ill luck to catch it. (Maybe I should revisit the concept for a clue as to why it seemed to be springtime in December.) I went up to the fifth floor, recalling a certain room where all the paintings were black. All different blacks—smooth shiny blacks, fuzzy-wuzzy blacks, blacks with brushstrokes sideways or upside down, blacks in squiggles over blacks in squares—but you couldn't escape the fact that every christalmighty square inch was solid black.

I sat on the bench staring at one whose title was *Black 14*—staring, it seemed, for hours. A guard came over now and again to see if I was still breathing, but he didn't bother me: my standard eye-glaze looks scholarly, and I'd brushed the dog hair off my pants. I was picking up recurrences of a brain-pulse from a Christmas party at the Shop where Lennie passed out tabs he called Big Bang—LSD heavily laced with catnip. Through these hours of the afternoon, *Black 14* began to shimmer, then sizzle, then sprout into faces, phantasms, and forms of Judith, Judith, Judith as contained in File #A10-242 ensconced in the subterranean vaults of ERP. That's where I knew her from.

At moments in life you feel you have super powers. It might be as you pitch off the garage roof flapping your arms in flight—just before you wake in the E.R. It might be when you finally bed the hot babe, flaunting your potency though winding up likewise on the asphalt. Now I felt the resurgence of that superhero aura. I had preternatural hearing through ERP's electronic buggery, a steady source of cash, forty-one years of expertise as a licensed fiend, and Turk was my loyal sidekick. I felt that eerie knack for the chance encounter that launches every crusader—Superman, Lone Ranger, Bugs Bunny—into the orbit of incredulity. With any luck I'd be a summer blockbuster.

That evening was the overture to the rest of my days. The Mahler concert pummeled me, blendered me, jazzed me into sweet oblivion. Surviving it, I felt fully prepared for all fortuities.

## —3—
## *Back in the Game*

The Mahler Seventh must have spurred me to action. The composer's instincts were those of General Patton: sending wave upon wave of strings against the redoubts, sneaking the oboes around the flank, carpet-bombing with kettle drums. All the way back on the late bus to Gravenstein, I reverberated.

At home, I found Roscoe comatose on my sofa. After dragging the stewed rodent down the hall to his room and sweeping up Turk's revenge—two rolls of toilet paper chewed into microscopic profusion—I logged into the files of ERP. Not directly, since they would surely be monitoring the cyber-hijinks of ex-agents, but I could usually hack into the Russian, Chinese or Israeli hackers hacking in. The back door was left wide open to hackers of files, real-time video bugs, phone sex, or HBO.

Judith: I knew I'd seen her before, or at least her photo. I had an eidetic memory for women with a specific geometry of curvature, whether in the small of the back or the nose or anything remotely visible. I recalled her as being younger, but then, at one time, so were we all. She was unlike other DIDs I'd studied in my days at the Shop, though none of them were ever quite alike. Her alter egos popped like popcorn: no one could hold the floor for even a minute. She was a board meeting without a chairman.

I was no computer whiz, but with a quick hunt-and-peck there it was: Case #A10-242 in the Tourist files, Judith Mae Weller, under surveillance since the age of three. I could log into her blood type and medical records, her high school yearbook photo, earnings for the past five years and this month's charges on her Mastercard, every website she'd ever clicked, her dental records and her prescription for an IUD. Her parents separated when she was fourteen. She married in her late twenties, had a son whose father deserted when the kid was two, worked a dozen different jobs over the years, had gone through a couple of boyfriends but nothing serious until this past year.

Judith at the age of three. All she remembers is a bright light, big eyes, fingers into dark places, the straps, the screams, so deep into pain that she can't feel it any more but really scared because she doesn't know why that distant little girl is screaming.

Judith, age five. She seems normal except Sweetie wets the bed and Mommy gets mad. She likes kindergarten, but her teacher is concerned because when she draws people, they have no eyes. Her mom gives her a birthday party, but when the candles are lighted she shuts herself in the closet. Those are the golden years.

Judith, age thirteen. Drucie comes on strong, and Marge shows up after Drucie suggests some filthy icky thing. She has a dog named Ragsie. She lies on the living room floor drawing monsters with a green Crayola while Drucie's whispering how they put their fingers up in her and it felt so good but Marge says shut up and Sweetie cries faintly, but Sweetie is always doing that.

Judith at fifteen. Raymond appears. He helps her cross the street, get her homework done, and negotiate with all the boys who are swarming around the hive.

Not long after, another voice, not bothering to introduce itself. Male, female, no way to tell. A voice so deep inside that it doesn't have eyes. It drones, drones, drones, and Judith breaks free from Raymond and runs crazy into the street, but the motorcycle swerves.

And then she gets a little bit married, has a baby boy, and childbirth fends off that nameless dark drone for a while. And suddenly she's thirty-nine, mildly insane but functional, meaning that she's pretty much like the rest of us. And she meets this guy.

One might ask how I know all this. It's all in the files, of course. They're working hard, day in, day out, to get inside our souls, while we try to keep our souls so well hidden that we forget where we stashed them. In fact, the more crap they have on you, the safer you are—your existence justifies theirs—unless they target you as a terrorist for reading *Where the Wild Things Are*.

But what could this woman have done at the age of three to merit surveillance? Obvious: she encountered the Tourists.

The early logs were missing: we were great at collecting data but lousy at filing it. And nothing much in the last five years beyond noting her recent sessions with a shrink and a relationship with a man of Middle Eastern appearance, which had likely spurred the planting of an audio bug in her apartment and renewed monitoring of the GPS device implanted in her left rear molar. That was outside the norm except for heavy security risks. I did a bit of computer clackety-clack, logged into her audio channel, and suddenly I was listening real-time to Judith in her apartment at 18th and Guerrero. Wonder of wonders: she's talking about me.

"Weird. This scrawny old guy— No, well, so— For a start, so they call me in for three hours' work, throw a pile of stuff at me that two other temps screwed up, all of which had to do with billings for work that never got done. I mean you'd think if a company was doing gutters and drain spouts for the United States Army that they'd know, or someone would, if the job was ever done."

"Mmh," said a quiet male voice across a table, it seemed, given the eating and clinking sounds. "An old guy?"

"I'm getting there. So I get off early— Three hours sorting and filing these bogus invoices into the bogus-invoice file, after which I'm told to take the files I've carefully filed and shred them. Then I make a pot of coffee for the supervisor—my contribution, I guess, to the gross domestic product."

"Mom, you're talking like a dedicated anti-capitalist." A teenage kid, it sounded like. High-pitched flippant voice—it must be her son.

"Well, tell me where to sign up."

I cringed. If you were on their watch list, lame jokes like that could get you an all-expense trip to a black site in Uzbekistan. But then she got back to the scrawny old guy.

"So after work I stopped at a coffee shop."

And this would have been about one o'clock, although at that point I was still mired in the black artwork at SFMOMA, except that was before I recalled I'd seen her before, yet that was before I'd come back to the coffee shop, but still it might have been an entirely different day— I gave up on chronology. Time was jumping the tracks.

I'd been sitting by the window, stealing glances at Georgeann the barista. I didn't know her name, but I dubbed her Georgeann because I once knew a Georgeann who was configured for serious wet dreams though dumb as a bag of hammers. This Georgeann was a bit gawky but had a nice swayback. I liked girls with swaybacks, that gentle dip before the buttocks rise up to make a statement. I thought about making an effort in her direction, but it wouldn't have been practical, living sixty miles away. The difference between youth and maturity is whether you think before you open your mouth, and that stopped me from hitting on Georgeann. Not that I was ever an unbridled jerk with women: an unbridled jerk doesn't realize the foulness of his behavior, whereas I usually realized it but did it anyway. Though less often with the onset of age. Such is life: improvement despite your best efforts.

I saw Judith come in. I knew it was her. She looked preoccupied, depressed, asked the barista for green tea. And then this throaty voice—was the name Drucie?—came slithering out.

"Love your tattoo." The girl said thanks, and Drucie went on. "Love to see the rest of it." You could see Judith screaming inside her own head for Drucie to stop flirting.

"Huh?" said Georgeann.

Over my short dry cappuccino I took the plunge. "I know you," I said to Judith.

Georgeann caught this and called over, "Sir—" but left it at that. She turned away and no longer figured significantly in the history of America.

"Call me Victor," I said, "an old nut rumored to be harmless. But never believe bad news."

"Sorry?"

"Come here, honey," I beckoned to her. She looked at me as if she'd just noticed a talking fireplug. "Don't be fooled," I said, and then I hushed. That's a line that you can't help replying to.

"What?"

"Well, you've had checkered experiences with aircraft. You flew from Fresno to Portland once, for some reason that wasn't noted in your file. And back to Topeka for your grandma's funeral. But at age three you had a really strange trip. You got picked up and waltzed around and, after some scary moments, put down." She looked at me funny, as if all her alters were lining up to take a crack at me. "They've got your number, Judith."

That got a reaction. "How do you know my name?"

I figured I'd better freak her out a bit just to earn her respect. "You're known in various circles."

And then in her eyes I saw Marge say, "Never talk to strangers," and Sweetie squeak, "He's scary," and Drucie murmur, "Scary might be fun." Or something like that: I've always been able to tune into people's eyes, but never word-for-word.

After a moment Judith said politely, as if nothing had been said, "Lots of stickers on your briefcase."

"Those are for camouflage. *MAKE LOVE NOT WAR*. People see that, they're pretty sure I'm nuts."

"Well, nice talking to you, Victor. I have to go."

"Watch it. Every shrink in America works for the Feds."

She stared at me, past me, through me, then spoke up in the pinched piping of a five-year-old, "You're funny-looking," and she was out of there without even sipping her green tea.

Listening into her that night, I was confirmed in my judgment that I'd made an impression, dumb as it was. The *strange-trip* stuff had its effect. I'd rattled her, but to what purpose? It took no special skill to act like a raving maniac. It gave me a little twitch of potency and then I felt pathetic.

"Guys are getting weird," she said. "I mean they've always been weird, but now they're weirder. Present company excepted."

"Thank you," said the guy.

"Look who's talking, in terms of weird," said Josh.

"You shut up," said Judith with a giggle. The kid would be in his teens, but they sounded like they got along okay. "And then this old guy, he's talking like he's got secret files or something— I don't know, he said some things— How would he know?"

"He said what?"

"Things that— Like my grandmother in Kansas, when she died. How would he know my grandma was in Kansas."

"Well, Mom, you kinda look like you'd have a grandma in Kansas." Josh was an irrepressible smart-ass.

"And then Sweetie said to him out loud, she said, 'You're funny-looking.' He really was. Like an old bleached chicken."

There are times when eavesdropping brings its punishment. I couldn't dispute her powers of description. Yes, I had overplayed my hand. Terror is a great attention-getter, but it has a history of unintended consequences.

"What happened then?"

"He sorta grinned and I left."

There were some kitchen clinks and then Judith asked her boyfriend, if that's who he was, what he thought. He said he thought they should finish eating dinner, and the teenage son agreed, and the guy asked, "All in favor?" And then in four entirely different voices—how the hell did she do that?—the creatures of Judith said "Aye!"

～

It was five months after my change of identity. The days would start out fine. Snap the leash on Turk, take the beast for a dump, then walk down to the square for coffee at Friendly Joe's, with outdoor tables where I could sit and look picturesque. I might go to the library to check the news on the computers, leaving the mutt squatting outside, then back to my room for lunch. Evenings, I could either watch TV or get blind drunk or both. But the span of each afternoon was a trek across Death Valley. I'd met the challenge of covering my tracks, but now I was trapped in the deathly wasteland of geezerhood in America. Your hair whitens and your face blends into the wall. Your beard bristles out and you're mistaken for a hairbrush. You walk down the street without a walker and some fortyish salesman with a belly chirps, "You're looking pretty feisty today, old sport!"

My golden years held many options. I could have robbed gas stations or put on puppet shows. I could have collected crippled children or rid my neighborhood of geraniums. I might have applied to one of those outfits that send out private killers to do deeds that would make regular soldiers vomit, but I'd have to give up my morning coffee at Friendly Joe's. I was like an old retired fool playing golf, only I was twanging my banjo. Turk was bored with my telling him how bored I was.

Definitely I could have spent time, perhaps with the counsel of some defrocked priest, discovering what stray crumbs of goodness lurked in my pigeon-pecked heart. Somewhere I possessed a moral center, I felt, but it was a moving target. I wasn't a multiple personality in the classic sense, but when I looked in the mirror I never met the same dude twice.

And I couldn't get this woman out of my head. In my past, relationships had never been highly successful ventures, and I had mixed feelings about getting interested, invested, involved with another being of my species. Rosella and I had a healthy bond: we were fun and entertainment, nothing more. Heaven preserve me from anything more intense than that. I had no hope of libidinous intersection with Judith, but there's nothing more boring than an orgy if you're just standing by the potluck table and nobody's even brought deviled eggs. Tuning into stray channels wasn't enough. For some reason this lady was a person of interest to the Federal ionosphere. There was panic in high places, and I wanted a juicy piece of it.

Maybe I was drawn to her weirdness? Or I missed the double shot of adrenaline that woke me up daily for forty-one years. Yes: I was addicted to that rush. I missed the action. I had seen that in guys who'd been posted to Afghanistan. When I was there, it was a piece of cake: I was ensconced in the Embassy with my stash of 18-year Glenlivet, premium cocaine, and a squad of federally-funded hookers. I could tell myself, hey, this is what we're fighting for: make the world safe for dopers and lechers. On the other hand, my friend Bradley was out in the field trying to avoid getting his balls blown off. He was a basket case—a basket full of slithering twitchy things. When we rotated back to DC, he acquired the hobby of dashing out in front of buses. He needed the rush. Poor Bradley.

And years before, I'd known an ex-Navy pilot with a great knack for dropping bombs on bad guys. A shining career lay ahead till he started thinking, concluding that his smart bombs didn't have that high an IQ, seemed to be wiping out souls not unlike his mom and little sister in Connecticut. He finished his tour, left his career, turned vehemently anti-war. When the next war broke out and we were blasting the living shit out of the evil hordes who perversely wanted to live where we bombed, he found himself watching the news in a state of twenty-four/seven rage. How could we believe our own lies? How could we kill, kill, kill? And then, one drunken night as we swayed on our bar stools like reeds in the wind, he said this: "Eddie, I just understood. Why I'm so fuckin' mad at this whole fuckin' war? Cause I wanna be there. I wanna be in the action. I wanna be droppin' those bombs."

Same with me. No more opportunities to mow down Russian mobsters, poison diplomats, chase zombies in stretch limousines, but I needed to feel the jazz. That's what drove me. Plus maybe revenge on the vile Moloch I'd served for forty-one years: to bellyflop into the pond and make a tidal splatter, to bring the temple crashing down. I wanted to throw a big party and invite all my friends and pull out a water pistol and everyone laughs at my joke until I start blasting and they see the blood. That was how I felt. Nothing personal.

And from that point on, this old bleached chicken was back in the game.

## 4
### *Moshe*

Next night in my Gravenstein digs, Turk lay on his back in the middle of my throw rug, stubby legs in the air, stoned on a hash brownie. I'd warned him that chocolate was bad for dogs, but he considered himself more walrus than dog and seemed to thrive on anything short of rat poison.

I meditated on my Judith options. Best choice was just to forget the whole deal. If I wanted a buzz, I could play video games. But the super-hero—with the powers of money, digital doodads, multiple identities and a funny costume—needed to take advantage. Like the playground bully: there's a magnetic attraction between the bully's fist and the wimpy kid's nose that weds the two. Whoever's got the magic twanger needs to twang it.

"Whatta you think, boy? I get involved, I'll be spending more time in San Francisco and you'll have to stay with Roscoe. Is that okay?"

Turk was a cur of few words. He made a noncommittal tail-waggle and broke wind. How many had he eaten?

"He treat you okay? He give you vodka or Scotch? Just one shot, I hope?"

Turk was in no condition to talk business, nor was I. Emotional involvement, especially female-centered, was the last thing I wanted to want. The best prophylactic was to stay far back. I could molder in my little room, tune into myriad feeds of hot action on the mattress, ride the high-test teeter-totter of uppers and downers, and live out my scrawny days in a feckless haze. Or I could…

~

I logged into an Oakland hacker hacking a kid in Newark hacking the Russians hacking ERP, which was bugging Judith. I picked up a throaty wheeze reminiscent of *musique concrete—*

earth movers growling and huffing as Congo refugees whimpered in their shadows, dissolving into New Age harmonics and the moans of withering cows. Then a sharp click: contact.

It was the guy—Judith's guy—on the phone. I recognized his hesitant soft baritone, crisp diction with a kind of Balkan/Brooklyn accent. I heard wind, a siren, a barking dog—he must be outdoors, which meant there was a second tap on his smartphone.

"Benny, hello. This is a minority report. I acknowledge and honor our mission. Yet I feel compelled to speak my heart." He spoke in the ponderous lingo you'd read in a comic book. Then some chicken croaks in the rhythm of a reply: an electronic rustle, tinkle and bleep that might be code for, "Go ahead" or might be a wayward garbage truck. I'd heard this before at the Shop. Our linguists made a stab at it, but how do you crack a language that sounds like the alligator munching Tinkerbell? We never got it precisely, and we certainly missed the punch lines.

Again, Moshe in pumped-up English: "Thank you. I ask that we reconsider Project Chemo."

Which was bizarre. A few years before my departure from the Shop, there had been an internal squabble. An intelligence analyst, Agent Skipper Kalich, assigned to perfunctory monitoring of the Tourists, came up with an intercept that suggested that these creatures had some scheme going dubbed Project Chemo, along the line of our dormant Greensleeves technology. Given the classic American paranoia that our chickens might come home to roost, his concern might have gained traction, but at that time our attention was fixed on a South American country that flirted alarmingly with democracy. And so Agent Kalich's notion became a standing joke at the Shop. Every serious boner we made was dubbed a Kalich/Cowlick—we loved that cutting-edge sophomore humor. And yet now I was hearing this foreign-sounding boyfriend speak of Project Chemo. Referring to what? Dope smuggling? A cancer cure? Bug spray?

A few inexplicable bleeps, and finally Judith's guy spoke. "English, Benny, please." Another spate of tinkles suggesting rebuttal, and at last a sharp nasal twang.

"Okay, okay, Benny here. Shoot!"

"Thank you."

"No problem. Is what they say? *No problem* or *No problem-o*?"

"Your choice."

This so-called Benny's accent was as elusive as his friend's. They were clearly not native English speakers: that crinkle stuff seemed to be communication, unless they were opening packages in heavy plastic wrap. Speaking English, Benny tried to pull off folksiness with forty-year-old slang, like some billionaire Congressman telling you he feels your pain or an opera diva blaring a Beatles tune. Yet here was an alien creature named not Mahfouz or Zifzox but a simple Benny. He sounded sincere and totally out to lunch.

"Names are big drag." Click, beep. "So I call you Mo-shay?"

"Indeed. M-o-s-h-e."

"Whack me not of alphabets, buddy."

So Judith's guy's name was Moshe, though he seemed less certain of it himself.

"That be your message? Whole hog?" asked Benny.

"Given that we have made tragic mistakes. That we have observed through our eyes and in our patterns, not in theirs. That we have drawn conclusions on scant evidence. That we have options other than—"

"Water off a duck."

"That is no response, Benny."

"Stars in your eyes. Doggie in the window. Singing in the rain." Was Benny a leftover from the Fifties?

"Be serious!" Which spurred another round of vehement squiggles and quacks and quarks. Strange that through the odd crinkles of their quarrel, I could sense a closeness between them—two brothers, perhaps, or two kittens tossing the rubber mouse. Religious fanatics? A murderous free-love sect? Turncoat entomologists? I was clueless.

The guy's reference to Project Chemo was surely raising a firestorm in our DC enclave, and it kept itching at me. Certainly, with our Greensleeves technology, we could wipe out any species with the push of a button. We might have adapted it to roaches and rats if they'd impeded our petroleum industry, but we'd never found a safe way to spot-target it on human demographics. Agent

Kalich had stood firmly by his warning of an indefinable threat, but we were convinced that he'd filched the idea from *Amazing Stories*. Whatever shit loomed in actuality, some sci-fi potboiler had done it first.

There was the grate from a sliding door—now I realized the guy was on an apartment balcony—and the next voice was Judith. "Moshe?" She said it with such tender love that I would have wept if my tears weren't freeze-dried long ago. There was a radio playing some golden oldie.

"Yes?"

"Coming to dinner?"

"One moment."

"It's on the table."

I found that very moving. The simple act of providing: whatever the world-historical event, somebody had to make dinner. Somebody had to wash towels, feed the cat, put out a new roll of toilet paper if your culture granted you the blessings of toilet paper. Superstars inhabited a different world. They never clipped their toenails, never stuck a finger of hemorrhoid cream up their asses, never woke at three a.m. to go piss and then try to get back to sleep. They lived magical lives. The rest of us…

These little cramps of sudden emotion, like alley cats slipping in the back door—these were new. They were utterly out of character to the Edward Funston I'd always known and loathed. On the balcony, silence, and I missed a snuffle that might have been a kiss because at that point Turk gave a twitch and began a slow trot, though he was on his back trotting in air. Unlike Eddie Funston, I was sprouting an affection for that pathetic beast.

I heard her shut the door, and the guy Moshe spoke a few intelligible words before he went in to dinner. A cluck, a wheeze and yaw of asthmatic whales, and then he repeated his words. And this really got me, maybe because I remember this girl I was with when I was young, can't remember her name, but after we did the deed she said, "Okay, now that's done, now I can get on with things." That wouldn't win first prize for romantic, but it seemed very sweet to me. She meant—at least I thought she meant—that she'd been thinking about me and now she didn't have to do that any more. That was it, I got it in one, she was satisfied. And that's what came to mind when Moshe said to his iPhone, blurting it to the Universe, "I confess that I love her."

A bunch of anxious crinkles and beeps: he must have hit a nerve. Funny that the obvious thing didn't occur to me, but I was off on a tack imagining him telling his Orthodox Jewish parents, who spoke in crinkles and beeps, that he was dating a *shiksa*. Strange how my brain took wrong turns even when no sex was involved. I'd had one of those hash brownies too, and though I wasn't on my back with my trotters in the air, I was hardly at the top of my intellectual form.

I switched off my hacked connection. Moshe sounded as if he were in some therapy circle where they massaged each other while spilling their guts. I'd always had a low tolerance for guys waxing poetically depressed, but I thought, well, maybe he's an unpublished science fiction writer. Then I thought, shit, he must be a *published* science fiction writer. The name Moshe sounded Jewish, but his surname—sounded like *Prokzabonajozik*—was more like running a Slovak through the blender. Even having spent forty-one years fighting multicultural terrorists, or being one myself, I couldn't pronounce it.

And then I realized, *Oh, I get it. He's a Tourist.*

It was so obvious. The first thing I had to accept was that he was an alien, but not an alien disguised as a human being, not a squid in a rubber mask. He must be shaped the way he was shaped: perfectly human. Well, it's obvious, it struck me: if God made humans, then why wouldn't He want to plant more than a single bunch on a cranky little planet that'd already been hit by an asteroid? Why wouldn't He set up experiments all over the Universe and see which ones didn't turn sour? Why shouldn't He follow the tactics of derivatives traders and bet against Himself? But then I remembered that I didn't believe in God.

∽

Next week I was in San Francisco, leaving Turk back in wine country with Roscoe. I intended to lurk at the coffee shop in hopes of an encounter. I could have readily hacked into Judith's location via her dental GPS, but it felt as if my involvement, starting by pure chance, needed to proceed … aleatorially? I was the frayed middle-aged lady on a bar stool hoping that Fate would seduce me into one night's entanglement.

No luck at the coffee shop, and the barista was a skinny guy with a puny roadkill chin beard: no Georgeann. Just sitting around with a cappuccino wasn't the way Eddie Funston would have done it. My leather hat harbored a passive soul that was worming into my brain.

On the bus home from the Bay, I found myself looking at passengers a different way. I had always felt there was some minimal eligibility for folks deserving to live, a grade-point cut-off to qualify as human and a ninety-four percent failure rate where you got pity or genocide, depending on whichever was convenient at the time. But if you started to look with newfound eyes, you might see that poor shambling stiff the way his mother saw him.

You noticed the ears. Rush hour, wall to wall in the aisle, you never could look at his face but you looked him in the ear: the complexity of the curlicues, like the labyrinths of labial folds. You feel a great rush of faith, hope, charity: if I saw this guy face to face I could kill him without a second thought because of his billion crimes, but I couldn't kill the miracle that's evolved this single flap of ear. Jesus must have caught the bus a number of times.

Same way that I'd started to look at Turk, that fireplug wad of meat that chugged along behind me in total faith—a beast that was once a pup that chomped onto a nipple and now eats, shits, mates if he has the chance, aspires, cries, dies. All these creatures born from one teeming womb, spawning its babies broadcast: feet trotting midair as the breath went in one end and out the other. These clusters of humans: each one a tryout, a sketch, a tangle of contradictions yearning to be loved. I looked at this sea of ears and noses and eyes with the wonder of a child. Not in character for me.

Moshe: I heard him tell Judith a story. After emigrating from Syria—he had this back-story down perfect—he'd met an elderly Rumanian Jew whose father was killed by the Nazis. The Yids had been rousted out, paraded down to the square. Just a formality, said a pleasant SS fiend. So they're walking there and his mother says not to worry, it's just a formality and, "Honey don't fret about death, it just hurts for a second, it's just a forgetting, like you forgot to feed the cat. Just a formality." *Formality! Formality!* The kid made a little song.

The machine guns rattled, the bodies fell on top of him, and under the bodies this little squirt survives. The gunners finished the work of another day, went back to their barracks, wrote letters home with lots of I-love-you's. The kid crawled out from under the bodies, whose faces look as puzzled as adults always do, ran back home, back between carts gathering up the dead. His mom's at home. She's escaped somehow. She stands at the mirror bleeding from the scalp. She takes little steps back and forth, and the boy sees his mother dancing to her reflection. Bleeding and dancing.

That was during the war that won a bunch of Oscars.

But according to Moshe, the old guy who'd been that kid—now in his seventies, eighties, a life of seeing atrocity—this old guy could say, "I don't hate anyone. What would I gain from hate?" The old guy told the story as if he'd found a gold piece in his pocket change, a glee at being alive to tell it. The old guy's name was Moshe and maybe that's why Moshe called himself that. With all that followed, I admired him and I hated him. That name carried the gift and the curse of loving the human race, though he was outside looking in.

"I confess that I love her," he'd blurted, followed by pops and yodels. "I applaud our intentions, our desire to heal wounds—"

"Whole ballgame, buddy."

"But I face questions that— And this woman sees me as a life-mate— Which cannot be, and yet—" When I heard that I wanted to kick his ass.

I wanted to kick his ass. He's not even human and yet he's getting his rocks off with this lady whose outlines obsess me, and not a sign that it makes him the least bit happy. He's schtupping her and I'm not and probably never will, and he acts like he's playing Hamlet. *I face questions.* Crawl back into your comic book, dude.

He finished the call to his muddle-headed buddy and went in to dinner. Turk seemed to have come down from his trip and was snoring softly. I followed his advice and ate another brownie, lay on my back in the bed to analyze the data. It occurred to me that

I should ask Miss Little. She had the kindest voice. She hugged you if you scraped your knee, and even when Jamie peed his pants and we all laughed, she made him feel okay. I remembered things I'd forgotten that she taught us in kindergarten. Then, after what seemed like hours, a little birdie chirped, "But she wasn't your kindergarten teacher, Ed. That was the former Victor." I'd shipped that old coot to Pocatello, but it wasn't far enough.

Still, Miss Little spoke to me. She was so sweetly round.

∽

At this point I sensed danger. Something was sending up shoots through cracks in my asphalt soul. It wasn't only the spurtle of geriatric lust aroused by this freaky lady. It seemed that Victor's soul—my original role model Victor—was seeping down from the droopy leather hat and oozing into my eyeballs. The former Victor was invading the former Eddie. Horror of horrors: I might wind up doing my first good deed since Boy Scouts when I threw an old lady into the street. Just joking with that one.

But I was feeling things—emotions, empathies, palpitations—and feelings were perilous. In cowboy movies of my boyhood, the bad guys were sent off to jail to get a Ph.D. in badness, but once in a while a bad guy got a twinge of conscience and did a good deed. Inevitably, he got shot: he couldn't be forgiven his sins, but he deserved a tearful death scene. I wasn't hot for a death scene.

And these feelings were a jumble. Moshe pissed me off, but when I heard him talking to Judith, he said stuff that opened her up, made her happy at least for five minutes at a time. That's what I always wanted to do when making love to women, to make them feel that it was something brand new, a whole new color in the box of crayons that nobody'd ever seen. That's what I wanted to do with Judith, but Moshe did it first. He was me even though I wished I'd been me before he was. At least somebody was.

One thing I knew from the outset: Judith never questioned who Moshe was. She just loved him and was grateful to him for loving her. He was the only guy who'd ever professed love that she hadn't felt that his saying it was a sign he was either stupid or unspeakably perverted. She felt his warmth. At least that was my sense from the way she said little things like, "Pass the salt, hon."

Once I got a clear fix on Moshe, I came to several conclusions about the Tourists. First, their technology was advanced beyond anything heretofore known in the Universe. Second, despite their dubious intentions in regard to humankind, they were basically good at heart. Third, they didn't know shit about covert operations.

## —5—
## *Project Chemo*

As I said, Project Chemo was a standing joke around the Shop. It was variously thought to be a disinformation plot by DHS against the CIA, or the FBI setting up a sting on folksingers, or maybe the sci-fi nuts at Defense Intelligence preparing the Broadway premiere of Armageddon after an out-of-town tryout. At that point it didn't involve the Tourists. More about the Tourists anon.

A few months before my retirement, my friend Jared invited me to lunch at a Korean place in Fairfax. Every restaurant in a fifty-mile radius of ERP Central was bugged, of course, but Jared signaled me with a Morse code eyeblink that we shouldn't be concerned. To maintain credibility, agents found it advisable to indulge periodically in bugged conversations that verged on treason without actually crossing the line. Otherwise you were automatically suspected of worse.

I liked Jared. In practice, he was as evil as the rest of us, but he had the grace to feel guilty about it. He was the one colleague I could trust, being eternally grateful to me for saving his life. In Serbia we were blind drunk in a bar, and for no particular reason I hauled off and smashed his nose—just five seconds before a bomb ripped seventeen guys to shreds. How I survived the blast I have no idea; possibly I've been dead ever since. But Jared was flat on his face when the bomb went off and emerged with only a bit of shrapnel in his buttock. When he recovered consciousness, he embraced me. "You saved me, my friend, and I won't forget." At the time I suspected irony, but he was true to his word.

Jared headed the legal department of the Shop, so he usually knew what was happening before it happened. Passionately devoted with covering their own upholstered asses, the big boys always requested counsel on the finer legal points of genocide, so Jared was privy to the deepest deliberations. And he was uncannily adept at separating fact from disinformation: it was standard practice at the Shop to keep everyone, even those at the top, totally in the dark regarding Reality.

"Well, Edward, I should inform you of a Presidential Directive, the implications of which are unclear, but it might be of some concern." He let it hang there. His necktie glared at me: one fiery duck's eye. His voice took on this very soft can-you-believe-it smirk. "Have you ever heard of Greensleeves?"

"The song?" Of course Greensleeves was old Shop news, but I knew Jared liked to hear himself talk.

"No, no. An experimental bioagent. You know our man in Brazil, our contact with the general who likes little girls? Can't recall his name. This was some time ago—

"Four, five years."

"In any case, Brazil approved testing within its sovereign territory. We needed a target, of course."

At that point the waiter came and I ordered *bibimap*, a blob of rice with an egg on it, veggies and little plops of anonymous protoplasm. Not bad. Jared ordered a Cobb salad.

"You were saying?"

"Yes. A target population was required, and this tiny tribe of jungle aborigines, the Amritkas, Salazar Province, they fit the profile perfectly: highly isolated, distinctive DNA markers. Forty adults total, give or take, and they were already dying out, so it was no ethical problem to expedite the process. Two British anthropologists were there on location, so they would serve as a control group."

"This was germs?" I asked, as if I didn't know. Jared knew zilch about technology, so he loved to talk about it.

"Not germs or chemicals," Jared continued, "but microwaves that affect only cellular structures with the appropriate DNA."

No surprise: we were always on the lookout for deadly new ways of spreading our democratic values. I recalled that the Shop referred to the technology as smart tweets.

"Jared, okay, but out of curiosity, how did this get past General Counsel?" (Meaning Jared.) "Aren't race-specific bioweapons pretty low on the political-correctness scale?"

"A contentious issue," Jared said, "but it was concluded that the President had the prerogative to destroy a race of people so long as the primary intent was to secure our national interests, not simply to indulge in racism. So it was green light go."

In fact, as I knew, it went very well. We boinked the button, inducing two transmissions: the first to target carriers of the gene, the second to stop their hearts. Within ten minutes all members of that tribe fell flat on their faces, dead. "Like a music-hall skit," one anthropologist reported. More important, only a handful of similar deaths due to random mutations were reported worldwide: a farm family in Vermont, a Siberian shaman, and a Chinese family vacationing in Puerto Vallarta.

But after the first wahoo, Greensleeves hit a brick wall. It worked fine for forty purebred Indians, but it was harder—given migrations, rapes, diasporas and trade routes over the millennia—to locate any significant bunch of purebreds worthy of slaughter. At some point everyone's great-great-grandpa had crossed the seas or mountains to snag a little nookie. The few appropriate targets they found were not sitting on oil reserves, so there was scant reason to zap them. We had this stunning piece of weaponry sitting alone on prom night, all dressed up with nobody to kill.

What concerned Jared was evidence of recently renewed interest in the technology. What were these memoranda crawling up the legs of his desk and across his mousepad and into his field of vision referring to Operation Chemo? More to the point, he was concerned that, since ERP had precise DNA samples of its agents, any of us who roused discomfort in higher circles might be offered instant early retirement. I was ahead of him on this. Modifying my own genomic profile to that of our esteemed agency director was a matter of simple arithmetic, but I thanked Jared for the warning.

We drank quite a bit of a strong rice wine that even the Korean waiter couldn't pronounce, and by the end of lunch we were pretty slobbery. It was then that Jared mentioned a marginal note in a recent memo referring to that old bugbear, Roswell Area 51. Were we about to go out on one more snipe hunt for the Tourists?

The Tourists. The Tourists had been a dead issue with the Shop since 1989, when it became clear they weren't allied with the Commies, there no longer being any functional Commies. Of course they didn't call themselves the Tourists—that was the smirky little term we used at the Shop. In fact they were pretty nice people as space invaders go, but being an astonishingly advanced civilization didn't guarantee that you wouldn't fuck up a lot. In fact it guaranteed that you would.

I'll quote the way I explained it to Turk. I often spoke with Turk to come up with my own answers to conundrums. I never expected specific suggestions, but Holmes often bounced ideas off Watson before arriving at his magic "Aha!" Turk was my Dr. Watson. He was worrying his squeaky toy, a rubber rat in its dolphin phase, Turk having chewed off its legs. He kept trying to gnaw out the squeaker, and I foresaw the day when I'd be hearing a windy concerto-for-dog-butt. He glared up at me, projecting thoughts of pork roast, then returned to his task.

"Here's the deal, fatso," I began. Again, he raised his pig-snout to me, like my ancient Civics teacher in high school, asleep behind open eyes. I commenced my spiel. "Okay, way back in 1947, I was just a kid, but the flying-saucer reports, the Roswell crash, that stuff, got the Feds' attention. Officially it was all bogus, but every half-assed debunking gave it more credibility."

*Sskrrrrk!* Turk continued his chaw. He had his own views on the matter.

"So the rumor, amid a dozen versions, was that they'd recovered some alien bodies from the wreckage. The Army said it was just a weather balloon. Which produced a bunch of exposés, which made a buncha bucks. What do you think, my fat furry friend?"

*Sskrrrrk!* "So fast forward to the 90's, and my buddy Jared clues me in: the bodies were in fact real, but shriveled from the heat of the crash. Space monsters, right? Wrong. With the advent of DNA analysis, the mystery was solved: the corpses were human. Some Air Force test that went bonkers or a plot by the Russians, we assumed."

*Squaawroughhh...* Turk had managed to gnaw off the head. He went on gumming the rubber. The beast had lost his front incisors when hit by an electric wheelchair running a stoplight. His former master had tried, to no avail, to fit him with dentures.

"Which proved nothing— Listen to me! I'll get you another one! Chew your bone! —Which proved nothing about the existence of aliens. We already knew they were real. At the Shop we'd set up the Tourist Bureau and collected data like kids collecting baseball cards, if they still do. But by then it was a joke. They'd find some guy naked in the desert who said he'd been buggered by extraterrestrials, and we'd all have a laugh. I wound up with a finger of the Roswell cadaver, still carry it in my briefcase." Turk whined softly. "I know, you can sniff it there. But absolutely no snacks."

I got off track. The question was why the Shop would have this renewed interest in the Tourists. Granted, paranoia kept the Shop in business, but space monsters—even those who might vote liberal—seemed much less promising as a budget stimulus than Islamist fiends, ecoterrorists, immigrants, or bedbugs. What looming threat did the Shop perceive?

As it turned out, it did involve the Tourists, and we were more than ready. For aeons we had practiced wreaking death upon humankind, so it was no big deal to zap aliens. They were way ahead of us on the Greensleeves technology, but they had the fatal disadvantage of having scruples. Eventually it came down to a race to save or waste humanity. That issue had never figured large in national priorities, weighed against the needs of Big Oil, Big Pharma, Big Ag, and Deep Pockets, but it finally penetrated the callused layers of bureaucracy's shriveled brain that the worldwide extinction of humanity—a legitimate threat—might adversely affect the Economy.

"So what's your take on it, Turk?" The beast was asleep. One good thing about the dumb animal: when he had nothing to say, he didn't say it.

## —6—
## *A Goddamned Moving Day*

    I suffer from chronic digression. Granted, this story is preposterous, though every day we fall for deceit like a fifteen-year-old virgin after three beers and a shot of vodka. And its theme—human survival—is admittedly frivolous. But the writing might save me from the ravages of drink.

    Human extermination… What's meant by being human? Certainly there's a good side to it. Everyone's nice to at least two or three other people in our lives, even if we piss on the rest. We listen to music—Beethoven and Mahler and Shostakovich make a merry ruckus—and lots of guys do the dishes without slugging their wives. I provided Turk with lodging despite his never doing a lick of work, and if it weren't for us, cats would never shit in a pan. We send out missionaries and Special Forces to get all God's creatures to shit in a pan. If you won't shit in a pan, you deserve to die: it's entirely your choice.

    In my years at the Shop, my appraisal of the human race plunged 90%—about to the level of pond scum. Not that I'd ever expected much of these sickly extruding guts popularly known as consumers. Anything this side of baby rape was a miracle. When a good deed hit the news, I was so shocked I giggled for days.

    Human race: a very fragile species. My old college roommate, Rosenberg—Orthodox Jew, pre-med—would get on this riff of suing God for malpractice. "See that ventricle, built to fail. Would the Japs or the Krauts ever design a piece of crap like the lower back? Hemorrhoids? Kidney stones? Aneurisms? The Messiah is coming, but not to save Israel: he comes to negotiate an out-of-court settlement." Porky, we called him, just for the anti-Semitic fun of it. "Your sense of humor is pathetic," he said. Quite true.

    Human race: those majestic little creeps. Of course philosophers have debated human nature since before the invention of philosophers. I haven't canceled my membership in the species, though I fantasize this huge explosion, one fiery fecal plume. Some Indian tribe got it right: a big bird shat us out and flew off. Blest be the name of the bird.

~

Forty-one years I was an operative of the Shop, mainly in Public Policy. You think, *Oh but the deep shit is in Covert Operations.* Think again: does the Shop put a wall plaque on their covert operations wing reading COVERT OPERATIONS? Granted that Public Policy sounds like a library talk on knitting Christmas ornaments, but as for the actual Covert Operations dudes, they brewed the coffee.

My qualifications were limited. As a kid I played Cowboys and Indians. In high school debate club we debated the war—whichever war—and I always did better *for* than *against*. Everyone does better that way. I got married for a while, then again, which honed my tactics for fighting dirty. Other than that, I was just your normal Midwestern cretin. But if I'd known I would get involved in ethical ambiguities, I might never have been an art major. People think the FBI or CIA recruit their new troops from computer geeks or football players or Young Republicans. Guess again: top choice is an Art Department MFA with Dadaist tendencies. It might have to do with our ability to justify, with multisyllabic opacity, why a repurposed urinal would constitute ground-breaking art. Rationalization is the name of the game.

My thesis project was a roomful of old-style electric razors on long extension cords. You flipped them on all at once and they'd scuttle around the floor like fibrillating mice. And all four walls of the gallery were blanketed with my rejection letters for teaching jobs. Maybe the ERP recruiters felt that I would take out my rejections doing nasty things with electric razors to dirty Reds. But with my ethical vacuum and massive student loans, I was fair game. They recruited me for the Shop's Graphic Arts division. I wondered what that was the code name for. I soon found out.

Lennie was my other friend at the Shop. His undergraduate major was in philosophy. "I jerked off to Hegel," he told me, and I think he wasn't kidding. The nature of Good and Evil, according to Lennie: if I do it it's good, if you do it it's evil. "You can't attach moral value to the deed itself. Lame-brains quote what God wrote in His sci-fi best-seller. They read *Thou shalt not kill* and try to work out the parameters of *kill*. Wrong. The operant word is *thou*. I shall do it, thou shan't. Simple as that."

So that's who I thought I was. We cling to our illusory sense of self, go out of the movie thinking we look like the stud or studress who's the star. The illusion lasts till we've dislodged the popcorn from our molars. We're not definable entities, just vast deposits of debris and seeds and yearning. Not the way our mommies saw us: more in the vein of *What hath God wrought?* Identity is like anchovy paste: a little goes a helluva long way.

∽

Now I faced another goddamned moving day. I needed to be closer to the action, whatever the action was. I rented a room in San Francisco, out in the Western Addition. I didn't make careful deliberations: I had always relied on sudden impulse to screw up my life. I was rarely disappointed.

The move had its complications. Here in sweet little Gravenstein, I was a comfortable freak, but in a city as weird as San Francisco, where I'd seen a photo of guys in public without any pants, I'd stick out like a DayGlo thumb. Rosella wasn't the love of my life, but she was convenient: at my age that counted for lots. And Turk loved waddling after the sparrows with no fear that he might ever catch one. Still, if I took the red bandanna off Turk and didn't spend a lot of time on the streets right away, I might not attract too much attention. I'd have to get rid of the turban that I'd flirted with, go back to my leather hat and forego my dreadlocks in favor of a frizzed-out gray ponytail. I had never been a master of disguise. At this point I had to rely on the invisibility that comes with geezerhood.

For reasons that escape me, I felt that moving was best done on a Thursday. And so, on a Thursday in late March—Time was doing backflips—I tossed belongings into a rental car and drove to San Francisco, listening to the classical station's diddle-dum-dum while Turk gnawed his seatbelt, with heavy traffic around Novato and again approaching the bridge. I tried to focus on Moshe's opaque reference to Operation Chemo, but all that filled my eyes was an image of sunshine on Judith's hair, how it would feel coming loose, flowing onto her shoulders. As if I would ever know.

Unlike countless moves, I had no need to pare down my possessions, check the holes in my socks, discard the ugly furniture that sprouted around me like a creeping sludge. Those times had posed the prickly question, *Who am I?* Which books would an Edward read? Did he prefer jockey shorts or boxers? Who the holy fuck was Edward Funston? But Victor had no such problem. His identity lay in his peripatetic hat.

I hated moving, but this wasn't really moving: I was extending. I kept my room in Gravenstein. I still valued my bouncy nights with Rosella, and the notion of separating Turk from Roscoe's loving care, given the beast's taste for good Scotch, gave me pause. If I'd actually given the whole thing any serious thought, I would have never done it. The story of my life.

∽

The plus side of electronic surveillance was that you got paid very well to do damn near nothing. More stress if you were in a damp cave in Somalia, but just sitting with coffee and donuts listening to the wallpaper curl in Fairfax, Virginia, wasn't a bad gig. Still, you got a new appreciation of how long five minutes could be. Even bizarro crazies spent the most of the day doing what humdrum people do. I squandered years of my life listening to people taking a shower, which the terrorists did a lot—some kind of metaphor, maybe. But doing it as I was now doing it, a lonely fossil pissing away his leisure years, you wanted more bang for the buck.

I was tuned in on Judith and Moshe day and night. Once in a while there were sounds with erectile potential—in bed, when Drucie was on top, it could get pretty gusty—but mostly I sat listening to people live their lives. Judith would come home, and her son Josh would be there. Josh was about fifteen and pretty much of a wiseass. He'd say hello and ask Judith who she was tonight.

"I'm your mother, bozo."

"Oh, right. It's my mother that's sleeping with a software engineer. Kinda sad: it totally deromanticizes cyberspace." He'd always try to squeeze out a punchline. I'd been like that, prior to senility.

"Are you having a problem with Moshe being here?"

"Mom, that was humor. Don't you recognize humor?"

"Not always when it comes from you, my son."

"Mom..." He had the inflection down perfectly: that universal teenage glissando of parental exasperation. When I finally met him we got along okay despite my conviction that fifteen-year-olds should be locked in a freezer for a couple of years, then thawed gradually. Caterpillars have the grace to adolesce inside a cocoon.

"Well yes, I admit it," Judith said tartly. "You suffer horrible child abuse, like getting fed dinner day after day." Silence, then she laughed. He sniffed out a chuckle, reluctantly acknowledging that his thirty-nine-year-old mother could match him in snarkiness.

"No, I mean he's great. Except it's kinda crowded, you and him and me and all your internal basketball team." He paused for a reaction. "But it's fine."

"Did he say when he was coming home?"

And I could hear the little girl Sweetie's faint whisper, "Never. They're gone. I'm lost."

I was starting to daydream about my own obnoxious teenage self when the door opened in this reality show between my earbuds, and Moshe came in.

Shuffle of an embrace. "How was your day?" he asked.

"I got through it. I'm alive." Several of her alters mumbled, but I couldn't tell what.

"I'm thankful for that."

"How about you?"

"Well, they're doing marketing analysis now. Who knows?" His story was that he programmed video games for an outfit in Oakland, though from ERP data I knew that was baloney. I had no idea what he did with his days. Browsed at the library? Sat behind the washer in the utility room reading science fiction? Fell into a coma? I never thought to track him down. My mania was Judith.

She narrated her further adventures with dormant invoices, and Moshe laughed. He laughed a lot to keep her cheerful, despite the fact that when alone he was gloomy beyond the call of duty.

"Well, that's day number seven hundred forty-two, if I'm correct." Meaning what? How long they'd been together? How long they'd talked about getting a cat? I'd heard a lot about the hypothetical cat. Sweetie wanted it, Marge didn't—citing statistics that cats were deceitful, diseased and hell on furniture.

Then Judith said in Sweetie's voice, "I can count good." That stopped the conversation for a while. Sweetie had a knack for saying stuff that came out of a Salvador Dali landscape. It was amazing how Judith could maintain functionality while being insane. The American achievement.

Judith picked up the thread. "Yeh, pretty good. I can stay friends with my buddies now. They're not causing too much trouble, even with all the noise inside. Sometimes they're helpful."

"Thanks loads," murmured Ray.

"You're beautiful." Moshe was close to her. He might be stroking her hair. I started hoping for activity that evening if things kept going that way, but I knew from my marriages that detour signs could go up with one wrong word. Once I was in a bar with this mutually drunken lady. We were leaning on each other to keep on our stools, getting horny. For some misguided reason I started to tell her my life, and the moment I said something sardonic about the USA she jerked upright and said, "Doncha luv yer kun-tree?"

I stared at her, got up, and reeled out the door. I wasn't in the mood for self-examination, but as I lurched homeward her question kept itching at me, and what came to mind was Aunt Effy. Old tub of lard, wispy black hairs on her upper lip, smelled like piss. Always driveling on about God this and God that and Uncle Bud's solution to the nigger problem and her kidney condition, and then my mom would say, "Now kiss your Aunt Effy," and I'd kiss my Aunt Effy because she always gave me ten bucks at Christmas.

Did I love my Aunt Effy? Did my heart go bunga bunga when I heard her wheezing up the stairwell? Did I hoist up her panties on the Fourth of July? Did I beat up little kids to make them admit my auntie was better than theirs? Would I jump in front of a bus to stop her from being smeared on the pavement? Not likely. But she gave me ten bucks at Christmas, so I kissed Aunt Effy.

How that relates to America is up for interpretation. I will say that I don't subscribe to American Exceptionalism: the vile shit we've pulled is nothing new. I like the scenery hereabouts, I like

Whitman and Twain and Vonnegut, and I've met a few people within these borders that I'm actually forced to admire. There's better coffee in Italy, but Italy's full of Italians.

I tend to wander off the subject. I listened on through dinner, dishwashing, then five minutes of TV with Judith's alters quarreling about what to watch, curtailed by Marge screeching, "Turn that shit off!" Josh went off to his room for homework or algebraic self-abuse, while Judith and Moshe settled back to read.

It was my fate to be surveilling a family of readers. A half hour of silence, then, "Tea? Beer?" then another hour. From Judith, "They say the climate's heating faster than they thought." Faint "Hmm" from Moshe. Could have been worse: imagine sitting in the Shop's sub-basement listening all night to your chief international thug soaking up game shows, reality shows, sports, reruns of Lawrence Welk and the cartoony chirp of dolts with cutting-edge hairdos reporting the day's atrocities as if telling the story of Goldilocks to two-year-olds. Better now that I spent a couple of hours with little more than that noncommittal "Hmm."

Later, after the sounds of making love, which simultaneously roused my feebleness and tore out my heart, Moshe would go out to the kitchen and turn on his device and send his messages. I wasn't always able to tune in. Clearly ERP monitored it, but sometimes there were better bug-jamming devices arrayed against us: their techies, whoever they were, versus our techies. Once upon a time it was the guys with the heaviest broadswords, then the guys with the most maneuverable fighter planes—think of the Jap Zero as a killer app—but now it all came down to the hacker with the slickest trackpad.

I passed the down-times feeding snacks to Turk at the speed of slow or slower. At that point he was into walnuts. It might take him half an hour to chaw his way through a single nut, but he seemed to enjoy the challenge. His native dentistry had been bred to chomp down on the nose of a bull, but having never been presented that challenge, he seemed content to worry a walnut. Two or three would fill a whole evening—just as well, given the next day's struggle of the walnuts to find the Northwest Passage through Turk. And watching him gnaw his nut, it struck me like a hammer: I was addicted. It was more than a peeping-Tom impulse. I had to be near these people. I was hooked on this little wad of sentient creatures. I was so lonely.

∼

The move to my San Francisco digs didn't bring me any closer to what I was moving toward. I fell into a drooling maunder, my hair growing into my brain. It wasn't the kind of plot where the foreplay builds up the heat and you cut to the money shot. This was more like the old cowboy movies where the Indians rode round and round the wagon train, getting shot off their horses, and you wondered why they didn't just charge in and scalp the honkies. I guess they had their reasons.

I had to admit that my natural sense of tempo—creeping or careening—might be the workings of residual dope. During those years of protecting our Way of Life, I ingested a shitload of pharmaceuticals. We got the best quality, so my vision may have skewed to a parlous degree of acuity. On one trip, I saw the silvery black merry-go-round horse where my mother set me at the age of three, hopped on, and flew to the moon. Those eyes return at times and it all looks new. Bad thing about the right kind of drugs is that when you come so near the center of the All, sliding back into your skin makes you feel like a bratwurst.

Suffice it to say that I couldn't tell if my brain was the addled Eddie or the banjo-twanging Victor. I just took my place in line behind the other souls. The story was playing out at its own steady pace, no worse than *Moby-Dick* where you had to read the full scoop on whale blubber before the action heated up. Eventually we would face the white whale, gaping its toothless maw to gum us to death. Though in fact this chronicle is about saving the human race, which some deluded souls still thought was a good idea.

Nothing much happened in these months or days. I'd moved to San Francisco, and I'd accepted that I was addicted. Addicted to these people, to listening in. Just listening in. All of which may have explained my grabbing the hot wire of Project Chemo.

## —7—
## *The Shrink*

I was back in action mode, though the action was pretty thin: listening to people canoodling while my dog ate a walnut. Fact is, we had lots of ingredients for high adventure: covert agencies, space aliens, and a woman who'd suffered trauma severe enough to split her head into small change. But why pump up the suspense? Why couldn't we simply tell the story of Judith on an ordinary day? What a miracle to get born and learn to walk and grow up and birth a baby and go to work and make love and fix dinner. What a miracle to live when you know that some day you'll die—the day when the great Rooster of Death comes down to Sleeping Beauty and pecks out her eyes. We could all relate to that. It's how we feel on Monday morning.

So we had all the components of a blockbuster movie, but there was a flavor missing. It required just a pinch of psychological depth, and for that we needed a shrink. Thanks to Moshe, Judith had one. He had gently persuaded her that therapy might make her life a bit less of a juggling act and offered to pay, given that his salary as a fake software engineer was moderately astronomical. While she would never accept more from him than splitting the rent and groceries, Judith regarded psychotherapy more like a trip to Reno than as life support, so she agreed.

Dr. Francesca Stipic was the kind of shrink who insisted you call her Francesca or Dr. Fran. She always played music in her sessions—New Age stuff with an angel choir, squirming harmonies, and a didgeridoo digesting itself. This was what you listened to while flushing your tank. Still, Dr. Fran was a very smart cookie.

I never actually saw the lady so I can't describe her, but she sounded like one of those very dark Italians who decide to be blonde and wind up looking like hell. She was in her late forties, and my research revealed a checkered past. She had been a biology undergrad at Penn State, but due to her intense researches into heterosexual mating habits, she flunked out. With the aid of a forged transcript, she transferred to Johns Hopkins, excelled, but eloped with a Haitian refugee who had a fetching limp. That relationship lasted until they were married, when she fell for an accountant named Stipic and moved to Dallas, a city she cited as grounds for divorce.

She migrated to San Francisco, where she worked as a call girl—though she hated the same-old same-old routine—until she'd saved enough money to enroll at Berkeley to complete her degree. Surviving twenty-hour days, she put herself through medical school, along with two abortions and a psychiatric residency, emerging as a licensed shrink with a specialty in dissociative identity disorders. Experienced beyond the call of duty.

The extensive detail of my research was thanks to the fact that she'd been recruited by ERP. To my knowledge, her office was bugged by at least three Federal agencies and possibly the Disney Channel, though the audio quality was third-rate. Thankfully my teenage hacker source in Tulsa had some neat way of enhancing the quality, so I managed to make it out.

Not long after our first encounter, Judith was in Francesca's office. "Would you like the music off?" asked Francesca, in a tone that made clear that if the answer was yes then that's what she'd harp on for the rest of the hour.

"No, leave it on, it's nice," said Judith. The music evoked a walrus with stomach cramps. "So how do you think I'm doing?"

"How do *you* think you're doing?"

"I knew you were going to say that." Judith laughed. "Okay, I think I'm doing a lot better. I don't get so bent out of shape when Marge and I disagree. Sweetie is behaving better, not so many tantrums. How do I calm a kid when she's screaming inside me? Give my left tit a time-out?"

"Go on."

"It was a question."

"I've never dealt with that." A shuffle and chair squawk. "And you're aware it's not my function to offer advice."

"Or anything else."

"As I said, I could prescribe a different antidepressant. You were taking Sertraline before?"

"It made me feel like a zombie."

"Well, Judith, as I've said, the best that medication can do is to make you a better-adjusted zombie."

Judith took a sharp inhale as if she were going to spit, but she must have thought better of it. "Okay, so I'm actually doing pretty good at work, with Ray's help. My current boss is a total asshole, but I guess he just does what assholes are supposed to do." She gave a tart laugh. "That was a joke, Francesca. Okay, right: it's not your function to laugh."

"You're a bit unsettled today."

"Well, dammit, that's why I'm here!" There was a heavy silence. I glanced at the news on my desktop monitor: we were invading some country where the civilians were greeting us by exploding. Then Judith continued, realizing perhaps that she paid as much for minutes of silence as for minutes of talk. "And I kinda wish it wasn't only Drucie or Ray that were making love with Moshe, and that Judith could have a turn, but—"

"Do you really want that?"

"I think I do. Yeh."

"That's progress."

"Yeh, it really is. Right. It is."

I gathered that when they made love it was a bit sad for Judith because in her mind it wasn't really her who was making love. It was her sexy Drucie persona or sometimes Raymond, the gentle-voiced guy who liked guys. They both seemed to enjoy it a lot, but Judith couldn't feel it. She liked it to happen because it made Moshe happy. He told her that these were just parts of herself and not different people, and so whichever Judith he made love with was fine by him. She didn't believe it for a moment, but he was beautiful when he said it.

Francesca scribbled something on a pad, though I could tell by the sound of the scribble that she wasn't actually writing a thing. "Does Moshe know who's in bed with him at any given time?"

"I think he does. He's very accepting. He sees us all as Judith." Judith sighed. "I wish I could."

Now, the background music was sticky sweet ooze. Francesca scribbled on. "So we talked about doing another hypnosis. Are you up for that?"

"Rummaging the attic?" Long silence. "Well, I get scared. Last time, when Sweetie peed the bed, that was pretty embarrassing." She took a breath. "But I guess we need to find what's in there. Okay, deep breath. Let's go fishing and hope we don't hook the giant squid."

"Ready?"

And then, maybe as a delaying tactic, Judith told her that she had this strange encounter with an old guy in a coffee shop. White hair sticking out under a leather hat and a briefcase with anti-war slogans, and he'd said that all the shrinks in America work for the Shop. Judith laughed nervously. "What, barber shop? Flower shop?" I listened for some kind of blurt from Francesca, but she played it very cool.

"Interesting."

"All right," Judith murmured, "I'm ready. Start up the horror show."

"Okay, counting backward from ten. Focus on the spot. Ten, relaxed, nine, very calm, eight, just very very focused, breathe, seven…"

I listened, one ear on the session, one eye catching the war on the screen where they were blowing us up and we were blowing them up like two-year-olds in the sandbox.

From Judith: "Like a dream where I'm… Like space aliens or… Like I'm on this table, strapped down. Very big eyes, there's some like normal people but some with very big eyes, and I just start screaming, just… Like some kinda monkey…"

Does that tickle your balls or what? It went about twenty minutes where she got into some pretty pornographic stuff. The media would love it, and I'd give it to them for a price, not that I need the money, but they're the type that only respect an orgasm if they pay for it. But in fact it was nothing new. All the alien-abduction stories had similarities, which you could interpret as verification of their accuracy or as evidence that the victims were echoing something they'd read in a supermarket tabloid.

The "some with big eyes," for example: we heard that a lot at the Tourist Bureau. As it turned out, the so-called "normal people" were regular humanoids while the bug-eyed midgets were robots that they'd designed in reference to our bug-eyed monster movies. The aliens, being thoughtful souls, believed that our movies reflected the stuff we craved, so they felt their abductees would enjoy a few bug-eyed monsters in the spaceship. Regarding the Tourists' complex stupidity, much more anon.

The session didn't accomplish much that day except a few screams from Judith in reliving the experience of a naked three-year-old on an examining table—nothing she hadn't disgorged before and nothing I hadn't heard from tapes of other abductees. Pretty much what you might perform on chimps if you were into chimp abuse: electric shocks, blood samples, orifice probes, lights in the eyes, though thankfully no vivisection. The terror was in her vulnerability and in the aliens' bland expressions.

After the hypnosis, Judith and Francesca chatted a bit. I couldn't tell that much had been accomplished, but perhaps it made Judith feel better simply because it was done with.

"So, Judith, what do you like to do for a good time?"

"Not this!" Sharper than she'd intended. "No, that was a joke, kinda sorta. I try, anyway." Deep breath. "No, I guess just be with my boyfriend. And my son, he's a handful, but we get along. He's smarter than me, anyway, and God knows I'm thankful for that. Which is more of a challenge, but maybe he'll go to college, something, I hope."

"Well, my prescription for the moment is just making yourself feel good is a vital therapy. Do what feels good. We'll get there." Squeak of a chair, footsteps, door opening. "How is it for you right now? You hear your voices?"

"Nope. They're laying low. They'll have lots of shit saved up when the time is right."

I heard the door close, and Francesca punched a recorder. "833-A43-D422. Quoting an old man in a coffee shop, Judith said, *All the shrinks in America work for the Shop*. Description: white hair, leather hat, briefcase with antiwar slogans. Hope this makes you happy, gentlemen." She clicked it off. "Assholes." She knew the bug would pick that up as well, but for them it wouldn't matter. She gave them full value for their stipend, which had allowed her to pay off her student loans at the age of forty-six.

Hearing this, I knew I'd have to get rid of my leather hat. It had kept me company. More than that: despite the droop of its brim when rained upon, it gave me a face that, checked in the mirror, looked nearly alive. That night I went to the kitchen and baked it in the oven. I'd have to go back to the former Victor's greenish-blue stocking cap, foregoing my image as *crusty old-timer* for the look of *goofy geezer*. History, in the long run, will find us all huddled under blankets.

~

Again I asked myself: why get involved with Judith? Why spoil my total dissociation from sympathy with humankind, that poor bare forked animal that God stabbed Himself in the eye with? Just for the diversion, the action, a faint hope of sex? Might it be that I was fatally infected with empathy?

Past midnight, after three shots of some sort of booze, maybe more, I dug into my briefcase to a secret compartment. I had been hooked on secret compartments since age eight when I sent in for a Captain Marvel Code Ring with a little slot where you could keep your coded message if you were smart enough to think one up. In my briefcase I had rigged a little slider that concealed a small stash of old cards, photos, memorabilia, and a tiny tin Sucrets box which shall be revealed in due time. I sorted through every scrap relevant to Edward Funston, including a dog-eared snapshot of his first girlfriend, nameless now. I replaced the tin box, took the rest of my stash, and flushed the whole jumbled wad of Edward Funston.

## —8—
## *Puzzling*

Granted this whole eavesdropping thing was slimy beyond words, though it was far from the slimiest thing I'd ever done. There were so many times when I'd be moving from a coffee shop to a park bench and then to catch the bus back to my little sardine apartment, listening on my earbuds to Judith and Moshe, when I'd think how wonderful the California dawn felt, or the twilight. This couple seemed to know what it was to be human even if one of them wasn't. A grim pair, but together they could laugh.

The morning after Dr. Fran did her shrinking, it was Judith's day off. Moshe said he'd work from home, a normal practice for software engineers. He didn't actually work for the company he said he worked for, but that company was clearly a front for another operation. Most companies are. You think it's a bank but in the basement they're wholesaling plumbing supplies. For all we know, Boeing and Northrop Grumman might be cornering the market in women's lingerie.

After Josh went off to school, they made love. A gentle calm followed, then Moshe sneezed. They started laughing and made love some more. Listening, I began to cry my eyes out for no discernible reason. I could imagine gazing into her eyes and hearing her breathe—the wonder of breath.

"Hey listen, didn't you tell'em you'd work from home?"

"I am doing so. I am involved in a complex issue of cross-platform connectivity."

In fact that was pretty funny. They laughed, then laughed at their own laughing, and that went on for a while. I could almost see them in the morning light.

"It's nice to have the morning," Judith said.

"Computers are my hobby," said Moshe, "but my profession is Judith."

"Oh yes, do that some more." I couldn't tell what he was doing, but I liked imagining it. I knew what I would have been doing if I still remembered how.

Silence for a while. I could never believe they didn't know they were bugged, but clearly they didn't have a clue. Normally you can tell: people who suspect it feel obliged to talk a lot so they don't sound boring. Then Moshe said an odd thing. "How does one open oneself to a stranger?"

"Stranger?"

"We're very close and still it feels like strangers."

"You're a stranger?" No reply. "Well, strange maybe, but—What should I know that I don't already know? I mean our whole life history bit took about half an hour and then we jumped into bed. Isn't that the way normal people do it?" Whenever she said something funny—which she often did—she sounded a little desperate.

"Don't you wonder if any of what I tell you is true?"

But Judith always wondered if any of her own life was true. When she started to remember stuff, she'd stop talking and ask Moshe to scratch her back, as if the memory was itching at the left of the spine, halfway down. He'd scratch her back and ask her what she was thinking, and she'd say how good the back-scratch felt. Which he knew was dodging the question, but he wouldn't pursue it because then she'd get very itchy. Some women have their own sense of time. Once I knew a woman—what was her name?—who if you just lay there stroking her breasts she'd talk beautiful stuff, beautiful funny stuff, as if time stood still. I never had the patience to continue it very long. Now I wish I had.

"No, really: what are you thinking?"

"I don't want to talk about it." She sounded proud that she'd asserted her right to keep silent, and then right away she told him. "Well, it's weird what I came up with today. Francesca regressed me, like I was really tiny and there's this bright light. I'm on a table and it's cold cause I don't have any clothes on, and people looming over me. It was like school, like dreaming you're naked in school. Or not people, but eyes, bug eyes like space monsters, and they're all over me. Which was all the same stuff, nothing new, like having this song in your head and it keeps going over the first two lines and you can't remember the rest, but then—" A breath caught in her throat.

"Then?"

"I got up to that point, and I'm like this little girl that opens her eyes and, *Oh, this is what life is like. This is the world. I have to live here.* Just knowing that. Seeing it. Seeing how many miles. And of course I freak out and start screaming and then Francesca wakes me up and scrapes me off the ceiling."

Sweetie's voice: "I get scared."

"And Sweetie was scared, but all my others, they just stood back and let old Judith scream her heart out. I hated to be the only one screaming. Reminds me of old relationships." Dry laugh. "My love, it's sweet the way you nod very sympathetically when you hear all this for the fourteenth time, but—" She loved it and she hated it. "But maybe I wish I had a guy who'd just scream with me. 'Whatcha wanna do tonight, honey?' 'Well, let's scream together a while.'"

He made a tiny cartoon squeak that stood for a scream. They laughed.

"Although Francesca thinks I'm making progress," she said. "I haven't tried to kill myself for two years now. I wonder now would I do a better job? My mom always said practice makes perfect." She laughed. He didn't.

"Have you thought about it recently?" In a serious mode, his voice was a swollen toe.

She sighed. "Hey, could we just go back to fooling around on a sunny April morning?" (The calendar kept backing up to the edge of a cliff.) Their breathing hinted they were starting to fool around, but Judith kept talking. Now and then she took a sharp breath when something like maybe a finger became a little too intense.

Her words rose to the top like foam on the surf. She talked about where she grew up, Iowa maybe, out under the cottonwood trees, feeding the cats and swatting mosquitoes. Words about other lovers, mostly lovers she couldn't remember except for cigarette breath or a scraggly fingernail or a funny smile. "I'm a sucker for funny smiles." She tried to remember anyone else who'd made her laugh, but she'd never heard them laugh—they all seemed to take it so seriously. She was always dead certain that as soon as they finished they were going to kill her, and the fact that they never did was proof they didn't love her. It was only Moshe who laughed, and only with him did she.

He spoke with deliberation. "I want to be very close to you, Judith. And honest with you."

She interrupted at the word *honest*. "Josh thinks you've got the funniest accent. He said you sound like Marlon Brando playing Dracula." They laughed.

"So I might say, in my funniest accent, that I would be greatly pleased if you were in love with me."

She replied flippantly, "That might be arranged." And then she began to weep, weeping in soft waves as if weeping the ocean. You could hear her shaking like one of those blessed drawn-out orgasms that go on and on, with seagulls bending against the sky. And a catch in the breath that's shameless, that lets your lover know that every pore is agape.

Abruptly, a snarl. Another voice within her, one I'd never heard, male in its potent force, female in its venom: "JUDITH WELLER: NEVER BE UNDER THE FAINTEST ILLUSION THAT YOU ARE LOVED."

This was a new one. Male or female, I couldn't tell which. But, oh Christ, it didn't have to say that.

～

That night I tried again to puzzle it out. Why would the Shop be monitoring the convoluted psyche of a loony temp worker in San Francisco? Granted, she'd had contact with aliens, and now possibly a Jewish one. If they were surveilling Judith it must have to do with Moshe, but what hot issue brought aliens back into their sights?

"What's your opinion, Turk?"

Turk rolled one eye up and stared at me. At that moment I felt his soul was very deep. It called to mind my second marriage, when we made an effort to be homeowners and I had to clean out septic pipes that were clogged with roots. I could have hired immigrants to do it and then have them deported without pay, but my wife was into Wicca and felt that might put a curse on our waste disposal system. That's what came to mind as I met Turk's gaze. Don't ask me why.

And still later that night, after too many shots of eighteen-year Glenlivet, I tuned into another call of Moshe to Outer Space. An electronic sizzle, a cluster of beeps, a squeeze-toy burp that sounded like *Shazam!* and then the familiar paper-crunch.

"English, please," Moshe said with some irritation. "As I said, I am out of practice." He had softened his comic-book speech. He actually sounded human, despite evidence to the contrary.

"Benny here. What is up?" Benny had the inflection of a wooden actor playing a farmer reading a poem to his cow. But he gave English a good college try.

"Benny?"

"Speaking English, yes? Subject, predicate, that stuff? You read me, Jack?"

Moshe spoke telegraphically: "First, request status of my petition. Second, status of Project Chemo. Third, my operational report."

"Busy, busy. Let us check thereupon." He emitted a cluster of pops like stomping bubble wrap. "Petition status: Under Review. Guess that means it's under review. Project Chemo: Under Review. Current Report... That is you, my man. Is my English well? I play American slang when I say *My man*? Often I sound cheesy, yes?"

"Well, Benny, Benny, Benny..." Moshe took the longest breath that could be taken. "I am torn."

Some clicks and squiggles, then, "Oh. Sorry."

"Torn between loyalty to our brethren and my love for this woman."

"They sing songs on that, yes? I did the crash course. *Achey Breaky Heart, All Cried Out, Baby Come Back, Your Cheating Heart, Heartbreak Hotel.* They got problems, it sounds, on the sex stuff, no?"

Moshe spoke as if into another world, high or tranced or heavily sedated, as if telling a dream so private it couldn't be voiced. "Her hair, the foldings, the arches to the feet, even the glide of her nose to the forehead. Remember the girl with blue eyes that we swam with once? A sharpness, a softness, the breath?"

A thin "Mm-hmm." They had a history together. I had never seen a movie where two space invaders were friends.

"I love her fingers. Not really good-looking: they're plain, stubby, useful. She cries, it's red eyes, rawness, grit. So much beauty in the grit. She's borne a child."

"Heavy. Is that what they say? Heavy?"

"These people: they kill, they betray, they enslave themselves, and yet they struggle, some of them, toward love. They dance on crippled feet, but they dance their dance."

It was a bit embarrassing to listen to. Raw words are too shameful, often, to share. There are times when men get so sloppy drunk that we speak our true feelings, but we have to be drunk enough to disremember, so that our friendship might be preserved. But if we actually heard the naked stuff, we wouldn't be able to look in each other's eyes. These aliens were different. I couldn't comprehend a brotherhood that included the sisterhood of truth. Benny's mangled syntax painted him as a loopy fool, but I felt their alien comradeship. Moshe spoke of a woman he loved to a man he loved.

Benny responded after a time. "What they say is *Remember the Alamo*." It's anyone's guess what he meant.

It had to be said, though, that Moshe's notion of honesty was about on a level with mine. He knew why he was here on Planet Earth, what was going on, and he reported back to his guys the same as I had done for forty-one years. The only difference was that he felt tormented, whereas I could tell myself lies and believe them right to the bone. Maybe it was his shortcomings that made him real to me. And I did like the Tourists, at least I liked Moshe, despite my slow realization that they intended to snuff out the human race.

~

I've told so many versions of my life that I don't know which are true, which are based loosely on fact, and which are straight out of James Bond. It was no big sweat for me to transform from buzz-cut agent of doom to weird coot with a banjo—just one more hoax along Memory Lane. Turk made no objection as long as he got fed. What startled me was that I was losing sight of my objective. My intention was to lay low, to wiggle my ass into a comfy cocoon, drinking good Scotch, romping with bargain-basement hookers if need arose, enjoying the sun and the shadow. No desire to save the world for plutocracy or to teach third-world countries how to waterboard or gerrymander or launder loot. Others could do that: not I. Now I had developed an addiction. Worse, a soul was creeping in. I was hearing Moshe's lyrical cadence without the ironic filter that had served me so well. Way too poetic for my taste, but he spoke a truth that resonated to the core.

A culvert had spoken to me that way. I was about ten, and my friend Vernon and I would wander out to the edge of town from the armpit where we lived, drawn by the river. During a dry spell, under a side road, we found this steel culvert, about three feet diameter. We crawled in. I could hear my own breath's echo. We started hollering—"Vernon!" "Ed!" "Pissypoop!" "Fuckityfuck!" "Wawa-woo!"—and the reverberations enlarged us, beefed us up into giants, brass bands, atomic bombs. Then we went silent and the echoes spoke, but not what we'd blatted. Their own words: *Enough now. Listen. Just be.* We were inside a breathing animal. We knew its mind. It scared us shitless.

I might have made this up. My memory is tentative. I do recall that at the other end of the culvert, staring up at us, we found a dead raccoon. It was all dried out.

## —9—
## *Caffeine*

Once I read a poem about dogs going on with their doggy life. That said it all. The more I felt drawn into this interstellar mystery, the more my tempo dragged. I was the hero in a movie directed by Turk: go here, go there, drink, flop down and dream of a hero that goes here, goes there, flops down.

Time continued its shell game. Jared's gnawed pork ribs had been cleared away two minutes ago, though my San Francisco dinner with Jared hadn't yet been scheduled. I ascribed my confusion to that extra round of beers we were going to have when we had them, though we might have had the beers at that Serbian joint long ago, when I hit him in the snout.

~

Time's dance: it might glide like a tango, whirl like a waltz, or bounce like an Irish jig where they hang in the air like scarecrows whose feet are a flock of chickens. The museum visit, the dinner with Jared, other tiny anomalies where Time performed backflips— Was it simple senility, the after-effects of high-grade drugs, the antics of space invaders, or maybe just that I'd wasted forty-one years in chasing my tail? Time was on summer vacation.

One night, as I shared a vodka with Turk, I recalled the workings of quantum mechanics, as explained to me by my second wife Trish. According to the uncertainty principle, she told me, if you knew where you were and you didn't know what time it was, like if you came in past midnight you were up shit creek. There was a cat in a box that might be dead or alive, depending on what a particle decided to be when it grew up. I asked if that meant a baby could grow up to be either an engineer or a trout. "It's nothing to joke about," she said. She left me for a Buddhist plumber.

I kept coming back for an answer. Perhaps it was findable in the ton of sci-fi I'd read. Perhaps it was Time that was all clogged up from letting it go to waste. Perhaps it was vengeance from losing my Mickey Mouse watch. Perhaps it had no meaning at all, just doing its dance. But these warbles in Time made me suspect that things were not proceeding in their usual doggy ways.

~

I went back to the coffee shop in the Mission. I knew there were no prospects with the counter girl Georgeann, who regarded me as an old worm with whiskers. This time, Judith again.

It wasn't mainly sex that was on my mind, though Judith held unmeasured attractions. Those thighs were spring-loaded, and I was pretty hard up despite my periodic frisks with Rosella, which was more like fox-trotting a friendly watermelon. Since Judith had four distinct personae and a dark one lurking, there was always the chance that one of them—barring the little kid—might have a letch for a scrawny old rooster with a knobby pecker that could sometimes be induced to point toward the mother lode. But my interest wasn't pure horn-dog. I wanted to feel—despite the sociopathic futility of my entire life—functional.

Going back to the coffee shop was risky. This lady was under surveillance by ERP, and it was my whole objective, simply, to care for Turk till I outlived him, after which I might calmly take a dose of a trippy toxin and go beddy-bye. I was taking a gamble, but I had to be in the game. You never lost your desire to be where the action is.

Judith walked into the coffee shop with that slight sway of the hips that said to me, yes indeed, that's where the action is. I longed to be one of those hard-boiled super spies that score before the end of Chapter Two, but I knew she only saw an old goat in a leather hat with hairs sprouting out of his nose. But hadn't I roasted my leather hat last night or the night before?

"It's the little lady with her entourage," I said. She stopped dead in the doorway and stared at me. I gestured to offer a seat. She came to the table and sat. Very pale, with clouded eyes.

I played a hunch. "Who you got in there? They want to talk?" Her face squeezed up and they all came rioting through the gates.

"Don't scare me," Sweetie hissed, "cause I'll tell my mommy and she'll cut off your thing!" Little kids shouldn't talk that way.

I looked at my shoe. Judith let out a gasp and suddenly she was this thirty-year-old gay temp. "Listen, Father Christmas, we don't really need your infusion of mirth," Raymond warned me. "You might overstrain yourself."

Judith wasn't done. Drucie loomed. She gazed at me, opened her lips with a glint of a smile. There were definite prospects with Drucie, though she'd be way out of my league. She eyeballed my nose, knowing where I'd like it to be.

"Don't even think it, mister!" snapped Marge.

I half expected them to launch into a Beethoven string quartet, but Georgeann's voice broke the frontal assault. "Is everything all right there? Sir? Ma'am?" I turned to her, raised my cup of fair-trade coffee, and that seemed to soothe her hackles.

Judith coughed, suppressing her flock at one gulp. "I'm sorry," Judith said with a shake of her head. "I have a psychology that emerges from time to time." Her eyes came open again as Judith's eyes. How seldom I saw women's eyes.

I might have spoken to those eyes, but I fell into character. "Right, you've got alters. Dissociative identity disorder. D.I.D. We ran experiments, got people so parceled out they could spell *cat* six different ways. It affects people differently. You, when the voices come, your face goes blank, you notice that? Like you sorta stare at the floor practicing your lines, but then, the funny thing, you react to what's being said. Your whole buncha friends are all totally poker-faced, except the sexy one." She looked away. "So where you work, are they aware of your hidden talents?" That got her looking at me, but not with the eyes that I wanted.

"Why are you talking to me?"

"Well, to put my cards on the table, it's out of respect for Our Heavenly Father's creating attractive women." In the old days, if I'd got that far, I could get'em into bed even on their way to work, but that's when I had the full testosterone of the United States Government boiling up in me. I gave a chuckle to imply that I was a honcho on top of things, "But I'm more harmless than I'd like to be." It hit me like a custard pie how ridiculous I was. I could have been a sit-com if they'd put a laugh-track on me. She just looked at me as if I were one potato short of two potatoes.

Sharp breath. "You ran experiments…"

"Experiments, yeh. Once I read a bunch of science fiction. That was my job, to see if there were messages in it." She looked up with a flicker of curiosity. "Our boss suspected there was encoded stuff in there, like space aliens, though I dunno why he thought they'd send messages in sci-fi instead of cookbooks. But it gets to you. You're lonely as hell, but there's a universe out there with trillions of creatures and not one pair of arms or tentacles to hold you."

"Sometimes I wish I could get lonely," she said.

I'd never thought of it that way. Even with her kid and her lover and her internal zoo, she struck me as the loneliest woman in the world. I connected with that. You're this little squirt whose only friend just moved away, so you go through your pile of comic books, *Superman* or *Donald Duck*, but then it's the last page, the superheroes or funny animals get off work, go to the bar, and you're left alone. Then you're twelve years old, you read about this high school football team, they win the big game, they're jumping around like spastic kangaroos, but you're alone. And then you're into Dostoevsky's guy who's killing the gross old lady cause he knows there's this classic novelist writing a book about him, but you're still alone. They talk about curling up with a good book, but you learn pretty quick that you can't fuck a book.

I gestured. She sat down at my table, though she was already sitting there. She sipped her coffee. She drank it black. When did she ever get coffee? Time was folding back on itself like an old gas receipt. My fault for killing Time?

I forged on. "Now you look at me you might wonder, what did that old fart do before he retired? Chicken farmer? Dope dealer? Bus driver for the Grateful Dead? Or how about a forty-one year veteran of the much-heralded Deep State, of legendary dimensions?" Her face was blank as death. "Oops, blew my cover. Course I'm out to pasture now. I was lucky. They give you these tests to see if you might cause trouble. If you get a bad grade, why, you die abruptly from natural causes. But I helped design the tests."

I must have been off in some alternate reality. I knew I was getting in deep. For sure she was bugged, and I'd just given our boys ample evidence that I was a loose cannon rolling all over Northern

California. Within a week I might be organic compost. But those guys never trusted what was blindingly obvious. Back when Saddam was suspected of having atom bombs, the utter absence of evidence was a sure sign that he did. And if this old blowhard was spilling his beans to a nutty gal in a coffee shop, there had to be more to it than met the eye. It would take them months to gear up their systems, analyze their data, convene their committees to determine that in fact I was as doltish as I pretended to be.

We sat there a minute in silence. I had an impulse to ask her straight out if we could go back to my room and she could make an old man very— I thought better of it. This lady had been through a lot, and one effect of my leather hat, even if I were wearing only its memory, was to give me a spurt of compassion. Never too late to get human. I took another tack.

"How'd you get that way?"

"What way?"

"Crazy." That hit her a slap. "Or your shrink might call you togetherness-challenged. But seems like distinct personalities, a lot to juggle. Four or five?"

"How do you know it's five?" She looked scared.

"Just a nice round number."

She got up, went to the counter, ordered a coffee, maybe the coffee I'd seen her drinking already, came back. Time had claimed a relativistic status, as they explained in high school physics: when you see the clock climbing slowly up to the top of the hour, it indicates either that you're approaching the speed of light or that school is driving you nuts. I sat there scratching my scraggly beard.

"What did you ask me?" she asked.

"Well, I asked if you recalled what they did to you?" I hadn't asked her that, but maybe in a minute I would. I was starting to see that whatever I did, I might not do it when I did it. Depended on whether the quantum particle took a sharp left turn and ran over the cat.

"What who did to me?" She was coiled to spring.

"That's what I'm asking."

This wasn't going quite right. "Honey," I said, "I really love those lattes, but they cut off my pension when I died. I'd really love a latte." I could easily afford it, but at times the best strategy is submission.

Judith called out to Georgeann, "Scuse me, ah—"

"My name is Georgeann," said Georgeann. She'd consented to be Georgeann without my asking.

"Georgeann, could we have a latte?" A hint of Ray's voice.

"Decaf," I said.

"Decaf," she said. That was nice of her. People are getting nicer now, despite the headlines. Nicer in small ways. Georgeann brought the latte to our table, though there hadn't been time for her to make it.

That Time thing again. Even *again* was a function of Time. My watch was running double speed, then slamming on the brakes and skidding. Time was elbowing into the movie—a wild card, a cherubic zombie, an endocrine spurt. At different ages you saw that shyster in different ways. It slowed each minute of the last week of school, ripped gobs out of summer vacation, slipped under your skin to drag wrinkles into place, grabbed your heart and squeezed, or ran like a centipede.

Judith was frozen. I rambled on, narrating a life story that you don't hear every day from scroungy old men in coffee shops. I swore that it wasn't us who did experiments on her. In fact we did do experiments on folks, but we always cleaned up our mess. Sometimes it was one hell of a mess.

Right then Georgeann set the latte on the table. "Here's your latte." I thought I'd already been drinking it. I looked again at my watch, and there was Mickey Mouse with little arms wig-wagging the minutes and hours: an instant of childhood regression, then back to digital reality. I sipped my latte. I loved those things.

"Hey, Georgie-girl, when we gonna put our fences down and let our fingers do the walking?"

"Sir, I'm sorry, but..." She didn't seem to remember what she was sorry for, or else there was so damn much in her sorry-ass life that she couldn't begin to speak it. Me, I was sorry for being such an unbridled jerk.

"Sorry, Georgie, just trying to behave myself. Which means I try to follow orders, and I issue pretty disgusting orders." I don't know why I bothered. Wit was lost on Georgeann, I told myself, but in fact my wit was overdue for a shave.

"What if you're just a bughouse old guy in a coffee shop?" asked Judith. Reasonable question: I was. But I told her a few old stories, as for example: once we had intelligence that the Russians were set to launch a biological attack on the United States—smallpox, likely—on a Friday evening just after deadlines so the news would get buried in the Saturday papers. We geared up to nuke them back into Pre-Cambrian life forms, all ready to go Monday morning so the President would hit prime time.

And then the imminent death of half the human race got one-upped: a school shooting that broke all records. Those days, if you plugged three dozen kids in a shooting spree you'd barely make the weekly shopping news. But that Friday when we were all supposed to be dying from the first assault, an elementary school custodian chained the doors, cut phone lines, then went classroom to classroom, K through six. In every room, he made the kids strip naked, shot those who didn't, then shot those who did, shot them all. Three hundred and forty-seven.

It was the strip-naked part that grabbed the headlines. The pundits noted the potential for the kids' psychic trauma, barely mentioning that the little tykes were dead. Plus that the janitor was known to the kids as Mister Buddy. Lots of commentary on violence in America, with proposals to arm all the kids or to require preventive castration of teachers and staff. When it was revealed that Mister Buddy had once smoked weed, all Hell broke loose. (I'd noticed that Hell broke loose pretty often those days.)

So we had to postpone the nuclear holocaust: too much competition for headlines. And late Sunday we realized that they hadn't attacked after all. The intercepted message we'd read as code wasn't code. It was the Russian Ambassador, who had funny tastes, reserving a couple of call girls to make his U.N. trip worthwhile. We cancelled our plans and passed his message through. He enjoyed himself and left the girls a nice tip.

"A bughouse old guy in a coffee shop," I mused. "Well, here's the bughouse reality. It's the Shop versus the Tourists. We called 'em the Tourists for the fun of it. But no joke. The reason that Truman dropped the Bomb, way back when, was on account of the Tourists. The fact was we had to stay armed and set up the CIA and the DDT and ERP to keep track of the Tourists. We don't know what they want here, maybe just souvenirs. But it gives us more monsters to protect you from."

She was getting my message but didn't know what to do with it. I could see her forehead bulging to keep her alters from blowing out the front of her skull. I'd maybe gone too far.

"But see, Judith, all those poor bastards who met the Tourists, whatta they know? How do we trust'em? They might even be fellow travelers. Or even lovers, you think?"

She sat there like a naked baby, looked at me and whispered, "Why am I so afraid?"

"Cause we did a real good job of scaring you shitless. It's the name of the game."

I could hear her souls screaming inside. *Get outta here, Judith! He's scary! Move it or lose it! Dial 911!* "What do you know about me?"

"Not much," I said. "You're a temp. You've got a fifteen-year-old son named Josh. Your birthday's November 11th. Your dog, who died when you were fourteen, was named Ragsie. You just have that look about you."

"Who are you?"

"I am your guardian lunatic."

And then she ran. Out into the street. Where the boys were waiting. You gotta love'em: they're always there.

## —10—
### *Lights! Camera!*

Onrushing traffic. Squeal of brakes. Door opens, hands grab. "Come along, hon." Muffled cry. Sidewalk scuffle. Door slam. Sweetie screams, "I don't want needles!" Judith is toast.

Almost. They didn't reckon with her protectors. That's what alters are, after all. They're created out of a survival urge, though like most bright ideas they have unintended consequences. But sometimes they work as advertised. The thugs were prepared for struggle and screams, but they weren't expecting Sweetie to pee her pants while Drucie reached to stroke their inner thighs while singing an orgasmic cadenza. They barked commands to their captive, but Ray's baritone burst forth with "I love Federal cock!" and Drucie shrieked, "No, it's mine!" One goon bellowed, "Hands up!" but a dark slutty voice warbled, "You wanna see my tits?" The driver looked around and slammed into the side of a bus.

An agent lunged out of the car and straight into the path of a 1921 Stutz Bearcat driven by an elderly classic car collector. In his dying spasm, the agent shot the old bastard dead. "Out! Get out!" roared Marge, and Judith scrambled through traffic, while the agents were scraping up their brains. Sweetie screamed for her dolly, lost in the handbag that Judith left in the car, but it didn't stop a broken-field run between taxis and delivery trucks, through a gaggle of teenage girls and into a pizza parlor. She staggered up to the counter and slapped it, gasping.

The pizza man stared at her. "You got a problem?"

"I lost my dolly," Sweetie sobbed.

The pizza man shrugged. Ralph was fifty-three and he'd had a hard day. He'd migrated west for a lady he'd met on the Web and missed New Jersey. He'd expected a thirty-year-old and she'd hoped at least for a full head of hair. He had bought the struggling pizza joint for the privilege of being on his feet fourteen hours a day and going broke. Still, the relationship held.

"So you want a pizza?" he asked her.

Next day I picked up the report from the surviving agent. He stated that the subject had made an unexpected movement which distracted the driver. True, though short on details. The agent complained that their briefing had left them unprepared for diversionary tactics. According to my private channels, the agent subsequently developed a perverse fixation on Sweetie's dolly.

In the movies, Action Adventure Time is a lethal ballet, but in real life it's a self-destructing mess. That's why cops riddle a dude who chose the wrong time to scratch his ass. That's why witnesses see it three ways. That's why when the Nazis machine-gunned a cartful of Jews there were a few who lived to tell the tale. If the Nazis couldn't meet high efficiency standards, what could be expected from the rest of us?

A transmission from Franny the Shrink reported her client's cancellation of an appointment due to attempted abduction. "Friends, we seem to be working at cross purposes. I am compromising my professional ethics; you are compromising the compromise. While it's not my position to advise you how to pursue your objectives, I do propose that for critical assignments, at the very minimum, you might select agents who have already seen a woman's tits."

I doubted the effectiveness of her precaution. I've seen many tits. Big tits, little tits, tits that sag or stand up to salute. Tits that you wouldn't write home about and tits that if you wrote home you'd cause consternation. Tits that you couldn't call tits, you'd have to call them breasts to accord them the respect they deserved, though perhaps at night in the heart of darkness you might call'em tits. Tits that were epiphanies of vibrant flesh to which you could croon, *You must remember this, a tit is still a tit*. Maybe Francesca was jaded, thought that if you've seen two you've seen'em all, but it didn't really work that way. They're so beautiful.

After the incident, Judith somehow got home. Ralph the pizza guy, despite his crappy day and his longing for New Jersey, gave her bus fare, patted her hand, and hopefully got some well-deserved dream fantasies. Now she was eating supper with Moshe and Josh. Moshe cooked supper most of the time, Judith being a crappy cook. That night he'd made some kind of stew with fish in it. He was like that. He had this instinct that told him when Judith needed fish stew.

Odd conjunctions. You've been near wipe-out, your mortality on the brink, and then suddenly you're back home eating fish stew. You're putting food in your gut and life goes on. I remember this Russian girl in Manhattan who'd lived near Chernobyl when it blew. She'd moved to the States, in and out of cancer wards, and she might be dead by now. Or it might be that she gets up every morning and stretches and pees and eats and smiles and does her work and goes on with the day, and I will never know. If we manage to achieve normalcy, we've achieved a hell of a lot. So these folks were eating supper, which was a pretty good deal considering the state of the world.

Judith might have concealed the abduction if Sweetie hadn't spilled the beans. She recounted the adventure in her thin piercing trill in the style of a Goldilocks puppet show. I don't think she knew what she was saying, but she still put lots of spirit into "Federal cock!" and "Wanna see my tits?" It was cute except for my worry that the little girl might be traumatized. Then I remembered that Sweetie wasn't a child: she was a leftover trauma.

Judith did her best to convince herself it was no big deal. "I guess it surprised me, yeh. Life is fulla surprises."

"Judith, eat." Despite his formal diction, Moshe had a practical side.

Josh, always the kid who didn't quite fit; Josh, the contrapuntal teen; Josh, whose presence drew Judith back to that night-long torment of his birth; Josh, who forced her to stay alive in her quagmire—Josh said, "You escaped by pulling up your sweater?" He would say that to his mom. Josh would say that.

"I escaped by Drucie pulling up my sweater. I was too terrified even to scream, and she's coming on to these guys. Yes, it is a fact, Josh, that your mother has something to flash."

"Spare me," said Josh. A pause for effect. "Maybe it's a reality show. You'll be all over YouTube."

At last Judith was chowing down on the stew, with no qualms about talking with her mouth full. "I'm feeling pretty shaky, guys.

I don't mean just you guys, I mean all my guys. Kinda my Secret Service, like the President. I mean, imagine if some guy jumped out with a gun, and the President yelled, 'I want my dolly!'"

I liked her for that. She had humor, not like belly laughs or chuckles or even funny at all, but more like the rubber duck that comes bobbing up no matter how long you hold it under. Moshe wasn't saying anything. He'd cleaned his bowl, it sounded like, but he didn't take seconds.

"No, Mom, you're doing a lot better. I would have expected your whole zoo would be loose right now." It wasn't filial deference, but for Josh it qualified as affection.

Under her breath Sweetie mumbled, "I'm not the zoo, I'm a girl." You never knew who would take offense at what: nonexistent tots getting riled at metaphors.

"Josh did the salad," Moshe said out of the blue. They talked about the salad and about the dinner which they all agreed was special, and Moshe told Judith she looked good, and Judith told him not to be fooled because there might be aftershocks. "Bring them on," Moshe joked, and from that togetherness, it exploded. Marge howled about ingratitude and Sweetie cried for her dolly and Ray said something really pissy, and then Moshe grabbed Judith, "Judith, please!" and Marge damn near bit off his nose.

"Do not call me Judith! Do not call me Judith! I do everything here. I keep her alive, I keep her decent, I organize this madhouse, this traffic jam, and I will not do this any more! I am not Judith! I don't care about Judith! Let her die!" Amazing what venom could spew from a face that would be slanted downward at two fish bones in an empty bowl, blank and unfocused.

"Mom!" Her son: "Mom, listen. You have to be here. I need you, okay? Mom, look at me!" Scuffle, clatter, then a deep deflating exhale. "Hey there, you okay?" She must have nodded. "Hey look, I'm fine with whatever complications, but Moshe doesn't make mac and cheese the way I like it, so you really need to stay alive. At least till I'm accepted to the college of my choice." A silence, then, "I hope you understand that was a joke."

"Yes. Right. Okay." Slowly Judith came back into herself. And Moshe said that he too had made plans contingent on her existence and didn't want to change his schedule. He was joking, obviously, but he was the type that when he told he had to laugh so you'd know it was supposed to be a joke. It was a bit ironic, though, that he knew at this point—which I didn't know he knew—that very soon she, along with seven billion people, would probably fall down dead.

Ironic too that this old guy a mile away in his little room was chowing down on a can of salty pork and beans despite a doctor having told him to cut out salt. And that he was listening to this sit-com dialogue on a surveillance device designed to save the Free World from anything that moved. And that he too would likely die sooner than he intended. And that, with all those anomalies, the only thing running through his mind was that these people were a family and he was not. He felt much happier in the good old days before he started feeling anything at all.

Judith spoke. "I always think it's me that's nuts. At least I'm trying to screw my head on straight, but the world isn't doing diddly about its own BS."

When I heard her say that, I clutched the tin can I was eating from and cocked back to throw it across the room. I didn't: I would have had to clean it up. But I thought, *Girl, this is news? You've lived your life under the dentist's drill and it's never occurred to you that the dentist is a Nazi? This is a clown show, babe, with fruit bats hanging from the high wire, the death squad juggling hand grenades, zombies fucking the elephant, a garbage truck growling its throaty lust for the fat lady's tonnage, and dancing bears prancing to a band called Apocalypse. To you this is news?*

Turk looked up as my innards ranted and then went back to his bone. My receptor started to fizzle out as they finished their meal. Later that night I tuned in to soft jazz in the bedroom. Before or after making love I couldn't tell, but I imagined them curled in a snuggle, and I cursed the Shop for not installing video.

"I wish we had a fireplace," Judith said. "But I guess you can't do that here, because of, I dunno, what, the smoke, pollution? Some kind of regulation?" She was placid now.

"There are gas logs."

"That'd feel fake."

"But you could think of them as genuine fake." They shared a chuckle, not so much at the joke as at Moshe's attempt at a joke. A crinkle, maybe a tickle, a silence, and out of the silence he murmured, "Your son loves you."

"He's all the good parts of his dad. I try to be honest with Josh, the good parts and the other stuff. But I don't see much of the dark side, if there is one. Maybe depressiveness, I guess, which he probably gets from me. Maybe there's hope. It seems like the human race gets worse and worse, but the people you know get better." Moshe made a faint nicker as if something was funny or something hurt. "Well, what about you, sir? Are you different than what you were, I dunno, ten, fifteen years ago? Better? Worse? You never talk about yourself."

Moshe thought about it. You could hear it in his breathing. "I am a very different being. The judgment of better or worse is not mine to make."

"Well, you still talk funny." She mimicked him. "*I am a very different being.*" He laughed. "At least you laugh better than you did when we met. It always seemed as if you were practicing."

"I suppose I was. My parents were very good to me. We had no reason to laugh."

"That's— Oh boy, that's just about the weirdest thing you've ever said. How could you stay alive, for godsake? You have to laugh to stay alive."

"Our people— Our family had no difficulty in staying alive. Until Time ran its course." Another silence. Talking about their histories seemed to be a difficult path to chart. "For us, I suppose, laughter implied a separation, some anomaly, incongruity, something out of place—"

"But that's life."

"And even directed toward oneself, a separation from self."

"Well, my love, I've been pretty damned separated all my life, but I wasn't laughing up a storm."

"True. For you, the fact that you laugh at all, this is new."

"So maybe we've got a future?"

Time had been playing hopscotch lately, and her words got me thinking. I had never doubted the future. I thought of it as a kind of septic system that the present flushed into. The afterlife might be a leach field to absorb the effluent. Definition of a human, according to my old buddy Rosenberg, the Jew we called Porky: "A human is an ape that believes there's a future and thus develops hypertension." Bad future: Yes, I'm going to die. Good future: My kids will survive. Would a human without the notion of a future be human? When I was young I started to develop a wall eye from trying not to see the future. But then I saw that the future would just be more of the same.

"Future? Well, I would hope," said Moshe.

"Well, so you're laughing too. We're both laughing, so that means we're more separate? I don't sense that, my dear, no way." A vague whiff of Drucie there. "Or maybe we're the exception that proves the rule."

"Judith, the exception proves the rule's intention, but in fact it disproves the rule." He was a very smart guy but no comedian.

"You're totally from Outer Space."

Good instinct, girl, though you knew not what you said. The alien, give him his due, was great at verbal ping-pong. "Well, in my extensive travels through Outer Space," he said, "I have encountered very few species as self-contradictory as humans." It was the old ploy of telling the absolute truth in order to be disbelieved.

Judith laughed, then sobbed. A questioning grunt from Moshe. "No, hon, just Sweetie having a nightmare." she said. But something had hit a nerve. "I've always felt, I guess, kinda like a specimen. Something freaky that nobody's gonna keep for long, just put me in a box and label it."

A whimper from Sweetie at the word *specimen*, and Moshe knew what Sweetie was whimpering about. She lay on a cold steel table. The sun was in her eyes. She couldn't move her hands or her feet. She knew she was going to die. She felt the bug eyes staring and thought how Mommy took the chicken's giblets from the big hole in its butt— Then black. One of the alters was there, maybe Ray, maybe Marge, poking off the TV before it got real.

"They take care of me, Moshe," Judith said. Nothing had been said about her alters. "Even when they tried— When one of them tried to kill me, the one I don't know its name, but it meant it for the best. It really did. I mean, hey, I'm well protected if I'm dead. It even told me be careful with the knife. It didn't want me to hurt myself before I cut my wrist." Her laugh was jagged.

"I only see Judith in all her colors." Moshe was close to her, I could tell. I would have liked to say that, but I was just an old hairy sourball.

Judith was joking now. "Well, don't you have some cute little lady space monster in every galaxy?" she asked, tickling him, and he gave a little wriggle.

"Judith, I want to be truthful with you. I grew up with … in a family where truth was spoken always. That seems strange to you, but yes, my species too—" He was laying it on pretty thick. He knew she would take the species stuff metaphorically, though there wasn't a metaphorical bone in her head. But I empathized with Moshe. There's a point where lying becomes so hard to sustain that it's positively heroic. "My species, like yours, sees the future, lives for the future, which means believing in the future, that there is a future, bending all to its service."

"So they all tell the truth in Sarasota?"

"Sarasota?"

"Where you grew up."

A fraught moment, till he recalled that growing up in Sarasota was part of his cover story. Clearly, the art of lying was a second language, for which they had to take an intro course in college.

For no apparent reason, he began to laugh. Maybe she tickled him or went crosseyed, but he laughed as if he'd just discovered laughter, and Judith laughed as if laughter made babies and she wanted a dozen. They laughed like the surf crashing in or the redwood grove springing out of the mother root or other similes in shameless embrace. It was one helluva laugh.

Then silence. I was a sucker for silence. I could listen to silence all night if you could hear people in it. That was new for me. A whisper of wind from my beloved Turk, and I poured the night's first shot of vodka.

After they caught their breath, Moshe said, "Would we be better, would we serve the future best, I wonder, if we never thought of it? If we did only what we felt in the moment, no plans, no sacrifice, no ideologies, no holy wars to secure the future, but only—"

"Only breathing. Touching. Loving."

"Like some wine?"

I heard him get up, give Judith the hug I wanted to give her, and she told him to hurry back. "Hey, c'mon, there's neat things about the future, maybe something hot and juicy coming right up." They laughed, I wept, or at least my eyes watered with the thought that it would be interesting in some future narrative if I wept. I always had that scripted feeling. If I could go backward in Time—

And what would they make of this scene at the Shop? Some junior-grade gruntling would be assigned to sit up on night shift transcribing it, knowing that at this moment his girlfriend Charlene was being humped by an M.B.A. with a thunderous dick. In thirty years this gruntling would run ERP and retaliate on every goddamned Philistine that pisseth against the wall.

∼

Footsteps, the hum of the fridge, and the track shifted to Moshe coming into the kitchen. Josh was there.

"Homework in the kitchen?"

"Algebra. I gotta stay close to the fridge."

"Just getting some wine."

"Gimme a hint on this one?" Paper shuffle.

In a nanosecond Moshe replied, "Cube root of negative A." Josh groaned, cursed, squeezed out a reluctant thanks. Moshe opened the fridge, poured wine, picked two chunks of fried tofu from the fried tofu container, closed the door and spoke at last. "Josh, I cannot say this yet to Judith, but perhaps if I say it to you, then I will have made the commitment to speak."

"Do I actually want to hear this? I'm like fifteen, okay?"

"A matter of—" From the glitches in his larynx I knew that, from every muscle of his soul, he was struggling to speak the truth. That he came from another place, of another species. That his name was not Moshe. That they had no names because they had no separation. That they found Gaia with a cancer bent on killing its mother. That they might bring blessings or death. He played four hours of *Hamlet* in twenty seconds, and he never could say it.

"Another time. You need to finish your algebra."

"No problem."

What would have happened if he had blurted out the truth? That he was an alien bent on killing all humanity? Likely not much. Most times in world history when some simpleton told the truth, nobody heard a word.

"So, carry on. Good night."

"Moshe?"

"Yes?"

"Listen, if you and Mom like … get together tonight, could you tell her I'm in the kitchen, cause sometimes she gets a little too loud for my comfort level?"

A truthful young man, thought Moshe. "We'll respect the acoustics."

## —11—
## *Jared Aroused*

I spent more time in San Francisco now, returning to Gravenstein only to divert suspicions by strumming my banjo on the square and parading with Turk. And trying to moderate my addiction to Judith, whose slender hips and the delicate curvatures of her question marks in adjacent neighborhoods drew me like a magnet.

At each return, when Turk saw Roscoe, his drunken dog-sitter, the beast went into spasms of delight—which for Turk meant panting a bit harder than usual. Indeed he was lusting for Roscoe's vodka or the ecstasy of Scotch, but there was a tenderness in them, a sweet bond between creatures of low intelligence that I envied. They needed some togetherness, so I bought a fifth of Glenfiddich and asked Roscoe to keep Turk overnight. Roscoe was all smiles, if rats could smile, and as they drank themselves into oblivion I scanned Google News for headlines from Niger and Cameroon. I was in a surrealist mood.

On that trip back to Gravenstein, a Friday it happened to be, I encountered Edyth. She had been the Former Victor's friend for many years, the Victor of whom I was a franchise spin-off, and it was a stern test that I was able to pass her needlepoint vision. It's risky to deceive an eighty-year-old lady with purple hair.

I did pass scrutiny, and despite my anxiety about a possible misstep, I loved spending a few minutes with Edyth on the corner of Main and Bodega. She stood there every Friday, noon till one, with *Women in Black*, which promoted world peace, the health of Mother Earth, and other improbabilities. Sometimes Edyth was solo, sometimes there were six or seven standing in silent witness. Passing cars beeped in solidarity or gave them the finger. I would walk away from my brief encounters with Edyth, my faith briefly restored in the viability of the future and the attractiveness of ancient purple hair. I don't recall how I knew she spelled her name with a *y*.

"Edyth, how's it going?"

"Well, don't you read the news?" Her voice was very fine sandpaper.

"What did I miss?"

"We're totally fucked up."

I knew that already, but it was nice to hear somebody sounding honest. She never failed to get right to the point. Nice thing about being in your eighties, I guess, is that you know you won't have to put up with this shit much longer. She almost made me want to last till eighty. We talked a while, musing on the viruses and toxins and Federal plans for waterboarding God, and we had a few laughs. "Well, they say it gets worse before it gets better," she said, "so we seem to be making progress." She was pretty bouncy.

We small-talked a few minutes, while I picked my nose—a means of sending an urgent message to Jared Van Mullen. Jared and I had set up the furtive code modalities that fans of spy fiction love. Nose-picking was a favorite. We evolved a complex vocabulary, and through his clearances he could tune in on my probing of mucus membranes at any hot corner in America. On this particular Friday, I probed with some intensity, despite having unseasonably clear sinuses, to arrange a phone call. I knew they'd be monitoring this old lady's every wiggle. It wasn't the peace sign she carried or the futile corner protest, but that purple hair might bring the Free World to its knees.

"Well, keep the faith, baby," she called as I departed. "Or I once told a pregnant friend of mine, 'Keep the baby, Faith!' And it turned out okay."

∽

We called on stolen cellphones, Jared and I—myself hunched beneath a 101 overpass outside Santa Rosa, Jared in an armored Pentagon toilet stall. We exchanged pleasantries and made plans for meeting face-to-face. I ditched my phone in a dumpster, which was blasted by a micro-drone within thirty seconds of saying bye-bye. Or there may have been a terrorist napping in the dumpster. Or it was a booby trap to deter the starving class.

On a pretext too absurd to be disbelieved, Jared took the next plane to San Francisco. We met for dinner at Tommy's Joynt, a bar on Van Ness with cheap fatty food and a loud clientele. We spoke in code, of course, supplemented by scribbles on a napkin, nail clippings, salt shaker shaking, and that old standby quest for the vagrant booger. Jared too had a Captain Marvel Secret Code Ring from a Fifties memorabilia shop, which he wore on his pinkie as a joke around the Shop. Old standbys, those secret code rings: you clicked its dial to the right for yes, to the left for no. We passed it back and forth under the table.

Yes, he confirmed that Judith was under surveillance, stemming from her contacts with the Tourists. The fact was that however much one might sympathize with the extraterrestrials, and I did, they had made serious mistakes. They arrived in the Forties and Fifties—attracted by our nuclear tests, we assumed—and saucered all over the place, leaving panic and B movies in their wake. They went out of fashion as the Reds grabbed the headlines, and when I saw our office Coke machine removed, I asked for a transfer. Two weeks later our Tourist Bureau got the ax.

What I didn't know, despite having worked in the Shop for four decades, was— But I should explain why I didn't know, though it might be readily surmised. Classified data was intended to be shared only with those whose work required it: the need-to-know concept. But ultimate security required that the facts also should be withheld from those who did need to know, as they might comprehend the relevance of those facts and leak them, thus compromising secrecy. The policy was to keep us profoundly secure in our ignorance.

Now, as I chowed down on meatloaf and gravy and my second IPA, I learned something new. We had always ascribed the traumas and torments that Judith and other abductees had suffered to one of two things. Either the aliens were mindless sociopaths, in which case we had lots in common and might negotiate some lucrative trade deals, or the victims had made it all up. But in fact, as Jared conveyed while dispatching his pork ribs with characteristic grace, the aliens had done intensive advance research. They were in a rush to fathom the human race—which we'd been attempting ourselves for forty thousand years—so they jumped to hurried conclusions. They saw how we treated our own lab animals, our protestors, our prisoners, and just made the natural assumption that we fully approved of the treatments we accorded our subjects. We wouldn't object if we ourselves were electroshocked, irradiated, caged or probed up every orifice with the respect accorded a lab rat. The Tourists were abominably intelligent, which allowed them so many creative ways of being badly mistaken.

"How are the ribs?"

"Very tasty. And generous portions."

"Hot sauce?"

"These are perfection. Would you like another IPA? My treat. Your tax dollars at work." The Shop loved jokes like that.

And further revelations. Judith was a guinea pig from ages three to five, with a few visits till fourteen, when the Tourists freaked out and formed a blue ribbon panel to study the mess they'd made. When they came to comprehend us better, they saw that we didn't enjoy being needled and thumbed and scared shitless. In fact they were inhumanly humane, heavily into non-violence, and their monkeyshines had produced real trauma. They were appalled to learn that they had ravaged a sentient species, though not nearly as rabidly as we ravaged ourselves. And they began to question the wisdom of provoking folks with 32,193 nuclear warheads ready to rock'n'roll. Old Chinese proverb: *Don't goose the elephant.*

Jared and I chatted a while about renovations on the Oakland Bay Bridge. I asked if he'd been to Muir Woods. We sighed about rent increases in the Bay and in DC. This was for the benefit of the Shop, should they be listening in, and they certainly should be. Do weird things like picking your nose too much, and they'd catch on that your mucus was code. Talk about pointless stuff with apparent nonchalance and they'd be certain that rent hikes and Muir Woods were code for something and spend weeks in the analysis, dedicating the world's most powerful computers to cracking the meaning of *pork rib*.

A stocky Mexican busboy cleared our plates. Jared beckoned him closer and whispered something to him. "No hablo ingles," said the busboy and hurried away.

"What was that about?"

"Oh, I just said, 'Fuck you, Lloyd.'" Lloyd was an analyst at the Shop who'd had a relationship with Jared. Jared had suspected him of swiping a treasured high school swimming trophy and took every opportunity to wreck Lloyd's life. It appeared that gays or bisexuals or wanna-be-anythings such as Jared weren't any more forgiving than straights in that regard. But Jared had a practical motive in his whisper to the busboy. The whisper would rouse suspicions and deflect scrutiny. They'd spirit Lloyd, and incidentally the Mexican, to a black site and subject them to what was termed midterms and finals—more of our infantile humor.

I couldn't blame Jared for these precautions. ERP would be watching his every move as he dined with a hairy old hippie at Tommy's Joynt. He was the rodeo clown waving his arms to distract the bull from the rump-sprung cowboy.

Having sent the busboy off to his fate, Jared went on telling me what he knew, clipping his fingernails in Morse code and forming Icelandic runes with the bones of his pork. The Tourists, having realized the extent of their bumbling, had accepted responsibility. After creating an identity, life story and hairdo, an emissary was sent to each identified victim to do whatever possible—friendship, therapy, job-counseling, love—to undo the damage. One such agent was the so-called Moshe. The aliens had distinct natures but no personal names.

As with Judith, some relationships had evolved more deeply, which aroused ERP's suspicions that the victims—two or three hundred in the U.S. alone—might be in collusion with their victimizers to perpetrate deeds too foul to be imagined.

"Like some dessert, Jared?"

"What do they have?"

"Heirloom Jell-0."

"Do they have mint?"

But questions remained. Why was the Shop focused anew on the Tourists, who had long been relegated to water-cooler jests. The wizened corpse from the '47 crash was variously referred to as the Roswell Prunehead, Flyface, the Turd of Arcturus—the wit was unstoppable. Did they fear that the aliens would contaminate the Master Race? That they might take our jobs or our potbellied pigs? That they intended to decree Sharia law or lefthandedness?

And this abduction attempt made no sense. The Shop never did things that crudely. Sure, we made mistakes—wiped out a cheerleader squad, lost fourteen tons of cocaine, slipped a laxative to the wrong ambassador in the photo op—but we did it like a stage magician, with elegance. We could engineer a Safeway line that led straight to Uzbekistan, and Judith would have found herself there without knowing how. But why did they want her in the first place? Granted that blame-the-victim is a hoary political pastime—it's probably in the Constitution—but Moshe and Judith hadn't spoken a word in the past two years that wasn't monitored and analyzed like a Pap smear.

Jared had no answers. He went to the bar to fetch two more IPAs. Upon returning, he informed me that the aliens appeared to be utterly benign—all the more surprising, as they'd perfected human shape and should exhibit at least a degree of anthropoid violence. I'd been curious about their physiology, but he assured me that they were humanoid all the way through, no toothy tentacled jellyfish under the outer skin. This should have led to an obvious conclusion, but I'd spent forty-one years in Shop-think, where *obvious* was not a word in our vocabulary. We were trained to think outside the box and often outside the brain.

Jared paid the tab. He would charge the trip to his interview with a senile ex-hippie as part of an ongoing probe—the pet project of a nonagenarian Senator—of a Beatnik conspiracy, dating back to the late Fifties. It was standard practice to allow agents to go off on their own demented toots, thus assuring deniability to their superiors.

Outside Tommy's we took our leave. Our emotion was heartfelt. Somehow, one drunken punch in the nose had bonded us as nothing else could. Among males it's a fact: assault each other—unless a lawsuit or death results—and you're buddies for life. Worst thing about the proliferation of guns is that bullets short-circuit male bonding. Long ago, in a drunken stupor, we two had sworn a mutual suicide pact against all enemies, including friends. Given the quirks of the Shop, it was a reasonable precaution. No torture could persuade one of us to betray the other if both of us were dead. We researched the options and settled for cyanide pills crafted as M&Ms. We each had a packet.

Jared clapped me on the shoulder, smiled his wheedling smile. "Did I tell you my mother died?'

"No, you didn't."

"Well, she did."

"Sorry."

"It was in fact a great relief."

I didn't know how he meant it, but I had no need to know. One learns over time that some things are better left clouded. Jared turned and sauntered southward. It was the last time I saw him.

∽

Later that night, in my San Francisco digs, I rambled to Turk, trying to roll back the silence. I had picked up another squeaky toy that seemed to please him mightily: a rubber rooster that gave out a *kratt kratt kratt!* like a cluster of startled farts. He gnawed it contentedly, not trying to kill it, more as if extracting information.

"So how is it, buddy, that my life's work has never involved a car chase, a shootout in the desert, parachuting behind enemy lines, or anything a petite lady couldn't do if she was degenerate enough to do it? Nothing more cinematic than a flail at playing the banjo? Why am I sitting here … evaporating?"

A rhetorical question, of course, and my mind kept gnawing mysteries as Turk gnawed his squeeze toy, but with fewer replies. Why had Judith's alien lover referred to Project Chemo, the Shop's technological wonder, useless to the tune of a half trillion bucks? Was ERP reviving it to wipe out Indian tribes and commandeer their casinos? Were we planning to zap mosquitoes or target dictators who turned against us? Could it wipe out purebred chihuahuas, those little yapping scumbags? What was the substance of Moshe's petition to his fellows? And what the hell was I doing getting involved in this old action-adventure? No answers were forthcoming. Only the *kratt kratt kratt!*

Wrapped in this tangle, I realized with a jolt that I didn't give a shit for the answers. My mind was absorbed with Judith. What was this perverse attraction? She didn't meet the hot-babe level of my previous wives and floozies, and the horn-dog hydraulic pressure of my middle years had slackened. She had none of that so-called inner beauty that poetic souls fall for. Yes, a kind of pragmatic humor, but I'd never been attracted to stand-up comics. And to put it bluntly, she was a nut case.

If I didn't know better, I'd think it was the nuttiness: being in bed with her would be a multidimensional orgy. But I'd been in a respectable number of orgies, and while there was always a twinge of pleasure in feeling, *Hey, I've been invited to the cool kids' party*, they never quite met expectations. It was more like five divas singing five different arias, all in the same shower stall. You crossed it off your bucket list but went off to pee in the bucket.

I went on jabbering into the night, thoughts trickling down from the pineal gland, while Turk interrogated the rubber fowl that clung to its alibi: *kratt kratt kratt!*

## —12—
## *Digression: Apologies*

At this point, I must issue an apology. My mockery of those souls who faithfully serve their country in federal intelligence agencies, branding them as incompetent psychopaths for the sake of a laugh, is unforgivable. I confess to these fabrications and affirm that this admission is not made under torture. Yet can a liar's confession be trusted? Do not all incontrovertible facts prove to be relative?

Following up my Hegelian colleague Lennie's observations on ethical standards: there have always been good guys and mean motherfuckers. Our American Century's achievement (though the Brits hold the patent on it) has been a genre of good guys who are also mean motherfuckers. (Not our own mothers: other people's mothers.) When I was a kid, my uncle got a TV, and we all went over to watch pro wrestling. The bad guys fought dirty but the ref—who represented America as we learned it in school, virtuous but stupid—never saw it. Nevertheless the good guy usually won, though if he lost we went to bed with churning guts. But once in a while, the good guy took it and took it until he saw birdies, but then came roaring back, hauling off and slugging the evil nazi or commie or musclebound fag. Justice was done. We'd been forced to use the Bomb. We cheered like hell.

They don't do it that way now. Now the good guy comes out from the corner, knees the villain in the nuts, gouges his eye, and they go at it hammer and claw. So what makes the good guy good if he's as degenerate as the skunk? His costume, of course. He's good because he's ours.

It simplifies things. Ethics could get you caught in a tangle of one-way streets where the only way out was to catch a lift on a scream. My friend Lennie—living proof that higher education has scant effect on innate savagery—once mused, "Philosophers make whole careers on expounding the meaning of meaning, and you still can't tell what they mean." The imperative is action. We'd often go off on a mission with sealed orders which, to preserve secrecy, weren't to be opened until we'd done what we thought they might be telling us to do. It kept us on our toes.

Although: if I put my deeds in a book, it wouldn't impress the public. You'd want to know, okay, who did I kill? (Sorry: whom.) Did I kill Kennedy? Did I kill King or that Minnesota congressman who was getting uppity or Malcolm X or a Beatle? But that would miss the point: it would be unprofessional to kill anyone whose name was known. The trick was to kill 'em before they got known.

Sure, there had to be some reason for it, though it was easy to find a reason. After every slaughter, the President would go on TV looking constipated with grief but tickled pink about the ensuing war. Meantime, the economy was going to hell, life on Planet Earth was getting flushed, civilization flopped like a headless chicken in the farmyard, so what was clearly required were bigger and better nukes. We all sat on our thumbs, waiting for a fart to launch us into orbit.

Of course, from childhood we'd practiced believing that God would protect us and that the egg laid the chicken. We learned to accept two or three contradictory things simultaneously the way a juggler learns to juggle—first one ball, then two, then three, and from there you're elected to the Senate. If we didn't make it that far, we could still appreciate the skill it took. Let's say you dumped your second wife when she came down with cancer and you were already screwing your third, but you're running on a platform of Family Values. What do you say? *My life is an open book but I'm a new man since I've found God and I'm grateful for His endorsement and isn't my new honey-bunch hot stuff?* It never fails. The time frame of my reference would be any day in the past seventy years.

It's hard to stay focused amid the blare. There was a story Reagan made up, or maybe some Leftie made it up as a story Reagan made up, or maybe Reagan was a story we all made up. Anyway: a guy's arrested for rape and murder. His lawyer insists on a lie detector test. They give him the test. "Did you rape her?" "Yes." "Did you strangle her?" "Yes." "Are you guilty of charged." "Yes." The needle never squiggles. They let him go. He didn't lie. He passed the test.

Nice thing about being a professional sociopath: you don't really care about objectives, you just do what feels needful at the time. Most of my darker deeds had some cracked logic behind them, but a few were gratuitous. The worst thing I ever did...

Early fall, nice weather, Fairfax, Virginia. This was ten, eleven years ago when my hairdo was a buzz-cut and I wore a suit and tie, but something about me looked disreputable, maybe my soul showing through. I'm sitting at a sidewalk table at Starbucks, drinking coffee from down the street. The manager—turns out to be the manager—comes out the door. He's a little fat-faced punk in his mid-thirties.

"Scuse me," he says, "How's it going?"

"It's going."

"Your coffee, you didn't buy that here, sir, did you?"

"No I didn't."

"Any reason why?"

"Yours is cat piss." Top-quality cat piss, though, I admit.

"Well, I'm sorry about that, sir, but these tables out here are just for customers, so I need to ask you to move."

"Well then ask me."

"Listen, I'm sorry, this is a public sidewalk, but the tables are private property, because otherwise we'd have, you know, like homeless people and junkies, so I'm sorry, but those are the rules." He's got this wheedle in his voice, must have gotten a master's degree in wheedle.

"Well, my friend, I'm sitting here, so if I see a junkie I'll tell him he's unwelcome." He takes that in, then repeats pretty much what he said before, so I ask, "The manager tell you to say that?"

"Well, I happen to be the manager, and I'm asking you to leave the premises."

"Wow. You're kinda plump to be a manager."

Then he gets very starchy. "All right, sir, I'm going back in there, and you had better get yourself out of here, okay?" Is he asking me if it's okay?

So I tell him I'm going and reach out to touch him. He draws back, but I say, "No, it's fine," and pat him on the arm. "My friend, I'm going to save you years of hypertension leading to a stroke and the need for adult diapers, lots of trouble for your wife if you have one, and so you'll want to thank me." He's frozen there like I'm a doc probing up under his testicle, telling him to cough.

"I'm sorry, sir, but—"

"Yes you are." I walk away and he sinks into the chair where I was sitting. I look back, walk a little faster. He teeters, sprawls face down on the sidewalk.

An artistic tradition dating back to the Renaissance. Not without redeeming social importance, but inexcusable in light of our humanistic heritage. He might have had kids and a wife who loved him and a girlfriend who understood him. He might have been taking yoga twice a week in search of enlightenment, and here I was sending this well-meaning soul to la-la land. In fact I bore no ill-will toward Starbucks. Their logo was soothing.

That's pretty pathetic. But what marks me as the ultimate sociopath is that I didn't do any of that. I just claimed it. A friend of mine did it.

⁓

I had set the clockwork in motion. Identity was frisking with Time, and everyone around me was somebody else. Moshe was under deep cover. Judith was a multiplication table. Benny was reluctantly talking with subject and predicate. Van Mullen was the ocean off Bodega: fifty shades of water. Judith's kid Josh was fifteen, the age where you try out new faces in the mirror every day. And for me, all bets were off. I was a sixty-seven-year-old wild-hair with a brain pacing back and forth like a demented chimp in a cage. Though if that sorry-ass ape saw what was happening outside the zoo, he'd be glad to stay locked up.

The only stable soul was Turk. Turk was solid. Turk gave no hint of self-doubt. Turk had only room in his skull for one word at a time: *eat, sleep, crap*. Who truly needs more identity than that?

## —13—
## *Death*

End of the vodka. I went to the fridge, nothing left but three beers. I never liked beer at night, but I didn't have to like it to drink it. Tonight was my regular assault on my putrid liver. I couldn't stand one more minute of listening to love. I tuned in for the sex, and instead they were making love. I almost wept at the tenderness. In my circles it wasn't natural.

Now it was three in the morning. I couldn't sleep. Turk was snoring like a cement mixer, doing my sleeping for me. Normally at these times I would flick on the computer, log into some Russian hacker channel-surfing between manga, machete slaughters, and hard-core porn. If you kept the sound off, it was restful. You had a sense that whatever happened in the world you were outside looking in. That's where it was safe to be.

I looked at my watch. It was only midnight. What kind of itchy monkey business was this? Chronology was hopping about like fleas on a kangaroo. I hadn't read time-travel crap since I was an adolescent trying to dream myself backward out of study hall or forward into Shirley Westerfield's pants. Turk was still on his belly snoring—maybe snoring himself backward in Time, and by morning he'd be the frisky lapdog of Eleanor Roosevelt.

My audio warning light twinkled. I heard a match strike. Moshe was lighting a cigarette. He'd presumably told Judith he was going out on the balcony to smoke, so in service to honesty he lit a cigarette to let it burn down. He'd be calling Benny, but maybe to help Judith feel less guilt for her own quirks, faking an addiction as evidence of his being only human, even if he wasn't. Soon the familiar clusters of *beep-chitter-crumple-cluck*—little alien blips that fizzed up like goldfish bubbles or burping mosquitoes.

"Benny, you speak too rapidly," Moshe cut in. I couldn't decipher a thing from those machine-gun burps. "I dream in English now, or various forms of Indo-European."

"It shall be so, Mo-shay, my man. What's happenin', bro?"

Of course I never saw Benny, but he sounded like a nice young man just doing his job, slightly time-compressed as nice young men are, or else a forty-year-old trying hard to grow up. I gathered that Benny had been Moshe's handler from the time he'd been first assigned to Lower Slobbovia, a.k.a. Planet Earth. His speech was rife with oddities, and when he spoke a name, he sounded as if he were naming dead Presidents. Later I recalled what I'd never learned. There was no *Benny*, no *Moshe*: they had no names. Not that they were blended into a cosmic mush—there was no mistaking Benny for who he was—but that between them there was no purpose to claim separation. For me the impulse of T*his is my money* or *This is my toe you stepped on* was always preceded, in effect, by *Me Victor!* For them, a name was like a bow tie: you put it on if you needed it, but why would you ever need it?

"Benny, please: current status?"

"Pronto, buckaroo, take hold of your horse."

Benny tried so hard, He wasn't dumb, just a bit too earnest, like beef stew trying to talk. Listening to him speak English was redolent of one of those old photos of a Zulu chief in a beaver hat. Benny and Moshe were earnest in different ways, but in fact I enjoyed their conversations. Of course my old buddies back at the Shop were hip to every word. One thing the Tourists never understood is that wars are won by information. For any normal foe making these transmissions, his goose would be cooked, basted, and every bone cracked for the marrow.

"Response to my report?" Moshe spoke like a Nebraskan using chopsticks, though he might have sounded breezier in beeps.

Benny let go a volley of burbles, got a sharp responding toot from Moshe. "So be it," said Benny. "I will practice American." What sounded like a shiver. "So. Status of petition: Sorry, nope. Status of Project Chemo: Rarin' to go and Hot to trot."

"When?"

"No tellin', buddy."

Strange frantic mix of beep-chitter and English. Benny got more rattled in the face of Moshe's implacable rage. Decisions, I gathered, were made by mind-meld of a council along the line of

Plato's philosopher-kings. It seemed blissfully utopian. Trying to explain, poor Benny sounded like the press secretary of a demented President rationalizing his boss's ramblings but not wanting to come across as a total fool. I had pictured these characters weird but harmless: your English teacher expounding on *Silas Marner*, your track coach riffing on the perils of self-abuse, your preacher preaching. Now I saw the deep menace of goodheartedness.

Putting the pieces together of Benny's sputtered fragments, the phonemes, the fits and starts, some confusion was answered—to my dismay. Indeed, Moshe and his fellow agents were on Earth to undo the wrongs they had wrought upon victims such as Judith. Non-violence was their axiom, and to their credit they were duly shocked at the monstrosity of their deeds. Unless they healed their victims, they themselves would bear the wounds. I knew this, having left my own trail of unhealed victims.

But the catch. Their explorations confirmed that Earth was a living being, sentient in a vastly different way than the normal human wiseass might fathom. It bore deep rivers of knowledge, miraculously calibrated biosystems, a circus of celebratory DNA, a self-crafted soul. Indeed, Gaia was the best argument for God's existence. It might even be God itself.

"Purple mountain majesties, amber waves of grain," Benny recited. "That's in the Bible, no?"

But Gaia's beloved children—us—were parasites. Cells gone mad. Viruses of unrelenting greed, toxins accreting, breath in hurricane gasps, carcinomas metastasized. We blotted out species by the dozens, hundreds, millions. We channel-surfed weather patterns, shattered the plate tectonics, cauterized the nesting grounds. The cancer was killing the mother.

To give them their due, the Tourists loved our music, our baseball, our comic books, but overall they saw humanity as a dumb blind swarm of pinworms. Flying over our cities at night, they saw arteries branching to feed the growth of the clustering melanoma. A cancer is a cell that can't remember, someone had written in a poem that no one remembered.

"Here is the big squeeze, my man," Benny percolated. "Gaia is going, going, gone. Project Chemo is our one serious big-time must-have-got-to-do-it." A raw muffled breath from Moshe. The cigarette burned his fingers.

The Tourists' plan, as I understood it, was first to smooth out the fender dents they'd made in the human race, and then destroy us. That's what would rouse the Shop into action to save our asses, realizing belatedly that those asses included their own. Changing the predatory nature of humankind was not part of anyone's job description.

From reading sci-fi, watching the movies, glimming the comic books, I couldn't help but feel that whatever the space monsters said they could do they could do. I saw curtains for Judith, Rosella, all the fine ladies I'd ever had or ever wanted, and then that snotty kid Josh, and Roscoe, Edyth, Georgeann, dear Van Muffin, Lennie, all my old partners in atrocity, even the primal Victor sipping lattes in Pocatello, unaware that he'd better drink up and flee to Mars. And then humans in general, without bias of race, color or creed: the passengers on the bus, the creepy skateboarding punk in Gravenstein Plaza, the refugees, the cops, the asshole bankers in business suits who were still beloved by their kids. Even the President easing himself on the crapper was suddenly precious in my eyes. And finally down to me, the star of the show, trooper, headliner, ham. No, ye gods, when it came to collective death, include me out.

Moshe was stirred to beautiful words, which landed in dead silence. "Their genius, you see, lies in their variegation," he said. "We see the cells going mad, the toxic accretion, the ravening greed. And yet they make music, they make love, they nurse their newborn, whatever the cost. Many races, and yet they struggle toward the oneness that we have reached. Now we see through a glass darkly, their holy book says, and a few of them keep straining to see. They walk a labyrinth, unknowable to us until we live among them, a complexity that they themselves barely grasp. Your metaphor of cancer, granted, but imagine a cell that struggles to remember, that yearns to heal itself."

"My kiddo, my chum..." For the first time Benny seemed moved to clearer syntax. "Here is quoted an explorer: *They carry death at the core. Their wealth is born of death; they devote their wealth to death.* The explorer was you. You spoke it. Two of Earth's years ago, yes, no? Your misnamed homo sapiens— Forget it, the series is canceled."

Echoes filled my head: *kaput! zilch! nada! outta here!*

"So for the first time in record we use violence against life?" Moshe's words were ice.

"All theirs. Theirs, my buddy. Formula theirs: *Do unto us as what we do unto you.*" Benny's syntax straightened out under the silence of his cohort. He explained it at length, but it boiled down to this. The aliens had wrestled long with the dilemma. To save Gaia, humanity must die, yet violence was counter to their blood, worse than the seven deadly sins to the power of ten. They could never kill, no matter the necessity. Yet at last they had come to elegant consensus: use the parasite species' own technology against its makers. Project Chemo.

"It is we or them. Someone is up shit creek without a metaphor."

The Tourists' plan presupposed that our paranoid vision of monsters from Outer Space would tilt us over the edge. Emissions would target specific DNA configurations and synergize the alien body's energy field to produce lethal dissonances. But our intended preventive strike would give the Tourists their opportunity: they had only to infiltrate one weapons station, juggle the numbers, tweak the target coordinates to home in on the DNA of human belly buttons, and perform a high-tech jiujitsu on the three-hundred-pound drunk with his fist in their face. The moment a Pentagon honcho pushed the button, the human species would zap itself. Death by public broadcasting.

"It's all on them, man," Benny repeated gleefully. "Do unto others, that stuff."

Indeed, an elegant solution, but for a moment I was relieved. This transmission would be picked up by every intelligence snoop on the planet, the scheme would be nipped in the bud, and I could go on trying to hit on gawky swayback baristas. But I recalled how intelligence worked. It passed through the bureaucratic gut like cement. Every other agency would work overtime to discredit it. Two months later it would poop out on the President's desk as he proclaimed the country's urgent need for more Mom and apple pie. By then we'd be toast. It was the race of the tortoise against the tortoise, and we could only pray that neither made it to the finish line.

Moshe asked to speak to the Elders. Some kind of appeals court, apparently. "I will speak to those who—"

"You know we have not authorities. We are network. We come to a mind."

"I have not."

"The decision is final and the fat lady sings."

"I dissent."

Sharp gasp. "No no no no no..." and a wave of burbles and squeals. Benny was stricken.

"I am aware, Benny: dissent is separation."

Benny made a frantic attempt at persuasion. He pointed out, in his preppy-gangsta style, that Moshe's dissent would exile him from the social order, the congregation of the blest. His voice would go unheard. He could appeal the verdict only if he concurred with it, though he would then have no reason to appeal. This was a mode of reasoning that I recognized all too well.

The words dribbled out and dried up. Benny was a whisper now, no longer speaking like someone named Benny. "I am sad, my friend." And I heard something in Moshe's voice I hadn't heard. Not that he ever sounded cheery, but that ponderous gravity was gone. In its place was simple grief. He was exiled. He was alone.

"I too." Long silence, with tiny crinkles I imagined might be their version of weeping. "Well, Benny, your English has certainly improved."

Benny burped. "True? Thanks oodles. I work but fear my slang is highly cheesy." A fierce squawk across the universe, and the echo, *Cheesy ... cheesy ... cheesy...*

∽

One thing about the Tourists: you could never detect a sense of humor. God knows how they ever reconciled their feuds if they didn't have a talent for laughter. From all I could tell, they were as fucked up as we are, though I had to admit they had good intentions and better manners. For the most part I admired them, though it takes true brilliance to be that wrongheaded. Hard to believe anyone could be simultaneously so smart and so dumb without having earned a Ph.D.

The Tourists' comprehension of strategy was like Benny's grasp of slang. The basic principle of strategy was deception—spouting flat lies—and that wasn't in their bones. For them, truth-telling was like excreting: you did it because the body required it. From childhood on up, it was never a question of doing otherwise, though it was hard to imagine total consistency. "Are you doing your homework, Bobby?" "No, Mom, I'm masturbating." "Oh, fine, well, hurry up." When duty called, Moshe could manage the same prevarications with Judith that any normal guy does with his girlfriend, but he had no models for it. Consequently, the Tourists' strategy was a shambles, and that's what did them in.

~

I had to make plans. Next day I would take a load to the laundromat so I could do some serious thinking. It was a little hole-in-the-wall and everything was tile, so the machines made a roar like a squadron of tanks. It was restful. I'd sit there thinking about Judith and the Tourists and my own pathetic life. I'd lose track, run out of quarters, come home with a wad of toasted underwear and three soggy pairs of bluejeans.

After that I could stay holed up in my room. Not that bad. One big room with a futon in the corner and a decrepit sofa against the wall under the windows, a rickety wooden table for eating, writing and setting a bottle of Scotch when I intended some serious drinking that wasn't vodka, and a little kitchenette that gave me ample room to open a can of beans. It offered a view across the street to a parking garage. I could crouch there and drink and eat beans and die without a fuss. It seemed like a plan.

It wasn't the first time I'd faced the prospect of death. Normally, in dire predicaments, you could concentrate on one thing only: shoot or get shot. But now it was all mixed up with Judith and Josh and Gustav Mahler, old Edyth with her fervent purple hair. Feeling that seepage of empathy oozing into my head, it struck me funny that, as it might turn out, the good guys wanted to kill off the human race while the bad guys wanted to save us.

Turk had popped open one eye at the burbles and beeps, and woozily gave his bone a single gnaw. I was gnawing my own bone: *What's dying like? How do I prepare? Will it hurt? Who gets my money? Will I make a mess on the rug?* To my final thought for the night—*who'll feed Turk?*—the answer was discomfiting. The beast gave one mighty snore, and I was out like a light.

## —14—
## *A Dog's Breakfast*

Next morning I leapt into action. I got out of bed. Disaster loomed and I had no notion what to do, but I'd surely get inspired after a cup of tea. Action heroes don't stop to make a list, they just hurl themselves off the edge. Impelled by urgency, I made my cup of tea.

Now I couldn't find it. I had started to drink green tea, which was rumored to be teeming with health. It tasted more like paper than like tea, little more than the sweat of hot weeds, but if I stuck my nose close and sniffed hard, I could get some tang and gulp it down. But just when I was starting to tolerate the stuff, I couldn't find my crappy little cup of crappy tea. I had brewed it ten minutes ago and set it on the counter while I brushed my hair and trimmed my beard and imagined death spasms, but when I came back it wasn't there. I checked the microwave: nothing. I opened the cabinet where I kept the cups, thinking it might have returned like *Lassie Come Home*. Half a dozen cups, two with cartoons of obscene penguins, more cups that I'd ever use, but none with tea. I wasn't senile, I told myself, only forgetful, and on the whole you do less damage with what you forget than with what you remember to do.

This death thing. Despite all rationality, what filled my head was, *Oh shit, I don't want to die!* Giving up life would be like kicking heroin cold-turkey. Genuine cold turkey just lies there in the fridge, to be spread with mayonnaise and dressed with lettuce and bacon for a turkey-club. But when my friend Stevie quit cold-turkey, he was all over the walls and clawing spiders off his face. With death, I imagined I'd be lying there in the freezer feeling a desperate need to scream but not remembering how. Few of us will volunteer to step up to the chopping block, and I was no exception. We're raised to desire that extra edge, and the fact is that those who survive have a distinct advantage over those who don't.

Briefly I mulled my options for saving the human race, after which I could make another cup of tea. But I had that coppery taste of mortality on my tongue and needed to flush it. I wasn't quite ready to leap to the mouth of the cave and spear the tiger. I'd work up to it gradually, hoping the tiger was in no big rush and might take a chomp from the dog before going after me.

"It's okay, buddy, it's fine." Turk looked doubtful.

Already I was doubting that I'd made the tea. I ought to forget it and put on my pants, so I looked for my pants. I couldn't find them. To be sure, phenomena were elusive, though science turned up new stuff daily by the shitload: yesterday, an ancient fossil, a baggy thing with a very big mouth but no brain, no eyes, no asshole. They said it was an ancestor to humankind. I could believe it.

I scanned all the counters for the cup of tea, checked the bathroom again to see if I might be sitting on the can. No, but I was standing pantsless in my plaid flannel shirt as Turk stared at me, waiting for breakfast. I thought I'd started to put on my pants but got distracted, and now I stood like a dithering bare-butt Hamlet, pondering the fourth-act enigmas. Wearing only boxer shorts, I felt unprepared for the death ray, but at least I stood on my own two feet, as Americans were supposed to do.

"You'll be okay," I said to Turk. He lay down, nose to his squeaky toy but not squeaking it.

Again Boss Death was calling me in to say," Sorry, bud, but we're downsizing." I felt a hot belch of panic, like when the ketchup comes splurting out. Surely they wouldn't start killing us until we had our pants on. You'd have to live that dream of being naked in algebra class, crouching under the equals sign to conceal your shame. I'd read that everyone had that dream of nudity, even bank presidents, nuns and legends of the saxophone, but when I looked around the classroom, I was the only one. I wondered if strippers felt panic at being naked in class or if they were more perplexed by the algebra.

Now Turk stood by his bowl, staring up at Hamlet standing there depantsed, a six-foot-tall Moebius strip. Nothing to do but feed him. Special day, maybe our last, so live a little, I thought, spooning out a full can of doggie-grade beef and liver. I checked the ingredients, of course, not wanting to feed him chemicals. Liver, bull parts, lard and salt—so far, so good. Plus the tricalcium phosphate, zinc and copper sulfates, potassium iodide, pyridoxine hydrocloride, biotin—seemed fine, and biotin sounded nutritious. *Fool!* I said to myself. The dog was wagging his tail stub now, but in three days he'd be locked up here, sniffing my cadaver and chewing off my ears. The phrase *a dog's breakfast* came to mind.

"Don't eat me, buddy," I pleaded, "till you're certain I'm dead." He wolfed his beef and potassium.

No question but that the Tourists had a point. You didn't have to love robins or whales to know that we'd perpetrated the most murderous century in the gore-splatted chronicle of human bestiality. We were wasting countless species while pondering the schedule of our own murder/suicide. I had a flash of my sister, who shopped herself to death, maxed out her credit cards, and had a stroke in designer jeans.

I found the tea cup I'd set in the fridge. My pants had fallen behind the radiator under the windowsill. It was going to be one of those days.

∼

At this point there should be a car chase. It's a bore that right when you sense the looming threat, where you finally get the picture, when your joints are popping on the torture rack, then all you see is a chicken-neck geezer pulling on his pants. You need a mad dash over the San Francisco hills in your Batmobile. You need Luke in his rocket ship. You need Bruce Lee dealing twinkle-toe death to the Hong Kong mafia. You need the Lord God Almighty spitting down His wrath on Jericho. For a start, I drank the rest of my tea and zipped my fly.

I couldn't figure where to start. In the movies they have a dozen scriptwriters to work out kinks in the plot, but I had only my hairy noggin. Turk whined and lay on his back, his short sausage legs in the air, squirming with tiny whines, begging a belly scratch. I rumpled his bulgy gut and sensed his thick suet brain do cartwheels in bliss. If I could only manage the same. I felt a sharp urge to pick up my phone and call everyone I'd ever loved, but I couldn't think of a soul.

But I needed to contact Van Mullen. It might be that he already knew, that the Shop was hip to the danger, that late-night comics were already cracking jokes on the death of the human race, but I needed at least to make an effort to yell, "The British are coming!" Whenever Hollywood faced Armageddon, there was always—among the last remaining humans—the lovers, the grizzled survivalists, the angry black and white dudes who had to find brotherhood to overcome the ultimate doom in a grim clipped dialogue. They always found the solution. Whether facing space monsters, vampires, supervillains or sauropods rising up from a nuclear casserole, we always won. It was us telling the story. If we weren't saved, who'd make the movie?

I tuned to my Peruvian hacker's channel-surfing, picked up an old Roy Rogers western. Spurred to action as Roy shot off a bad guy's hat, I sent a code message to Van Mullen, asking him to goose the news up the chain of command to the top of the garbage heap. We had worked out a sophisticated code: my entire report contained in the phrase *The Red Sox look good this season.*

He replied with an extended technical description of the science behind Project Chemo, the specific locator genes, the etiology of electrochemical disintegration—I couldn't follow a word, but it sounded damned scientific—all contained in *Depends on how Yankowitz' arm holds up.* I hoped the Red Sox had a pitcher named Yankowitz.

Yet surely the Shop had already tipped to the news. Why else would they go into gear on the Tourist issue when they'd be so much happier tailing pedophiles on the beaches of Waikiki. They had to be way ahead of me. They would already have the President, his Cabinet and his major donors in a lead-lined vault replete with jacuzzis and bimbos, sending out condolences to the rest of us. There was always hope.

A shaft of morning sunlight glinted off Turk's ruddy eyes. It calmed me as I finished dressing, fastened his leash and led him down to be emptied on the sidewalk. As I emerged from my building, a Chinese lady passed, listening to her phone. Her face was contorted, and I couldn't tell if it was pain or something incredibly cute that her granddaughter said. Leave it to the Chinese to make us wonder. There were dense clouds in the sky, lying like heavy pudding over the city. Over the parking garage, they thickened. Dread crept up my spine with glacial inevitability.

In the face of the imminent End Times, I walked to the Haight, stopping to rest whenever Turk's belly scraped the concrete. Both of us bore that dull zombie stare, as if Death were too boring to give it a moment's thought. We walked the length of Golden Gate Park down to the western end, once around the windmill, then caught a taxi back. Maybe I wanted to be under California skies when the fist came thudding down, so that Turk might break free and run with the wolves. It would do the fatso good.

It was time for dinner by the time we returned—alive—but I wasn't hungry. I opened a can of pork and beans, dumped it into the dog dish. I needed to spring into action, I told myself, but I was prone to these digressions, which followed close upon greater digressions, which had followed close upon birth.

I tuned to Judith.

~

They were in the kitchen fixing supper. Braised lamb shanks, I gathered. Judith was no whiz as a cook, but they worked fine as a team. I could almost smell the lamb shanks. *Razzle sizzle spit*: those lamb shanks were teasing my glands. I watched Turk gobble the pork and beans.

"How was your day?" It was a question Moshe rarely asked. He could usually predict the answer.

"Not bad. It was okay." The way she said it, it sounded pretty bad. "No, it was okay. They gave me a stack of customer complaints to file. I don't even know what the company does. I thought it was gutters and drain spouts, but they seem to be branching into airlines and breakfast cereals and cluster bombs. You can't tell by the complaints: people are too pissed off to make any sense. I just filed'em for future generations. Satisfaction guaranteed." Something clattered. "Funny," she added, "I never ask you how your day went."

"Well, you may if you wish, but my days are quite predictable. Today I sat at the keyboard, I worked on a bit of code to enable another bit of code to access another bit of code. The result of which, when I succeed in doing it, will be that another person sits at the keyboard all day doing something he doesn't really care about but which is relatively harmless."

"You're funny."

"And I had a tuna salad. It was delicious."

"What are you doing?"

"Braising the—"

"Oh. Fine. Okay. Well, mine was pretty routine. Supervisor making cute little come-on remarks, but they're using me someplace else tomorrow, so I'm out of his reach. Although I had to stop my alters from tearing into him, which wasn't easy."

"You're getting control over that."

"Hear'em? Not a word. They're sulking. Or else they're looking forward to the lamb shanks. Guys, I know you're in there." Her voice was held back as if she were afraid of being heard. "Yeh, some control, I guess. Oh and there was an angry ex-employee came in with a gun, but he didn't get past Security. The receptionist said it happens all the time, but still it breaks the routine. Otherwise just another day."

And then, amid the kitchen's quiet scrape and scuffle, he came out with it. He told her who he was.

There are moments we choose to reveal our deepest secrets. That we've been fired. That we've had the affair. That the doctor says six months. That the indictment is coming down. That we were the one who left the light burning for three weeks in the attic. That the time has finally come. And we rarely cue the fanfare and fling open the door and— No, we try to slip it in so it's barely noticed. *I come from another planet, hon.*

I can't think how he phrased it. Some stumbling circumlocution that brought him to the edge and tipped him over. And of course she took it for a joke—clearly one of Moshe's dumb jokes. Normally she would squeeze out a laugh to encourage his efforts at humor, but she hadn't slept well the night before and she was in no mood for nonsense.

"Yeh, right."

But the dam was breached. He poured out the story. The abductions, the grotesque mistakes, the search for the victims, the assignment of emissaries, his creation of an identity, and the detailed planning of their own chance meeting. I empathized with his struggle: it was hard enough to confess that you'd made hanky-panky with Miss Kissyface in Personnel—and you'd surely fall into that let's-be-rational tone, hoping your gal wouldn't brain you with the skillet—but it was more of a challenge to pop the news that you came from another planet. He droned on, hoping that she'd be lulled into acceptance, the way we do with new wars, new plagues, new crimes in high places. It's not that hard to accept the unbelievable: we do it every day.

As he spoke, I could imagine her alters on the verge of riot, but later she spoke of a numbing, a fatigue, the peace of drowning, or what she remembered from some story in school, how a guy in the snowstorm tried to build a fire but his matches kept going out and he sat down to rest and felt a great comforter tucked over him. He froze to death, the story was, but Moshe was fixing dinner and she couldn't die when lamb shanks were so expensive.

Moshe faced her, holding her by the elbows. "I am telling you this. Judith, hear me. This is no joke. I love you."

She heard him say it. He said it often, but now it felt insistent, demanding, desperate. He held her firmly, and she felt Ronnie's hands on her, Ronnie, Josh's dad, so different from Josh, so angry, so hard with his bulging eyes and taut lips. Her lover went on talking, talking, talking in that low pragmatic phrasing intended to calm all waters, to assuage all pain, to suffocate the waffles with thick molasses. He had chosen the right time to tell her: the lamb shanks were nearly done.

"Where's Josh?" asked Moshe.

"In his room."

"Will you tell him?"

"Okay," she said without knowing what she said. Like most of us, she heard only what she wanted to hear. She caught every crisply articulated word, but the words had no meaning attached. At some point it might penetrate, what he was telling her, but right now she saw only that sorry guy in the snowstorm.

At that moment I hated this Moshe whatever-his-name. Yes, I admired his gentleness, his rationality, his love, his courage in telling the truth, and I had seen the gaunt pain of his exile from his fellows. But he'd been schooled in the ways of our world, including our skills in selective honesty. In his gallant blat of truth, he neglected to mention the chemotherapy intended by his cohorts to kill us all. I hated that sweet empathetic loving sonofabitch.

Anger made me ravenous. I regretted dumping the pork and beans into my tail-wagging dumpster. I opened a can of mackerel, found half a head of wilted Romaine to make a salad, and sat down to a feeble last meal. But as soon as I started to feed my face, I began to have comforting thoughts—a frequent side-effect of feeding your face.

Despite my terminal jitters, there was no reason to think that anyone would be in a rush to push the button. The Tourists' social order smacked of bureaucracy—as evidenced by the absurdity of healing humanity in order to destroy it—and they seemed to have evolved a system as byzantine as the U.S. Senate squared. As with us, it spoke of commissions, blue-ribbon panels and competing agencies, all one prodigious dog's breakfast. That might give us time. Like the old lady in the post office line, either side might take years of fumbling in their coin purse for the last three cents of postage.

That was my hope, anyhow, as I watched Turk guzzle the last dollop of pork and beans while I forked my health-ridden salad. The beast looked up and gave me the faintest hint of a grin.

## —15—
## *Appointment at Four*

Judith had an appointment at four. She needed to see Dr. Fran. She needed to talk, to cry out, to get rid of the tremor in her hands.

She had worked at Blecher & Huddle for a month and was on the verge of becoming a permanent temp. Low wage, no benefits, but flexible hours—meaning that you never knew your schedule more than a day in advance. The up-side was that the work was brainless. She had no desire for meaning, for self-expression, for career—mere survival was sufficient challenge.

Today she was filing again. She hadn't been scheduled, but Ellie had called in sick and the crap being filed couldn't remain another day in its three-year-old stack. She said she could do it but had an appointment at four that she couldn't break. Mr. Pinkel extruded a reluctant "Okay, sweetie, fine."

The afternoon was routine, except that every time she went into the hallway she expected the goon squad's armed assault. She had seen too many of those movies. Ronnie, her ex, loved horror flicks, cop flicks, war flicks, anything with big bangs and grim-eyed iron-jawed guys, the fewer words the better. Like himself. Not much different from her dad, except for her dad's cold-fish car-salesman smile. When Ronnie tried to smile his eyes went dead. The only guy she ever felt safe with was her uncle Henry, her mother's brother, a big jolly lunk of a farmer. She loved when they visited the farm. Except for the time when she was very small and wandered out into the cornfield, and funny-looking guys— This I knew from her sessions with the shrink.

All she wanted— Well, she'd fantasized about being a nurse and started to college a couple of years after high school. If her new internal buddy Raymond had been more helpful at the time she might not have dropped out after three weeks of utter confusion. Maybe she could have healed herself, as she'd read in some self-help book with a blissful lady's mugshot on the cover. But now all she wanted was to be with Moshe and get Josh through school in one piece. Lovemaking was good, but she could hear the desperation in her cries of passion. She loved him best when he was in the kitchen cooking, when he spoke gently and smiled his secretive smile.

She kept waiting for the ominous music to swell. Her alters had come to her rescue in the abduction attempt, but since then they'd been strangely silent. She had expected an onset of nightmares at the very least, if not a total breakdown, but she noticed only the tremor in her hands and an impulse to look both ways when she stepped into the hallway. The abduction hung in the shadows like some goofy YouTube thing that Josh had pulled up. He loved to crow at the nuttiness of the world, like watching the antics of kittens before you've felt their claws. Judith had felt the claws.

Filing the dead invoices, she tried to sort her own jumble. It hadn't helped that Moshe babbled some nonsense about feeling alien, like from Outer Space—who didn't feel that way? He was fishing for sympathy or to get a laugh, but she just didn't have it in her. She couldn't listen when he got weird. Josh was weird all the time, but that, she knew from experience, was just being fifteen.

∽

I slept most of the day, stumbling out a second time for Turk's benefit. God created dogs to force us to get a bit of exercise every day. But then, though sensing that the fate of the world was in my hands, I snuffled and snoozed till late afternoon. Once in a while I tuned in to Judith at work, just to check that she was okay.

Well, not precisely. In fact I was obsessed by her. Why? She wasn't sexy in any conventional way, no more so than Rosella, and it truly wasn't some perverse attraction to her mental state: I was never a fan of crossword puzzles. Like finding a piece of taffy in your trick-or-treat bag, no delectable burst of enchantment, just plain taffy—and yet it was what you'd always longed for. Five years ago I wouldn't have noticed her, yet now I was lusting with the fiercest kind of lust, that I-know-it's-never-gonna-happen lust. Hopeless attraction gains force because you never have to calculate the logistics, the stratagems, the consequences—all you have to do is sit there lusting. It's proof that you're still alive, and it takes your mind off stuff that really matters.

I caught only snatches of her workday. She spoke as little as possible to the office staff. Perhaps she felt if she opened her mouth to ask a question, Mr. Pinkel would hear, "I want my dolly" or "I love your fat lips, Pinkie." She could normally rely on Raymond to get her through the day, but he was in one of his pouty moods and would comment only if she made a mistake: "The McCorcorans go before the rest of the M's, my dear." At break time in the Staff Lounge, Marge cut loose with a vicious mumble—"What's wrong with you? What is wrong with you?"—as if she expected a straight answer. Judith stood by the growl of the coffee machine to drown out Marge's imprecations. The notion of employees being termed Staff was as absurd as that sterile tile jail cell being called a Lounge.

A girl from the front desk came in, stood waiting with Judith for the coffee to finish its dribble and smacking her chewing gum hard enough to dislocate her jaw.

"Hi. You're Judith, right?" *Sklurt. Squissh.*

"Right."

"Kathy. Reception. How's it going?" *Kasweetz.*

"Fine. Kinda pressured." Judith hated the sound of chewing gum. If Kathy talked, maybe she wouldn't chew. "So there was something happening down there, yesterday was it?"

"No, happens all the time. Some guy gets fired, comes in with a gun, but Security's there right away. They get shot before they get to my desk. At least they don't stink like the homeless types." She was chewing as if to pulverize the homeless types. "Hey, I wanted to catch you, let you know. Just a little while ago—"

"Scuse me, Kathy, but I have this funny thing about—"

"These guys came in, asked for Personnel, and I pointed and—

"Guys?"

"Two guys. Suits. Sunglasses. Funny. Sorta like the movies or FBI or— And they went down the hall, then came back, left. And later, Gracie told me they were asking for your file."

"My file?"

"Your records. Your— Whatever they've got at Personnel. And Gracie said—

"Kathy—" She suppressed a subvocal Sweetie, who was begging for bubble gum.

"And Gracie said no, she couldn't do that, company policy, and they got real pissy and left."

"Kathy, do you mind? I have this thing about chewing gum. It's a phobia. I mean—"

"Well I thought you'd wanna know."

"I do. I mean, but it just sends me up the wall—"

"Well I'm sorry! I thought this was a free country! I came in here for a cup of coffee and you're hogging the coffee machine and I try to—"

"There's coffee. It's done. Have your coffee."

"Never mind!"

Sudden explosion: "Well, lick my pussy, honey! Make it smack!" Depend on Drucie for the punch line. Kathy ruffled her feathers and went clackety-clack out the door. The gum was gone.

I could picture Judith's hollow eyes. She was terrified of the two guys, yes, but more at Drucie's outburst. If Moshe was right, all these guys and gals were Judith Weller, a brood of ducklings that she was the sum of. Of course she clung to an illusion that somewhere there was one essential Judith, a Judith coherent to the core. But in her heart's occluded ventricles she knew that was crap. She was a swirling muddle, as were we all. She half-filled her cup, took a tentative slurp and poured the rest in the sink. At least at Blecher & Huddle the Staff Lounge had a sink.

Of course you may know you're an ambulatory traffic jam, but it's not so easy to accept it. She might have to wait till she was my age before she'd be at peace with cold facts. She could see where Sweetie came from, that innocent little where's-my-dolly kid. She could understand Marge's acid tongue. Drucie's sluttiness she might ascribe to her violations, but where Raymond got his gayness, she had not a clue. Know thyself, said some ancient bozo, as if it were so damned easy. As for the other voice, the voice that said *Die—*

"You do very well, Judith," mumbled Ray, emerging from his pout. Well, thanks, she wanted to say, but her alters liked to have the last word. She saw that her break was up. She went back to her filing, finished *Nyquist* by 3:15, took the bus to Potrero and was early to her appointment.

～

This whole identity thing. We ask a kid what he's gonna be but never who he is now. Maybe we're scared he might ask us the same and we'll forget the oral report we've cobbled together. Maybe there was no answer: you just buy a Barbie doll or a superhero T-shirt or a ten-inch dildo and pretend it's you. At most checkpoints it's adequate identity. And most of us define ourselves as who we aren't rather than who we are. That's why we need celebrities: I know that grinning baboon with the haircut is definitely not me, even if I wish it was.

For me, the question was a challenge. For forty-one years I had an identity attested by a little plastic card. Now, with my hair sprouted out and my resurrected leather hat, I wasn't whoever I'd been. Was I now the accumulated rubble of my misdeeds, or had my soul undergone a makeover where all warts disappeared and my hands were clean?

People go to extremes in search of identity. They wear flowered shorts on vacation. They join the Mickey Mouse Club. They buy a cap with a Dodgers logo, clueless as to what the Dodgers are dodging. They plaster their name on their mailbox, their forehead, or their skyscraper. They give the barista explicit instructions for their organic decaf soy-milk latte, dark roast please, with a sixteenth-inch of foam. They compete with their victims for victim status. They say *shit* and *fuck* with greater frequency than they actually shit or fuck. They vote for the angriest candidate: rage ratifies identity.

Judith, on the other hand, was grateful simply for having more voices in her head than the one saying *Die*. She loved her son, she loved her weird lover, and she put up with her job. Whenever she started to feel sorry for herself, to grieve that she was Judith, she glanced at the sagging eye-bags of Mr. Pinkel.

I envied her complex simplicity. However loony she was, she possessed a dignity that transcended the dreary files of Blecher & Huddle. Once in a while, I was able to look at human beings with an unfamiliar eye, as I could sometimes see Turk as a beast who was once a pup, who ate, excreted, mated if chance might ever allow, aspired and burped and would some day expire. I could see these creatures born out of one womb. Three or four billion wombs, in fact, but all one; the form, the structure, the chemistry, the implacable urge the same—a single billion-wombed goddess spawning her creatures broadcast.

It wasn't I who said that; it was some guru on the remainder shelf. But it struck me in the heart. Every human is a tryout, a thumbnail sketch. The nose could be shaped this way, the lips pursed like that, the jawbone at different angles. It could live its life by whatever illusions, embody whatever paradox. One grows up to write an opera; one to rob a Quik-Stop; one to toddle into the path of a truck. And having seen one actor's audition, the Producer calls in the next. Every once in a while there's a breakthrough, a creature who embodies what's truly possible. We applaud them or crucify them or both, but things are never the same. And whatever kind of shit you pull, you're part of the experiment.

~

"Where's Mom?" Josh had been in his room playing a video game, something with lots of snorts and beeps, but I caught his subvocals: *God, I need to stop this, it's addictive, it's so stupid, it's rotting my brain—I can't help it.* All the stuff we used to tell ourselves while jerking off. Nowadays they do guilt-free jerk-offs but rot their brains with gizmos.

"She had an appointment at four," said Moshe. Josh came into the kitchen, opened the fridge, rustled around, found some cheddar and cut off a hunk. Moshe was starting preparations for supper. When Judith had a date with the shrink she would come home drained, so he tried to fix her something special. Josh sat at the table.

There was always a distance between them. No unfriendliness, no tension, but they felt the absence of the woman who united them. They could only think of her. It wasn't right to talk about her behind her back, so they floundered for a subject that might grease a flow of words. A common predicament for males, and the prime reason for the invention of cars, football and politics.

"Funny thing happened at school."

"Yes?" Moshe turned from dicing the onions to look at Josh. The boy never talked about school except to ask for a hint on algebra.

Normally, when Josh spoke at all, he spoke in little bursts like the speech balloons of comic strips. Now there was something different in his voice, a casualness that hid a deeper current but didn't quite manage the concealment. "So I got called to the principal's office. And I thought, yike, what did I do?" A breath.

"Well, so what did you do?"

"Well, nothing. Mr. Stuelke called me in, said there were some guys came to the office, asked to see my files. They've got files on all the students, I guess, and these guys wanted to see my files. Made some kind of excuse about a summer job application I made, which no, I didn't. So Mrs. Lawson, the office lady, gave them a form to fill out and said she'd talk to the principal. They acted kind of pissed off, but they left. Kinda creepy. Two guys." He took a deep breath and a bite of cheese.

Moshe went to dicing the onions. "Well, let's see what your mom has to say when she gets home. She has her appointment, and then she'll be home. We're having goulash tonight. She likes goulash."

That evening Judith did not come home from work.

## —16—
## *Getting in Gear*

Another round of blazing action. Cue the kettle drums' rumble as a swarm of fiddles tremble and the woodwinds toot. But this would be low-calorie action. No engines revving, armpits sweating, flights through back alleys or ackety-acks from bare-chested jocks. Instead, we'd see sharp zooms to fingers tapdancing the keyboard, code flashing up on the screen, then heads exploding at the Pentagon. That's entertainment. These days, most of the action is just dudes sitting on their asses till their asses get blown away.

I was slouched at my monitor, drinking green tea laced with vodka, listening to Josh wash the dishes. It was the ERP audio bug, hacked by a perverted greengrocer in Kyoto whose usual fix was listening to women use the toilet. Somehow he fed to a kid clattering salad bowls. Josh was unsettled: he knew his mom was nuts, but she was reliably nuts, punctually nuts, never late, and his panic unsettled the silverware.

Hesitantly, I took a plunge into activism. Flipping to another hacker, a precocious ten-year-old in Burkina Faso, I picked up an ERP video feed—video this time—from the office of Dr. Francesca. The vid-cam was focused weirdly, offering a panoramic close-up of the therapist's gray sweater over protuberant breasts. She could have kept ham sandwiches under there. Someone may have found it attractive, but for me it suggested a pair of hefty ICBMs poised in North Dakota, targeted on the Kremlin. You could almost hear that bosom singing the national anthem. I knew the ERP flunky monitoring the feed could control the camera's focus, so he clearly felt those boobs posed a threat to national security.

The office music was running, of course, with the swan songs of countless species making their farewell tour. It was backed by a placid New Age belching, perhaps a Buddhist bullfrog. Judith was in mid-session. I could have told her, before she'd walked in the door, that it wasn't the best place to be, but historically, when faced with the prospect of saving lives, I didn't like to interfere with Darwinian selection. I was either too scared or too lazy. If you started saving all the people who needed saving, you'd never have time to make one quick squat on the can. Hard to imagine how Jesus Christ found time to relieve himself.

The camera pulled back to a wide shot. Judith was leaning back in a black vinyl lounge chair, eyes closed, head nodding right and left. She was narrating her bout with the goons again, her shrink adding a dutiful "Mm-hm" at intervals, or sometimes a "Right, right" in that comforting way she had, as if listening to someone's recipe for cranberry muffins. More chit-chat, and they launched into another hypnotic regression. I started to zone out, but suddenly Judith was Sweetie again and screaming her little screams.

"And they're all round me, round the table, they say *Judith*, they say *Judith*, in my head they say *Judith*—" It was a thin wafer voice, like talking to your kitty-cat.

Francesca sat in her padded chair near Judith's head. She wasn't taking notes: it was all being monitored. "It's okay, Sweetie, you're just seeing it, they're not really doing it, you're just remembering. You're safe. They're not really there, they're just—"

"Who's Judith?" Sweetie was an only child.

"Go on, Sweetie," Francesca said with a soothing warble, "what's happening now?"

"Real bright lights. In my head, these clicks and beeps and— Needles. The needles hurt."

"Okay, Sweetie, but it doesn't really hurt because they're not really here, you're just remembering, okay?"

They'd been over this territory a dozen times. Searching for clues, it seemed, though I'd known a lady who'd seen *Wizard of Oz* thirty times, just couldn't get enough. As Sweetie was close to running out of screams, Francesca croaked, "Judith!" Sharp gasp, deep breath, and Judith was there. The shrink spoke with practiced authority. "Now, Judith, tell me what's happening to Sweetie." And Judith, in the flat voice of a taxicab dispatcher, said okay.

"Okay. Room. Low ceiling. Bright light. Table. She's strapped down. She's naked. She looks about three years old. Funny little bug-eyed men, like midgets, like in the movie I saw, and then some that look like grownups. There's a voice close to her head, very soft, *It's fine, not to worry, we love you, we're here to learn.* And her face looks like a smile but it's not a smile, she's pulling her mouth huge and the light gets brighter and brighter and the man looks puzzled and the scream starts up and she's nothing but screams—"

Same old stuff. Was this therapy or interrogation? She was stuck in a mud rut, spinning her wheels.

"Can you describe the man who's talking?" Francesca asked.

Something clicked in the subconscious storage bin, and suddenly all the alters were screaming out in a wad—"Toosislebadbet imaguskeylaxenhit!"—the garbled shouts coming out of this plain blank face that showed no more emotion than if she were checking her credit card bill. Or voicing cartoons, dispatching taxicabs, slitting her wrists. She was so out of it she was way deep in.

"Judith," Francesca barked in a shrill Pomeranian yap, "Count of five, wake up. One, coming up, two, three, see the room, four, right at the surface, feeling good, five, hello. Hello, Judith. Are you here?"

Her eyes popped open like a fish. "What?" A flash of terror behind the face, then, "I'm here."

Elevator music in the room again—flutes cooing, whales in labor pangs, the didgeridoo digesting a marsupial. I was hearing what Judith heard as she found her ears again, then her breath coming back in a hiss like an old radiator or an angry cat.

"I'm here."

"How do you feel?"

"Fine."

"Truly?"

"No." Another breath. "Well, as fine as can be expected. Give me a minute, for chrissake."

"That's good." "It's me." "You're fine." "Odious! Vile!" "I'm fine." I couldn't tell who was talking.

Wisely, Francesca shut up. In fact I was impressed with her. She was a rare combination of assertive, gentle, thick-headed, wise, and replete with ethical anomalies that matched my own.

They were silent for a while. Right then I was getting pretty good video despite a time-delay that put face and voice out of sync. With hacks of hacks of hacks of bugs, you didn't have great quality control. I went to the fridge and got a beer. I didn't often drink beer, but sometimes I felt it was the right occasion. I took one sip and let it set. It might still be flattening there, for all I know. I tried to remind myself: no one had intended to hurt her. The aliens had simply modeled their experiments on what they'd seen of us. As far as they knew, humans didn't feel pain: screaming was just something kids did to gain attention. As for the agents of ERP, they meant no harm: they just did what, according to the latest departmental memo, had to be done. The world was filled with good intentions: warm beer gone flat.

Francesca asked Judith if she remembered what had transpired in the session. Yes, she remembered it all. Did she believe that the memory was factual? Judith said yes, then asked, "Was it?"

"Well, I'm asking you. I wasn't there," Francesca said. We were back to a close-up of the bosom. She adjusted her position to make it less aggressive. There was a thirty-second silence. The alters must be taking their afternoon nap. I hated dramatic silences. That was always a problem I had with women.

The vid-cam swung to Judith's face. Her eyes flickered from ceiling to window, the camera following her gaze to the huge wall tapestry, a flaming dragon in greens and reds who did not exude benevolence—might be the shrink's subconscious. I read the label on my beer: *twelve fluid ounces ... malt, hops, yeast and water ... women should not ... impairs your ability ... in mortal combat upon the battlefield of your palate*. It really said all that. In my lifetime career of reading between the lines, I had never actually read the lines.

"It's true," Judith said at last. Another voice—low, objective, murderous—echoed, "True..." Was I the only one who heard it?

The vid-cam had returned to a simple two-shot. Francesca leaned across to sit on the edge of Judith's lounge chair and gazed into Judith's eyes. With anyone else, it might seem a seductive move, but Francesca, despite her bosom and diverse life journey, had all the seductiveness of a plumber cleaning the sink trap. "So,

Judith," she said with portent, "I want to know if you trust me? You've done really well. This is very important, and you're so brave to go through this and face up to the whole thing, which I know is very painful. But I think we're on the edge of a breakthrough and I need to ask if you trust me. Do you trust me? Really really truly?"

Now at that point any four-year-old would know it had better hide its toys and yell for Mommy. There were times when Judith seemed to be a very smart cookie, but this was not a time. You wanted to roar at the cute blonde bimbo, *No, don't open the fucking coffin lid!* But Francesca knew that the wide-eyed bimbo would say, *Hey, it's just a coffin lid.* Judith hesitated, shuffling through her minds, and finally she said, "Yes, I trust you." This was another problem I always had with women: they trusted me.

Francesca took a digestive pause, then recited what they'd written for her. "Well then," she continued in a buttery voice, "if you truly trust me, then you need to trust my friends. I have friends who want to help you. You have to make a choice, and you're totally free to make the choice. Do you really want help?" They wrote this stuff by committee. It would never win an Oscar.

I saw the tension at the corners of Judith's lips and recognized the effects of the drugs the shrink had prescribed, elegant penny candies the Shop was expert in—risopratodol, cyclobenzaphetamine, maybe atroxate—a whole pharmacopeia for dissociations, inducing trust, cooperation, stupidity.

"Yes," flat voice. "Yes, I want help. Of course I want help. Dammit, that's what you're being paid for!" She sounded a little shaky, gritting her teeth, biting down on her other voices. "Sorry."

Francesca eased into her hypnotic tone. "That's wonderful, Judith. So I'm bringing in some consultants of mine, their names are Monte and Clyde, they're very competent, they're here and they want to help you. They want to know more about the people who hurt you, so they can help you. Do you trust me?"

"Here?" Now Judith was shaking hard. *Get out of there, babe. Get outta there fast.*

Dead silence except for a very thin whine that came from someone in Judith's throat. Must be Sweetie under a heavy blanket. Then voices—

"Hi, Judith. I'm Monte."

"Judy, hi. I'm Clyde."

—From a duo in trench coats, reflective sunglasses, trim haircuts, two hundred twenty pounds of solid muscle each, not counting that between the ears. Therapists, undoubtedly. I brought up my face-recognition app, but it told me what I already knew: goons from the goon squad. ERP was scraping bottom. Monte had a wide smile-crack on an ass-shaped face and a shiny blue suit that barely contained his bulges. Clyde had pig eyes, a needle nose, no visible nostrils, the slouch of a necrophiliac tax accountant.

It always started like this. One guy says he's Monte, the other guy says he's Clyde, and often they believe it themselves. Part of their training is remembering their names while abandoning any surname that might connect them to a family, a neighborhood, a race, creed or national origin beyond what's detailed in the job order. They're to be very polite, to speak in firm but quiet tones, interchangeable and implacable. No one is Monte more than three days in a row and then it's time to be Clyde. If they remember when they were little kids and their mothers tucked them in with a goodnight snuggle, those weren't the names that got whispered. But somewhere along the line they got those names assigned and then they forgot their mothers.

Judith didn't like to be called Judy. "Judith," she said.

Clyde didn't like to be corrected. "Let's go, Judy."

"Francesca!" she screamed.

Francesca tried to intervene. "Take it easy, guys—" But one thing those boys knew for sure was the chain of command, and she was outside it. "For God's sake that's not the way—" she cried, but she was wrong because in fact that was the way. The camera zoomed in on her bosom: the flunky in Fairfax must have hoped that it might burst its bonds. Judith cried out for Francesca, Francesca made little hiccups of protest, and the door banged open.

"Kill her! Kill her! Kill her!"

That low demonic voice within Judith. For a moment it startled the goons: a nameless dark voice that rose to protect her by urging obliteration. But the guys knew their business. This particular Monte and Clyde were much more experienced than the previous Monte and Clyde, and experience paid. "Come on, Judy, we're Santa's helpers. We just want to talk." Judith tried to scream through the hand that clamped over her face like a slab of beef. She was dragged through the door and down the hall.

Francesca stood breathing leftover breaths. "I'm sorry, Judith," she murmured. "Oh God, I'm sorry, I'm sorry. But it's for the greater good, and all that shit."

This was a major turning point in Dr. Francesca Stipic's life of turning points. The vid-cam jiggled its focus, and I saw it in her eyes. Her lover Samantha, a gastroenterologist, was moving into a new specialty and had invited her to join. Francesca had felt ethical qualms about cosmetic botox, but now she was ready. She was useless in healing the madwomen of the world, but she might at least help to make them a bit more cute.

༄

Once upon a time, people exhibited a wildly diverse range of motivations. They might want to save humanity while making some money doing it. To serve God or someone like that and become a famous bigwig. Maybe they longed to fuck a celebrity or just to have a nice spouse and kids, to eat breakfast and die. None of that now. Now we all lusted to sell the movie rights to our sorry lives: grab the illusion of immortality. Somebody ought to be interested in the story we had to offer. Our daily dog-eat-dog, our playing the penny slot machine, our cleaning the cat pan, our mass murders. Problem is, with dog-eat-dog you need a special hook, like if you're a quadriplegic and mass murder isn't as easy as it looks. The fallback tactic is suicide, but that's only salable for published poets, which takes a lotta grunt work with adjectives. Still, we all keep up our hope. Hope is cheap.

As far as this story goes, nobody was going to get rich from the movie rights. So I should get on with it, as the whore said to the dwarf rabbi. I forget the rest of the joke.

༄

I couldn't just sit there. I had to gallop to the rescue. I could handle these guys or die trying—probably the latter. Then I saw Turk lowering his belly slowly to the kitchenette linoleum so as not to bruise his bowels, and it occurred to me—I kept coming to these insights when I'd already started to gird up my shoes and lace my loins—that I was a mile away from the action, no wormholes, no Batmobile. I sat down on my stool by the table frozen by a surge of common sense. *Stay out of this. Nothing to be gained. Jigger your moneybag Arab's bank account and buy some premium dope and Yellowtail Merlot, Australian wine, cheap but good.* For that matter, Australia was sounding better every day.

But seeing Judith's wide eyes, I couldn't escape involvement. I tied my shoes. I made sure that Turk had a spread of the *SF Chronicle* to use as needed. I lurched out the door and slammed it like a shot heard round the world. Old Mrs. McClafferty cracked a slit in her door as I strode past. Her radio played *The Flight of the Valkyries*. The game was getting in gear.

## —17—
## When People Disappear

What do you do when people disappear?

Well, that's absurd. People don't disappear. This is America. We've got guns, security cams in every toilet stall, two million citizens in prison, and a shitload of nukes. Crooks vanish, of course, but they always get caught at that motel in Tulsa on South Mingo Road. That motel always gets them. And those pathetic kids on milk cartons—do they still put those photos on cartons?—there can't be that many disappeared kids. Even psychopathic perverts have to work for a living and can't abduct kids at all hours. I had to stop drinking milk.

But in fact people do disappear. Judith doesn't show up at dinnertime. Josh and Moshe wait and after a while they snack a bit, but Josh is hungry and Moshe feels he should keep him company, so they eat. Then it's nearly two hours and Moshe considers calling the cops but decides it's best not to stir up the hornets. He calls Judith's smart phone and work number: no humans on tap. He hits her therapist's voicemail backed by the whimper of dolphins. He questions Josh about friends she might have or places she might have gone, stuff he's asked half a dozen times. They're going around circles inside circles.

As an enlightened species, Moshe has a deep empathic bond with all humankind. Josh is only human, so he tries to feel what he feels he should feel when his mother's disappeared, but he just feels guilty for not knowing how to feel. His life might be making a sharp turn, just a day after Sherry Nybold smiled at him in Algebra. He has a vision of Sherry easing his head to her breast to comfort him for his mother's death. He feels deep shame at the fantasy, but it clings—he's fifteen, for chrissake.

I didn't read minds. I was only guessing. At his age I hated myself for thinking stuff like that, but I couldn't help it. I was no different from millions of other kids who only wanted to survive finals week and get laid. Christ died for our sins, but He'd have to do a helluva lot more dying to work down through the dumpster.

Josh had a sudden mid-gulp thought. "What about the old guy she was talking about? Coffee shop by the place she works? Or maybe they're closed by now." He was starting to shiver and wanted Moshe out of there so no one could see him falling apart. "Victor, I think his name was." Moshe grabbed his hat, an old fedora that made him look like a refugee who'd fled Hitler but not fast enough. The moment he was about to rush out the door, I buzzed the buzzer.

I didn't want to get involved. As a kid I'd found how to stand at the edge of my nightmare and slip out the door as soon as it got too hairy. Whether falling in love or doing a job, I could tell myself it was only a story, an unreal fantasy subject to revision. That's why they invented erasers. Or you could flip to the end to see if it turned out okay, and if it didn't you could pick a different book. You could choose which dream you took for a joyride.

Yet now I was at their door. The intercom squawked, "Yes?"

"Is this the residence of Judith Weller?" They buzzed me in. Up two flights. Moshe stood outside an open door at the end of the hall.

"Yes? What is it?"

"Lemme sit down. I'm outta breath."

"Who are you then?"

"Father Time." This business was urgent, but I didn't like to be rushed. I walked past him into the flat, nodded to Josh, and perched on the arm of the sofa.

"Where's my mom?" The kid stood frozen, his back to the door of the fridge. His eyes were a little boy's.

"Where is Judith? Who are you? What's happened?" The tall alien loomed at the door—dark eyes sharpening into points, his face tense as a hand grenade. They weren't expecting this relic from some two-bit Summer of Love.

I fell into my just-the-facts mode. "So: Judith. Blonde? Kinda weird?" He nodded. I guess he hoped I'd open my briefcase and she'd be there. His eyes were lethal, but his half-open mouth was that of a toddler looking for Mommy through the legs of the

Christmas shoppers. How wondrous that this creature from some civilization advanced beyond the wildest dreams of our science fiction fans could be so helpless. Finally I said, "Okay—"

*Whatta you mean by that?* crossed his face. But he knew, and he knew that I knew, that we didn't have a clue what we meant.

I took a dramatic pause, then proceeded. "Okay. They took her bye-bye. Her dentist was on the take, as was her shrink, so she's got a GPS chip in her molar that allows us to find her. Check this address. The front is a video store, the back is private. If she's not there, she's three thousand miles away and fading fast. Be careful they don't tear your face off. These guys love their country."

Moshe was torn between faith, hope, and common sense. I wasn't the type you'd see as having an inside track to the centers of power, and he hardly resembled a guy you'd send out on a mission of lethal force. Why didn't I make a move to go with him? I must have assumed that advanced aliens would have killer weapons far beyond ours, or I may have been scared shitless.

"Look," I said, "you don't know me, so you might as well trust me because my grandma always said it's your own folks that do you dirt. I'll freely admit that all my life I've been a louse, but now I'm retired. I'd like to do some good in the world, if that's remotely possible. But you don't have time for my life history right now." He started for the door. "Take your jacket," I said. "San Francisco gets chilly for space invaders at night." He grabbed his jacket and left.

Josh stood, back to the fridge, gaping at this mad old scarecrow as if seeing a cross-eyed wallaby perched on the arm of the sofa, uncertain whether to be amazed at the wallaby's presence or wondering how it knew to buzz the buzzer. But he kept his cool. He had that teenager's saving grace of disbelief in Reality.

"Josh, here's the deal. Pack clothes for everybody, toothbrush, that stuff. Remember your school books."

He made a try at speaking. "Listen, I'm— What's—"

"Right, you're asking what the hell in this. It's time to not ask questions. So you're fifteen and you're not ready for it, but it's time to grow up fast, like they have to do in Africa or Detroit. This is the major leagues."

"Where's Mom?"

"Either she'll be okay or she won't. So I'm getting a car, and you pack up stuff, two suitcases, and be out there to meet us at the southwest corner of 18th and Guerrero in exactly forty-five minutes. Clear? Southwest corner, 18th?"

Josh wrinkled up, on the verge of crying, then took a breath, blank face, and repeated, "Toothbrush. Clothes. Car. Road map. Snacks. Laptop. Algebra II." Under stress people pack more than they're told. "Sir? Scuse me?" he muttered. "What the fuck? What— What's happening?"

"Life. Just life. You'll get used to it."

At that point I wasn't really engaged in serious thought, just speeding ahead of my headlights. I called to reserve a Zipcar, walked over to 16th and Shotwell to pick it up, sent a text to Moshe whenever he'd tend to his phone: *Waiting at 18th & Guerrero. Make it quick.* I had dropped an audio gizmo in his jacket, fumbled with my earbuds but no point in following him into the cab, onto the freeway, off the exit to Daly City, into the shopping plaza—though they'd do that in the movie with quick edits and throbbing cardiac music. The tumblers were falling into place. Give the aliens their due: once they weren't utterly clueless, they moved at warp speed.

For me in my Zipcar, a half hour before the appointed rendezvous, there was nothing to do but wait. I pulled in by a fireplug and sat. My life flashed before my eyes, and it wasn't a pretty sight. Strange things run through your head when you're keyed to a state of panic but find yourself forced into patience. I could have turned on the radio but didn't: they might play a song that roused a memory so sharp I couldn't stand it. I stared at the *No Parking* sign.

∽

What was to be lost with the death of the human race? There's a diehard constituency to save the rhino, but we don't have much sympathy left for ourselves. We've worn out our welcome. Of course we'd lose Shakespeare, the Yankees, YouTube, and all the aspirations, the pangs of dispriz'd love, the novels of Dickens, the cheap but stylish double-knits on sale at Walmart—the sum of the human condition. But what a comfort it would be if tomorrow and tomorrow and tomorrow just stopped dead in their tracks.

Our bellies were ever-expanding, and it'd be blessed relief to see them explode.

I remembered a college philosophy prof who joked about a possum that committed suicide because it wasn't sure if just playing possum would keep him safe. The prof was making a serious point, but I couldn't see the relevance. I've always had houseflies in my head.

Still, I had trapped myself in these people's destinies and I felt obligated. Simple as that. All my life I had avoided responsibility except to myself and belatedly to Turk, who looked up at me with the rheumy red eyes of a dissipated child. I could be kind to innocent creatures if there was no way to avoid them.

So now it was time for action.

∽

For the action part—upmarket, high concept action—we'd need a taxi screaming, skidding, leaping over underpasses and under overs, veering into five oncoming lanes with flames shooting out of its gas tank. But Moshe's species were hopeless with histrionic testosteronics. Nevertheless, they had a strange relationship with Time. One of those things I recalled from high school physics: as you approach the speed of light (if you ever do), Time slows, so the faster you go, the longer it takes to get there, and when you finally arrive you can barely climb the stairs. Something like that, anyway. So, with Moshe telling the taxi driver to take it slow, he got there pretty fast.

He pulled up to the video store, gave the driver a nice tip and walked in the door. The video clerk was a guy in his early thirties named Pudge. Pudge had a fat ass and a belly like he was pregnant, a baby face and protruding upper lip that wept out a teeny blond mustache. Later, checking records, I learned that Pudge was named Rex by his parents but didn't look remotely like a Rex. Recently he'd suffered a major life crisis: after lengthy soul-searching he'd come out as bisexual but found that nobody cared. Pudge was in a grim mood that night.

The video monitor was playing a loud cartoon, something about chickens starting a revolution, which could happen, I guess, as they certainly suffer oppression. Pudge had seen it three times that day and kept rooting for the chickens. Moshe went up to the counter.

"May I help you, sir?"

"Yes. You may show me the door to the rear. You have a storage room, yes?"

"I'm sorry, sir, no, I mean, no, I mean—" Moshe walked toward a hallway. Pudge made frantic clucking sounds in solidarity with the chickens. Moshe turned to face him. Pudge came around the counter, his face bulging with the rage of a rampant fowl. "That's it, mister!" he cried. "That's it!"

Part of this I heard from the bug in Moshe's pocket, part he told me later. The startling thing was that no one got shot. He had some kind of gadget which he never really described, but whatever he had, he had it. A whistle in the air and a high-frequency pulse for two seconds. The chickens froze.

Pudge stood fixated for a moment, then leaned on the counter, relaxing against its firmness. His lips parted in wonder. His face cleared like a shoreline lapped by the sea. His eyes focused on the tiny ecstasies of distant stars.

"You can sit down if you like," Moshe offered. "Feel okay?"

"Good. Fine. Yes. Great. Oh my." Pudge lowered himself to the floor, curled into a mellow lump. "It's great. Better than great, it's terrific. O-o-o..." His voice stretched into timelessness.

Even hearing this from five miles off, it freaked me. That wad of misery was rendered happy. No drugs, just an electron pulse, a flurry of feathers, then bliss. He lay wilted by joy. "It's beautiful..."

Moshe walked down a long bare hallway to the back of the store, its fluorescent tubes making sixty-cycle hums offset by quarter tones. I knew that hallway. A walk down that hallway lasted for years, with the throaty yaw of Time twisting and whirring up like the cotton candy swirls at the county fair, where I knew at the end I'd have to be fully grown.

A guard loomed ahead. "Hold it right there, buddy." A throaty old coot: in his voice you could hear he'd been screwed out of his pension, picked up this gig, sat there every night yearning for someone to charge down the hall so he could yell, "Hold it right there, buddy!" and blast away. He leveled a shotgun.

Moshe stopped. A pulse. The guy must have been near seventy but more enthusiastic than Pudge. "Oh hey! Hey! Hot dog!" His eyes went wide in awe, his body shivered, and he started to drool. "Big … beautiful … bouncing … boyoboy! I never knew… Oh hey!" A thin falsetto laughter trailed away like smoke.

Moshe walked past the enraptured old man. At the end of the hall he opened a door marked STORAGE. Typical setting: small room, gray walls, naked light bulb glaring over a chair in the middle. The Shop had gone back and forth on room decor. One school of thought was to recycle those old ingrained Nazi clichés and let them work on the victim. Others held that elevator music and a soft-focus mural of mountain meadows would create a cognitive dissonance more effectual. Right now, the Nazi theme was in vogue.

The duo were intent on their work and didn't notice his entrance. Judith sat in the chair, eyes closed. Clyde was speaking. "Miss Weller, as I said, we are needing information, and currently you are not being helpful. If you can assist us we will be grateful, whereas if you will not then we have our orders. You have a son and we know you would like to get home and fix dinner for your son, who will otherwise be hungry as well as concerned for your well-being—"

Monte interrupted. "Shut up and get to the point!"

"So as I said," Clyde continued unperturbed, "we would like to know about your friend Moshe. He is in no danger if you will cooperate, whereas if you will not cooperate it will limit our options, but that is entirely up to you. That is not a threat but it is a fact that I am authorized to tell you. I am being factual." It had taken him a long time to learn that speech.

Monte broke in. "Judy, listen up! Look at me, lady! Look!" She didn't. "We know about this guy! Hear me?" I knew I'd seen this movie but I couldn't quite recall it.

Without warning, Sweetie screamed, "Don't look at me!" Marge yelled, "Shut that kid up!" and Ray whispered, "Stay calm. Do what's asked," and Drucie, breathlessly, "I'm all a-tingle!" Abruptly the dark bass voice rose up out of Judith's throat, "Go for his gun. If he kills us, we're safe."

Monte and Clyde pulled back an inch. Moshe took a sharp breath. The goons wheeled to face him.

High-frequency pulse, and the walls held their breath. Suspended in Time, the duo issued C-major farts in perfect unison. They wafted, suspended by threads of moonlight, and their voices flowed like warm honey.

"Clyde, is that great or what?"

"It's beautiful, Monte. Beautiful."

"Not just beautiful. It's great."

"Great and beautiful. And so … great!"

"Like whales."

"Yeh, whales, big whales."

"Big, hairy, but they do good stuff."

"Like they eat mosquitoes."

"And kangaroos."

"Kangaroos hop."

"Up and down, they do. They love it."

It was good to hear them sharing their thoughts, not just the idiot drivel of musclebound Cub Scouts but the flow of surrealist poets. They sank to the floor like seaweed. They had never known such peace.

"Yeh, over cactus, they hop right over."

"Cactus, I mean, think about growing a cactus? Sticking on all those prickles?"

"Think what it takes to grow a whale!"

"You said it. Beautiful! Awesome! Great!"

Indeed, there was something truly beautiful, awesome, great in seeing men reach their lives' epiphany. A later background check revealed that Monte had flown the classic arc from high school football star to thirty-year-old shelver at Walmart, almost before the shutter snapped on his yearbook photo. Clyde was a bookish type, wanted to be a writer, but spelling was a challenge. His numerologist said that in three years he'd have a best-seller, so he didn't fret about actually writing it. When the numbers flipped him the bird, a fellow drunk told him a high-tech enterprise was recruiting. The high-tech enterprise was the Shop. Both men were hired for the snarl in their eyes. Deeply wounded men, yet now they drifted in a Disneyland of oneness, embracing each other, weeping, baring their souls, and Judith and Moshe were gone.

They ran down the hallway. For millennia, all races, colors and creeds have run down hallways. They're chased by Nazis, by the Cossacks, Red Guards, the death squads, running down endless hallways one step ahead of the goons. Their feet won't move fast enough, so it's plod, plod, plod. But this was a first: the goons lay dreamily in each others' arms, watching the clouds floating upward in tangerine skies.

My feed was cutting out, so I only caught flashes of words and heard a couple of screams from Judith or her understudies. Women scream better than men because they've had more practice. "Through here!" yelled Moshe, which was what they always yell. They ran out to the street, jumped into a taxi, headed for 18th and Guerrero. They saw Josh on the corner and skidded to a stop. Timing my arrival, I swung by, heaved their bags into the trunk, and we squealed into the night.

## —18—
## *Into Hiding*

Strange when you've awoken in one world expecting normality and find yourself in another. It was the third day of our escape from San Francisco. I had gone back to visit Turk, whom I'd left in the panic of flight, and now I was driving back to our hideaway.

I tuned my iPhone to the intestinal eructations of our intelligence community. On the second day, the cops had been called to the video store when a customer couldn't get the babbling clerk to wait on him. They found two other dehydrated occupants, lips fibrillating with the wonder of it all. "It's beautiful, awesome, great," was the chant of the blissful goons. "Get a life," said a cop.

I turned from the 101 onto Highway 1 toward the coast and channeled into an audio feed of Monte and Clyde being flown east, euphoric.

"How you doin', buddy?" The reception gave it a brassy twang.

"Not bad, bro. Strap's cutting into my shoulder, but that's cool, it reminds you you're human, right?"

"That's deep, Clyde, that's fuckin' deep."

"It's deep, it's like … awesome."

They seemed to have attained an enlightenment of sorts, which I found moving, though it hadn't broadened their vocabulary.

"So whatta you think? I mean about life, God, that crap, you know?"

"I know. Hey, do I know or what?" Their voices were mellow as milk toast. "So first, what we say, we tell'em what it's really like. The straight dope, the true goods, the real deal. We just tell'em how beautiful. They gotta know. So fuckin' beautiful."

"Life, the only life you got—"

"Can't just piss it away—"

"You can't piss it away. And what I'm gonna—"

"What you're gonna do—"

"I always wanted to be a priest. All the candles, the music, that deep shit. I'm gonna be a fuckin' priest."

"No shit."

"I'm gonna do it. So help me christalmighty, I mean just do it!" Peals of laughter, and a bark from up front to keep it down. "How about you, my friend?"

"Librarian. School librarian. Like junior high, cause age thirteen, that's when I started becoming a total asshole. Keep all the books in their place, dust'em and tape up the pages and cross out the dirty parts, cause Mrs. Malloy, she always had a smile…"

"It's beautiful," they kept saying as they were flown straitjacketed cross-country. People say that it's beautiful and sometimes really mean it. I said it once looking at a newborn baby, those eyes floating up to me, but then its mom got mad because I'd called it an *it* which she thought was an insult considering that it was my own daughter. I wondered where the girl was now, or the mom. I had to turn off to the edge of the road and sit for a while.

The agents dithered on, and after a while, I started up again, plinking my iPhone into ERP's innards, listening as I drove:

"Subject escaped interrogation. Agents exhibit no memory of encounter, repeating phrase, 'It's beautiful, it's great,' and similar reports. Video reveals no procedural irregularity. Intrusion of unknown party preceded loss of cognitive functions.

"Agent Tolliver appears cooperative but hums an unidentifiable melody, off pitch. Agent Snerd grins broadly, even under duress.

"Escape confirms subject D422 to be supportive of Alien agenda. No trace of D422, her son, or suspected companion. Search continues. Recommend sustained procedure on detained agents."

Nothing surprising. I was about to tune out, but we get addicted to our devices. I listened on:

"Off the record, George, the screams are getting to me. I'm two doors down from the (ha-ha, funny) Restroom. Like the poor bastards think they're on carnival rides, they'e so high they don't even know they're screaming. What actionable intelligence is forthcoming from men reduced to shrieks? Gotta break eggs, fine, but break them into a frying pan, not into my ears. Or let me change offices with Andrew, who's more the happy-go-lucky type."

Just a normal day at the Shop. Comforting to know that some things never change. I had hopes for Monte and Clyde. They knew peace.

Three days earlier, I had driven this route with my refugees, the space invader to my right in the passenger seat, Judith and Josh behind. I reached back, handed Judith a stick of chewing gum. "Chew this. I'll explain."

A squeal of delight from Sweetie, objections from Marge, who said it'd rot her teeth. "Do what he says," said Raymond.

"I'm sorry, I don't chew chewing gum. I—"

"Chew it, Judith," repeated Ray.

"It's just a thing with me, it's nauseating, it's—"

I detailed its properties: genuine Guatemalan chicle, not the gummy polymers of the postmodern chew, and embedded with nano-particles to disrupt GPS transmissions from the filling in her molar. "It loses its taste pretty fast," I granted, "but otherwise the helicopters are on their way." I didn't explain the technology, since I didn't remotely understand it myself, but I assured her that she needn't chew more than half an hour a day to confuse the entangled quarks, their bosons fused to their gluons. "You might sprinkle on a little cinnamon or mint," I said, "and stick the wad on a clean spot overnight." I handed her the rest of the pack. "Each one should last three weeks," I explained, "though they get pretty disgusting after a while. But you've got more serious worries."

She chewed.

Across the Golden Gate on the 101, I was heading toward Bolinas, this little coastal town just north of the Bay. Bolinas' claim to fame was its residents' resistance to being found. Whenever the state put up a sign to mark the turn-off from Highway 1, it vanished overnight. You had to locate the little road by Braille. A few tourists managed to achieve the three blocks of shops and the spit of sand, but most gave up and settled for tourist-ready Stinson Beach. With the advent of GPS, its days of isolation were numbered, though I expected local diehards to place jammers in the hills. For now it seemed the place to take cover.

I turned off the 101 toward Mill Valley, then Panoramic Highway. My night vision was getting dicey and I couldn't use my own

GPS for fear of getting tracked, so I had to watch closely for the turn, which I missed. I turned around and hit it on the second try. On the little noodle road toward town, I became aware again of my passengers' silent presence, Judith doggedly chewing her gum. Yes, they seemed to be all in quantum fibrillation—now here, now gone, now here, now gone—in sync with the fortunes of Schroedinger's cat.

"So this should do you for a while," I said, turning off on a lane that veered up into the hills above the town and trickled back down to the cabin I'd reserved. "Some years back, on a trip to California, I struck up acquaintance with a lady my age, as desperate as myself, I guess. We spent a weekend in Bolinas. Memorable. She was…" I lost my train of thought, then hopped back onto it. "But I found the landlord's number. This cabin, it's right on the beach. It's good for a week or two." I remembered the fork in the road, sharp downhill to the left. "The lady moved to Seattle. They all move to Seattle." I don't know why I said that.

Bright moonlight, and I saw the cabin. Mustard yellow in the daytime, I recalled, though now it had an unearthly glow above a rough-hewn beach, framed by a stand of scraggly eucalyptus. Clapboard siding, a stack of firewood against the snaggletoothed fence, a wooden bench—my lady and I had thought it'd be great to sit out there at sunset overlooking the ocean, but it rained that whole weekend. That kept us inside, for which I had no regrets.

I located the key under a pot of succulents, placed to make it easy for burglars to find, and the migrants trooped in. It was unchanged. A wood-beam ceiling, an open-space arrangement of kitchen and livingroom, a leather pull-out couch at one end, where I figured the boy could sleep, and a sterile white bedroom not much larger than its double bed. They would find it cramped, but much less so than a cell in Guantanamo. By day the yard was a salad gone crazy—shrubs and granite outcrops and opulent plants with big jagged flapdoodle leaves that looked as if they did strange things with each other by night.

My troops entered in a stumbly slow motion like the first explorers on a newly discovered planet. On one wall of the kitchen nook hung a leather thong strung with clamshells, a flyswatter on a hook, and a luna moth in a frame. A carved Balinese mask: a slit-eyed girl with a mouthful of secrets frozen in her smile. A painting above the bed: a huge red dog surrounded by spindly trees and looking very guilty. Rosy throw pillows on the bed, inviting guests to an intimate pillow fight. In the bathroom, a clawfoot tub with paws of a mythic species, and above the towel rack a bas-relief of a whale with one fervent eye. Throw-rugs all over the place, some kind of Mayan design, or nouveau-Mayan. With my long-lost Seattle lady I'd made a joke about the rugs, but I couldn't remember it, nor could I think of her name. Then it came to me: Lynnie. Bouncy huggable faraway Lynnie.

On the bed I saw three pillows, two with watery stripes, in the center a Prussian blue. For a moment I had a glimpse of a triad with Judith in the middle, her blonde hair spread in the tide. Alas, no time for fantasy. "You're right at the edge of the continent, so don't fall off," I said to no one, but I needed to hear a voice.

Moshe brought in the bags, Judith started unpacking. I showed the boy how to wrestle the pull-out sofa and where to find extra bedding. I put the list of household instructions—recycling, stove, wi-fi, no smoking, no pets, enjoy Bolinas—on the kitchen counter. After a while they settled. Josh sat mid-sofa, Judith on the edge of the bed, Moshe leaning on the bathroom door jamb. I gave directions to the half mile's walk downtown, said I'd phone to check in every now and again. They were not talkative.

"So here's what maybe happens." Saying that, I had no idea what I was going to say, so I didn't say much but took a while saying it. I explained the situation as best I could, but it was mostly babble. *Stay here till it blows over* was a cheap line burped up from some movie. In my experience the only thing that ever blew over was marriage. There was nothing to say except to beware the boogyman man, but they got the idea. For myself, I had no idea what to do except stay one step ahead of Democracy's hobnailed jackboot.

They hadn't moved. Like me playing chess: I knew that whatever I did would have implications down the pike, and my pawn would be trapped in the crossfire though he'd only grabbed that square because it was vacant. But I hoped that when they saw the ocean in the morning, felt the sunlight pour through the windows, walk in the mad flapdoodling garden, they'd come alive gratefully, go on living life one gasp at a time. That's what I wanted to hope.

"You didn't bring my teddy bear," Sweetie wailed, and the silence wrapped us again.

I didn't like to drive in the dark, but that's what my life had always been. I left them staring into space and carted my carcass back to San Francisco. The moon had been out, but now the sky was clotted with clouds. I reached the 101 with no roadblocks, no floodlights, no helmeted robots with incisors set for the chomp. My paranoia was going to waste. The bridge glowed ruddy in the dark, and I looked forward to waking Turk and sharing a can of tuna with the lonely critter. Heavy action gave me an appetite.

The downside of my nonexistent plan was that I had no communication with these people. No transmissions, no hot wires, no bugs. I could only imagine the moment when Moshe came to Judith, embraced her, whispered, "Yes," whatever that meant. And the boy would get up from the sofa, come over to join them, put his arms around them both, sob once, then chuckle at the silliness of their plight. And Sweetie would whisper, "You're silly!" Sweetie was always honest.

I hadn't thought about food—Judith had been spirited away before supper—but I expected they'd find some crackers, cans of sardines, apple juice, and they'd sit in the breakfast nook. Moshe would break the silence, speaking of his mission, and Judith listening like a mother to her child's first attempt at writing a poem—*That's nice, honey*—but never hearing a word. How would the boy react? Most likely the way my own teenage self reacted to anything spoken by a grown-up: boredom, disbelief, disgust that such crap roamed free and ruled the world. But maybe tolerance, even some wonder that this guy Moshe believed what he was saying or that it might even be true. Josh was unusually tolerant of the human race, except for his mother, and that might extend to aliens. I didn't hear Moshe, in my fantasy, speak of plans for mass extermination. He wouldn't want to hear himself say it.

After a while, Judith would say they'd better get some sleep, tomorrow's another day, all that maternal stuff that women are born knowing, their mitochondria inherited from the mother. I saw her looking out the window, hoping the moon would show itself again. And then Moshe would tell her he wanted to smoke, so he'd go out on the porch and call his friend Benny, who would no longer answer. Judith would come out to the porch and embrace him with all the fierceness of the beings within her, and they'd cling together among plants with elephant ears. They'd sack out exhausted, leaving one glowing light in the range hood over the stove. That's what I saw them doing.

Later, Judith told me the bed was very comfortable. Which brought back memories of Lynnie, and yes, it was a perfect bed when occupied by myself and that pungent soul. A pleasant thought, that Judith and I had shared the same bed—though with different mates, different bedsheets, a different me.

Back in my room, I woke Turk and shared a can of tuna. There weren't lots of thought bubbles rising from his brain to clog the ether, so I could think more clearly in his presence. Turk ate his fill and then parked his bulk in his box. He took a minute rundling around, as I'd changed the blanket which had grown funky with dog sweat and drool. He wasn't a fan of clean, but at last he snored.

I tried to give the matter some serious thought. I was in way too deep. Judith's wiry curvatures were alluring, but there was little hope of pay-off in that respect. I might have felt pity for their high-concept dilemma—lovers of different species, stalked by the callused fist of the state—but I had to recall that I was a lifelong sociopath with minimal experience in the pity department. And I was too—*Oh shit! Oh fuck!*—too goddamned old.

At this point, the top-grossing hero would see the whole chessboard, the Achilles' heel, the chink in the poop-chute of the Death Star, and set his one-chance-in-a-million plan into operation. All it took was one bright glimmer, but my brain was as blank as my smelly canine with brains of Jell-O.

I refilled my glass, saw the time: nearly six a.m. on the previous Tuesday. No way could it be that late or that early, but it was. Time was doing its double shuffle. Some line from a story came back to me: *Ticks from clocks that tell another time.* My ticker was playing bebop, but I flopped into bed and squeezed it into submission.

∾

So now, third day, I had driven up from the city to check on my stowaways in Bolinas and then sacked out at a motel in Stinson Beach. I faced multiple issues. How to provide for Turk if I suddenly croaked. How to heal Judith, assuming she'd like to be healed. What to say if Josh should ask me for the wisdom of elders. And how to carry on with my life. Could a slug become a butterfly, or should I settle for being a housefly? Could I bring the scions of Baal to their knees? Not to mention how to save humanity's sorry ass.

I knew that moment of teetering on the edge of sleep. You never want to let go of the day. There's something looming, something you have to solve, to fight, and the hours are dribbling away. It's got a fingerhold on the ledge, but the fingers are slipping, clawing, giving way to the plunge. Tomorrow's another day, your mommy says, and you have to give in. But the first thing that hits you upon jerking awake is, *Omigod, now it's today!*

## —19—
## *Stumbling toward the Light*

Having no coherent plan of action, I went back to Gravenstein to think. People do think in San Francisco, but Bay Area thought balloons float over the traffic blare and rarely sink into the mundane wad of the brain. Gravenstein, still nominally agricultural, had trees. Plus, there might be a message on my microwave.

To explain: some years ago my aging mom complained about her washer. "Everything's computers now," she'd say, fearful she might launch into a game of Grand Theft Auto when she only wanted to wash the towels. But she was right: everything was computers now, and that offered options. Van Mullen and I thought ourselves fiendishly clever to work out messaging by microwave oven. Panasonic worked best. You punched in a number code, scribbled down the beeps that came beeping back. Simple and elegant, though I always felt I was conversing with my lunch.

Returning, I didn't want to rouse suspicion by arriving in a rental car—Victor was inconceivable in a Hertz—so I opted for the bus. What to do with Turk? Sidekicks could be inconvenient: what would the Lone Ranger do with a drooly-eyed beer-bellied farting Tonto? Dogs required more care than kids, since kids grew up, would graduate, get into drugs and out of your hair, whereas Turk just got fatter, and smelly dogs were disallowed on Golden Gate Transit. I thought of carting him aboard in a suitcase, but I worried that my suitcase might start to whine. At last I went online, scored a white cane, next-day delivery, dug out my old pair of sunglasses and hoped that if I held him, Turk would pass muster as my seeing-eye pig. It worked fine, except I had to lift him up the steps of the bus.

Riding northward, I had a chance to think, or at least to think about thinking. Pleasant just to stare out the window at the mighty cinnamon-colored bridge, the houseboats of Sausalito, the flashes of river and exit ramps, then at last the tawny crouching-lion hills of Sonoma County. It would make a nice snapshot: crusty old guy with a buffalo-nickel profile staring out the glass at the wooly haunches of Mother Earth. I kept imagining my life as a movie: just edit out the endless spans of boredom, reshoot the scenes where I came across as a total fool, and give it a zippy title. If the flick wound up as an utter bomb, it might still become a cult classic for midnight shows. If it's bad enough, it's good.

Nearly to Petaluma now, I was blowing my chance to think. My mind was fizzing up sluggish bubbles, like a lava pool. Here were alien monsters bent on killing us but wanting to be nice. Here were vicious federal bastards trying to save us. Here was interspecies sex—an extraterrestrial with a crazy lady, plus a snotty kid—though the snotty kid had his good points, as did the crazy lady, as did the space invader. If that wasn't an up-market high-concept flick, what was? The only character with no redeeming allure was the prickly wilted fossil who'd cast himself in the lead.

One thought buzzed in my ear like a midnight mosquito. I could just give it all up. Let my little throng of refugees piss away their days in Bolinas. They'd work it out or else they wouldn't. No reason to worry about humankind being wiped, as long as it wasn't painful. If we died, all our problems were solved, and at least it wouldn't be so hard to find a parking place. Civilization might survive: most of your basic jobs could be readily filled by roaches.

By the time we pulled into Santa Rosa, I had almost resolved to pay no mind to my humanistic flirtations, the budding of sticky empathies in my heart. Anything I might do would be pissing into the wind. No point in trying to make up for a whole life lived in a toxic dump by one good deed. In grade school we used to do paper drives to raise money for some worthy cause. We brought old newspaper stacks from home, and the pile got bigger and bigger till the truck came to haul it away, and they tossed us a couple of bucks for the worthy cause. But for me, that vast accumulation of outdated pulp embodied my utter indifference to life on Earth. Which grew, truckload by truckload, over the days and years. Let all worthy causes go down the shitter, and the world would little note nor long remember. Quantum physics pays no mind to moral or ethical absolutes, except perhaps one axiom: *It's all jazz.*

I got off the bus, saw that it would be a three-hour wait for the connection into Gravenstein, so I opted for the seven-mile hike. I could use the exercise and so could my porky canine. In fact the hike took nearly three hours, stopping at intervals to let my sidekick die and resurrect. It was past eight-thirty before I climbed the stairs to my little room and waited for Turk to ascend in a frantic slo-mo scramble.

Nothing had changed, but yet it looked strange. Time changes perspective. When my grandparents' farmhouse burned down, I thought I might visit and deepen my soul. I took the plane into Des Moines, drove down to Red Oak. But when I stood on the concrete step up to the absent door, I could only think how small the charred foundations appeared, not enough square footage for all the sadness hung over a Sunday afternoon. I remembered setting out my lead soldiers and throwing a pencil at them. I remembered shooting a sparrow with my BB-gun. I remembered swatting a fly and beheading Grandma's geranium. No space for all that. Every room that I came back to looked close to coffin size.

Still, it was good to be back in Gravenstein. I found a fifth of Scotch and four cans of sardines. I opened two cans, forked one out to Turk, the other into some lonesome boiled rice that lurked in the back of the fridge, and warmed it in the micro. I sat down to eat and think. The eating worked fine, but the thinking had its challenges.

In my rush to eat, I had forgotten to check the micro for messages. I sat on the kitchen stool, poised with a pen, and punched. The intelligence came through: *ERP sees victims allied with aliens. Expanded abductions to black sites. Crisis as fear tactic in next budget cycle, as Islamic fanatics have not fulfilled early promise. New tests on Pruneface. Keep you posted.*

I took little comfort in his news but I always enjoyed his style. Action heroes have scriptwriter squads, but I had to proceed at a more stately pace. Next morning, I hooked my beast to his leash and walked downtown. A pimply kid, River his name was, skateboarded on the Plaza. It was forbidden there, and two blocks away was a skateboard park designed to maim kids in more graceful ways, but he was claiming his Constitutional right to be the exception to the rule. "Yo, Victor!" he waved. I waved back and sat on a bench, half in the sun, half in dapple. Turk crouched under the bench.

Time at last for grappling with serious matters, but I saw a distant flutter of purple hair. Edyth, supported by a gnarled walking stick, once more over my life's horizon, came stumping over the Plaza, balancing a coffee from Friendly Joe's.

"Morning, Victor," she called. "We wondered where you were."

"I exist."

"Well, glad to know it."

I nodded a nod in my dotty-grandpa mode. She stood before me. Her ancient child's face, her blue needle eyes, I felt I was being scanned by Mother Time, found wanting in some respects, adequate in others. And then she stumped past into history. Every soul I encounter seems to stump past into history.

I turned my mind to the matters at hand, shifting my butt on the bench into a splotch of sun. A flash of my mom: "Always look on the bright side," she'd say as she stood in the dark. I sat there ten minutes, my mind a blank. Turk farted gently as if to encourage this becoming a major motion picture, should the human race survive. I squeezed my brow to force my head into focus. Turk outgassed again, doing his best to rouse a shout of *Eureka!*

"Victor, hi!" It was little rat-faced Roscoe, my neighbor from down the hall, trotting across the Plaza past the pimply kid who stood staring down at his skateboard—the whole human race faced challenges that morning. I readied myself for Roscoe. Once started talking, he wouldn't stop. Last time, he had an inside scoop on the Illuminati, the source of all other conspiracies—climate scientists, evolutionists, abortionists, Copernicans. Roscoe was the most openminded guy I'd ever known: he'd believe anything.

"Hey, bro, who were those guys?" He scratched Turk's mangy head.

"What guys?"

"Those guys asking for you?" He looked as serious as his pointy snout would allow. "Yesterday afternoon. They knocked on your door a while, I came out in the hall, said you hadn't been there, and they asked who I was. They were kinda scary, hats and shades and trench coats, like in the movies." Turk rolled over on his back, and Roscoe rubbed his belly. "Hey, little doggie, how you doin'?" Roscoe had little driblets of kindness in his soul. He would have made someone a lovely pet, and not that expensive. I could imagine him in his next life as a shopworn dachshund.

"They identify themselves? Show you identification?"

"No, man, I didn't ask."

It all came clear. The obvious reason why ERP had been so clumsy in Judith's abduction: it wasn't ERP. My first guess was right: the CIA or one of the dozen clandestine agencies, sprung up since that bunch of Arabs decided to bring out the worst in us, was trying to discredit the Shop. It was evident that the Shop had a file on Judith and had traced me to Gravenstein but hadn't yet put their cards on the table. If the Shop ever came after us, whatever they did, they'd do it right. But I had to tell Roscoe something. "Okay, can you keep a secret?"

"Hey, man, you know me." He gave a final belly pat to Turk.

"Okay, so before I moved to Gravenstein, I was forty-one years with a clandestine agency which, in order to stay clandestine, frequently kills their agents upon retirement. So I changed places with the actual Victor, and I'm currently tangled in a matter involving the annihilation of the human race by friendly extraterrestrials. That's the God's truth."

I saw this news dig its way through Roscoe's cranial digestive tract. He grinned. "Hey, man, you don't need to hide stuff from me. I know better. It's the Illuminati. Right? The Illuminati?"

"Well, in fact no, but you're close: it's the Freemasons." He darkened. "But they try to make it look like the Illuminati cause they want to discredit them. It's dog eat dog out there." He brightened. "So if they come back, tell'em I moved to Denver."

"Did you?"

"Safer for you not to know."

He darkened again. Playing it safe was not part of Roscoe's self-image, but I'd given him something to chew on. "Yeh, but how is it you know this stuff?"

"Those websites you told me about. They were a revelation." I had never checked out the six hundred seventy sites he'd recommended, but I knew they would contain facts so transrational they must surely be true.

Roscoe walked on. Turk gave a whine. The ratty little dogsitter had enlisted him as a drinking buddy, never failing to dole out the vodka or Scotch. Turk was learning what it was to be human: expect a premium snort but settle for a belly-pat.

Back to Square One: James Bond sitting on his ass. None of my higgledy-piggledy thoughts had heavy-duty Velcro. I wandered around the town, said hello to a few acquaintances, gave the finger to a white pickup that tried to run me down—just a normal day in the autumn years of life. I walked north on Main Street to a diner where they didn't mind a stinking fat dog beneath the table and you could get old Iowa-type food like meatloaf and mashed potatoes without a parsley twig or a rose petal gracing the heap. Then I went back to my room. The goons had made their point and wouldn't be back for a while, I assumed. Just for security, I set my little vial of nerve spray on the bed stand—potent enough to floor a bear, if they sent a bear.

I knew this was goodbye to Gravenstein. I liked the town, I liked being Victor, I liked Friendly Joe's. But my cover was blown, and I would have to say goodbye. Goodbye, Gravenstein. Goodbye, neatly gardened town square with scroungy kids. Goodbye, old ladies with purple hair. Goodbye, cute boutiques on Main Street. Goodbye, posters for shamanic gymnastics. Goodbye, our certitude that we lived in the very best spot on Planet Earth. Goodbye, my flirtation with flowering things. Goodbye the sweet belief that Spirit shall keep us safe. Goodbye.

By now Judith would be bugged by ten agencies, six countries, and Northridge Shopping Mall in the city of Kenosha, so I texted a message to the boy: *Keep up your hopes. Great muffins at the coffee shop.* I was actually suggesting hope. As I did with my pop-up toaster: stick in the slice, set it to Medium, and stand there in hope as it burns to a crisp.

Turk looked up with his own dreary hopes and a glimmer of drool. The sardines had not entirely scratched his itch. I looked in the cabinet to see what else might be edible to a dog. Pickles? No. Dish soap? No. In my briefcase I had half a Snickers bar, and all the better for Turk that it was petrified. Reading my mind, he began his subterranean whine. I snapped open the latch, found the hunk in the rubble, plucked off some lint and a penny stuck flat in the goo, and tossed it to the floor. It vanished up the dog. I shut the briefcase.

Then opened it again. Among the debris of forty-one years was a tiny box. I had found it many years ago in the kitchen sink of a house that hosted a departmental strategy session that turned into a drunken orgy. This two-by-three-inch blue tin box: what use would it be, and why was it in a sink? I pried it open: empty. But I had a keepsake, a souvenir, wrapped in a crumpled napkin, for which it would be the perfect home. That's what led me to filch it. Now I pried open the tin. Snuggled in its nest, unchanged from decades ago, lay a small withered finger.

## —20—
## *Beach, Waves, Gulls, Finger*

Driving back to Bolinas next day in a rented camper van—Turk stashed with his buddy in Gravenstein—my mind rambled back to the *fugitive* stories I knew. What clever tactics had the screenwriters devised that might serve an old man and his swollen mutt? Earlier, I had stepped over Turk, rapt in the throes of digestion, went to the microwave, and composed an urgent message to Jared Van Mullen. I preferred Panasonic for reliability, but no question it was kludgy. I should try Westinghouse again.

I had paid two months ahead for my rooms in the city and in Gravenstein, so it would be a while before I was missed. I obtained a new ID as Mr. Albert Weatherlee of Mitchell, South Dakota. In Bolinas I would change into dull casual garb and shave my beard. No way could I revert to a crew-cut, but I banded my long gray hair into a neat ponytail. I had ditched Turk's red bandanna in favor of a simple working-class collar, though he remained my most conspicuous feature. I stopped in Mill Valley for groceries, dog food and booze.

I had no idea what my people were doing, but I saw them more vividly than I saw myself. Moshe would have walked down to the grocery store for provisions but couldn't recall if Judith drank whole milk or two-percent. Superior intelligence was useless on issues like that. Judith would be sitting in the garden. When one of her voices emerged, she would hum some chirpy tune she'd sung in grade school, and the alter would bite its tongue. I imagined Josh walking on the beach bewailing his fate to be stashed in a place where all that happened was to live from day to day. Perhaps a fissure might open for him to glimpse a world that included living. Maybe he found the bookstore and bought some Buddhist meditation thing. I had tried that route, but it took me three days to unfold myself. My brain was on a ramble.

I saw the three of them standing together in the night. One stepped out to the porch, another followed, the third came out to see what was going on, and all fell under the spell of the moon. A full moon was veiled in light fog. A pathway offered a trek down to the sand and the rocks and the fragrant scum of the sea. Despite all tumult and terror, they couldn't resist its beauty.

"I didn't know there'd be seagulls at night," Judith would say. The gulls cried over the crash of the waves. "How do they see?"

"It's beautiful, Mom." Josh's first words since arriving.

Instantly Raymond chimed in, "It's lovely," and Drucie, in a mellow mood for once, added, "The moon."

"We're safe now, Judith," Moshe reassured her. "You must believe it." She continued to wonder, I imagined, that seagulls flew at night. Who were they calling to?

I thought of her thinking this. I don't know if she actually thought it, but I felt it was real to me. I might have been picking up acid flashbacks from Victor's leather hat, or it might be poetic license or a blurt of horrorshow. But I felt this crazy woman curled inside me, shivering, as clouds flickered over the moon.

Josh made a crack about his grief at missing Algebra, and his mother laughed. She was startled at his lightheartedness, but she might be remembering that blindered world called high school, where survival meant passing the test, getting a date, or dodging the daily indignities. Kids committed suicide to save themselves from failure, which had so many faces. Her son might view the equals sign with the same cold dread as when long ago she felt the electrodes clamped in place.

They walked a while longer and then turned back. Now the moon was a silvery blur in the fog. Earth seemed too vast for humans ever to find one another. They might signal across oceanic gulfs but never touch. The gulls howled out like mad prospectors striking the mother lode.

"Beach cabins are amazingly cheap off-season," Moshe said. He didn't know what else to say. His training had been state-of-the-art, spanning nine thousand years of human history in numbing detail, yet it got down to the basic fact that every school kid knows instinctively: whatever you learn, it's not what you need to know.

"Glad to be informed," said Josh, who'd been thinking unrelated thoughts related to age fifteen: how to get laid, and with whom, and where, and how many years would it be?

"Josh, could I talk with your mother a bit?"

"Sure. I'll stagger off into the dark."

He walked over the wet black sand, carrying his shoes like school books, his socks tucked into the shoes. Judith watched him disappear. Moshe turned to her. They lunged into a fierce embrace. Embraces were so much easier than speech, but they come to an end. At which point one had to find words.

"So what's to say?" Judith asked.

"I am uncertain," said Moshe, "whether I should be speaking to you or to one of your entourage?" He tried to say it jokingly, but he never got the timing right.

She took a sharp breath, and there was Drucie. "Let's not talk, baby, let's have fun right now. Nothing matters except what we got going. It's me you feel good with, not Judith, it's me that you have fun with, it's me—"

"Judith!" he cried.

Sharp gasp, and Raymond was there. "Judith is under a cloud at the present time."

"Raymond?" ventured Moshe.

"Well, my friend, at your service." Raymond never quite managed to be a slut, but he tried. It was one of those kinky moments between two men who were lovers of a sort, possessing the woman between them as a time-share condominium.

"You never speak to me," said Moshe.

"We're both strong-willed. If we came to blows, Judith would suffer the bruises." The gulls echoed agreement.

"With our species, we know violence only once in our lives." Moshe averted his eyes from Judith's vacant stare, speaking to her innards. "On our fifth birthday, we have a party. A simple children's party with cakes and soda. At the end, a stranger appears. He comes to the birthday child. He places his hand on a shoulder, explains—lovingly—that it is time for the child to feel the pain of violence: its startle and humiliation. Openhanded, the man strikes the child in the face. Of course the child cries, but is embraced by parents and friends. Then the child knows the nature of violence. In our world, this is the one violation we ever know. It suffices."

"And the stranger?"

"Departs for a month of cleansing." Raymond was silent. "I must speak with this woman now."

Raymond recovered his lemon tartness. "Well, right now our contract specifies that you talk with her manager. That's show biz." Judith was staring blankly at the floor as the voice came through her.

"Then we'll start from some distance back." His words seemed to come from afar. "When I was nine years old..." It was a lie, or so I imagined. Moshe's childhood was a blur, even to himself. Tales of his childhood would have been written by specialists so that when people asked him what his childhood was like, he could answer.

But then what was a lie? However much the aliens valued truth among themselves, they had no more qualms about lying to us than I had misgivings about feeding Turk his dogfood. He was a dog, he ate dogfood; humans were liars, they fed us lies. For that matter, don't we all edit our memories, polish our facts, embroider them until they're pure embroidery?

And so Moshe told Ray, as Judith listened behind Ray's eyes, all the memories that had been composed for him and the memories he'd rewritten. And he spoke of his missions to Earth, the mistakes, their debates about such utterly baffling behaviors as laughter. Our movies revealed that Earth had been invaded hundreds, thousands of times by monsters of all shapes, appendages, ideologies and digestive tracts, who were always foiled by human ingenuity. Their researchers were embarrassed to find that these stirring sagas were bald fictions, intended to amuse us through abject terror, and that our films showed people really dying when they didn't, while our religions preached we didn't really die when we did.

Moshe met Ray's cold stare through Judith's face. He spoke of his assignment to establish rapport, ascertain the nature of her trauma, and take remedial measures. With hesitancy he told of the dawning of love. As he declared it, Ray's presence dissolved and Judith was there again in her wide green eyes.

Later, they lay in the double bed of the cabin's cramped bedroom. Josh stirred on the couch, then went silent. They heard distant gulls careening through the hours, late for their appointments. The whole time she hadn't spoken. She had heard his low methodical voice spin out his various tangled skeins but couldn't unravel the words, could feel only the movement of his lips. He spoke over the wind and the gulls, then finally he was silent. He embraced her, and she understood it all.

She expected one of her voices to speak but found her own. "I wish I could sleep like Josh. Any place, no matter what." Not really much else you could say if your boyfriend told you that he was from Outer Space. Of course most women suspect their boyfriends are from Outer Space, though the boyfriends try to hide it.

"Outer Space is not a meaningful term." Moshe spoke as if he'd heard her.

Judith lay listening to the wind, wondering how she might react. She pondered what reaction Judith might have when her boyfriend talked that way. She vaguely remembered a movie like this. There were movies about everything, and if you had time to watch you'd get the equivalent of a college education. But her reactions were almost never her own—so much safer to let one of her alters do it. She would wait endlessly at the reception desk of Limbo before someone would take responsibility, and then she'd see herself kissing or crying or throwing the honey jar at the kitchen wall. It was all like watching an old TV sit-com with its zombie laughter echoing in her armpits.

"What about now?" She spoke in a deadened whisper. "The future?"

"The future? The future is the future. The future is uncertain. That's what makes it the future."

"You said that your people told the truth. Do your people tell the truth?"

"To our people."

"Not to me?"

Curious concept: if truth-telling to your species defines a species, then we must be billions of species, since no one tells the truth to humans. The wind answered me with a whispered *Yes*.

"I will tell you the truth when I know the truth," Moshe replied. "Will Judith hear me?"

"She'll try." Her best guess, anyway. She asked him to hold her. He put his hand to her heart. Deep within, she heard muffled voices. Marge barked about table manners, and Sweetie chirped a prayer for a kitty-cat, but the voices sounded as if they were in mothballs under blankets. Judith stroked Moshe's cheek. He hadn't shaved. In their time together, only her alters could look at him this closely, never through eyes she knew as her own. A panic spread through her like surf on the sand and then shimmered into wonder.

Up to this point, the scenes on the beach and in the cabin and in the bed were only the meandering fancy of an old man with bad night vision on the winding road to Bolinas, his trusty brute beside him, snoring, snuffling and a faint exhale that sounded like *Whaaa?* The vision splintered with a sharp knock at the door.

The couple listened a moment. Moshe got up quietly, picked up a small device, approached the door. "Who is it, please?" he called.

From outside the door, chilled to the bone, I said, "Mayhap the Messiah."

I didn't get the warmest welcome. Chalk it up to tense vibes and the fact that people just don't like the company of old guys. They let me in. I sat at the kitchen table. Moshe latched the door and remained standing by it. Josh roused himself from the couch, said hi, went back to a little desk and pretended to do homework. I waited for them to talk. They waited for me.

Silence is power. I had never used torture unless the guy was a doddering mule that you had to whack with a bat to gain its attention. I would sit there with a receptive look on my face and wait. If he had anything to tell us worth hearing, he already knew the questions, so why insult his intelligence by trying to second-guess? It didn't always work but more often than not. Once a guy broke down babbling about his grandpa, how when he was a little kid he wanted his grandpa to molest him because his grandpa molested his sister, but the old guy never would, and this led to significant information about the grandpa, who was barber to a major terrorist. And it was cathartic for the prisoner. Which demonstrates why people avoid old guys: they ramble.

Finally Judith had to say something. "What do you want?"

"Scotch."

She looked at me a moment, then went for the bottle. I always concentrated better on the business at hand if there were perks attached, a free meal or sex or maybe just a scenic view. If you waited for pleasure till you got to the bottom of the worklist, you'd have a very long wait. It was excellent Scotch.

"You knew where I was. You knew where they took me. How?" she asked.

"People don't realize that everything gets heard. Used to be only God heard what you uttered in the privacy of your perversions, but now it's all public knowledge. Thoughts spray out. And I told you about the GPS chip in your molar." Of course she thought I was crazy. It takes people quite a while to realize that crazy is normal. Two-year-olds know this instinctively, but it's all a muddle from there.

What I had to tell them—show them, in fact—was relatively incredible. I led up to it with incremental doses of lunacy so it might not seem so bizarre when I got down to brass tacks. People don't brandish mummified fingers just for the hell of it.

I nodded hello to Moshe. He nodded to me. He was looking at me hard. The plot was moving ahead by leaps and bounds. After a while he pulled up a chair and sat at the table. Judith topped up my Scotch. Josh got up from his desk, approached, perched on the kitchen counter. The silence was doing its job, drawing the troops tight around the campfire. Time to spring the news.

"Thanks for the Scotch. Appreciate it. Tuck in some serious boozing amongst the festivities." Now they reversed it, turning me on the spit of silence, and I couldn't keep my mouth shut. "Thing is," I groused, "I can't go back to my favorite coffee shop. That's a real loss for the coffee, not to mention Georgeann. Cause it might seem improbable, but she had a certain attraction in the eyes of this knobby old vertebrate." I tried to get to the point. "So I can't go back now. They got these vibes-detectors. You heard of good vibes, bad vibes, but now it's refined down to vibes as specific as DNA.

Your psyche sends out beams like a cell phone signal, same principle. Like a guitar string that picks up a sympathetic vibration, so it looks for the vibe that turns it on and, tallyho, contact. Once it's got your vibes it can find you anywhere on the planet. Pretty sure they're laying for me at the coffee shop."

They drew the obvious conclusion that I was a lunatic. "No danger," I said. "Just carry these." I dug in my pocket and pulled out three iPod knock-offs, which I handed across the table. "The classic pattern: the only way to defeat technology that cost billions is with stuff that retails at under a hundred bucks. Keep one of these on auto-play, so it puts out a signal to out-vibe your personal vibes. *Pink Floyd* works great." Josh looked at me, hoping I was kidding, but he knew better. Kids age fast if they're anywhere in my vicinity.

I glanced around the cabin, hopeful of recapturing a whiff of my long-gone Portland lady Lynnie. Same ratty furniture, gas range with the smell of gas, the same throw rugs, the sad red dog over the bed. Strange how the light would change the decor from one time to another. And there must be— There it was on the west wall: an oil painting of the ocean, same ocean you could see out the window a hundred yards away. But no one to go to bed with, and that made all the difference.

"And so what are we doing here?" Moshe asked. He didn't really want to know. Well, he did and he didn't. I didn't really want to say. I did and I didn't. But seven billion people's lives depended on it, so I worked my way to an answer.

"Why are we here? Well, apart from basic precautions in the face of madness, we're here to check out my briefcase." I set it on the table. One sticker said *PEACE NOW*, and others equally futile stuff.

"Briefcase?"

"Well, it contains information. This is the age of information. World economy used to be based on gold, now it's all about the data, getting the lowdown, knowing the score, grabbing the facts by the short hairs." I talked like that sometimes because once I saw a movie where the tough guys talked in non sequiturs and babbled about all the doughnuts they'd eaten in life, and it sounded very intimidating. From me it sounded like having a screw loose. Which of course I did.

Judith and Moshe sat silent. Josh fiddled with a salt shaker, shaking salt into his palm and licking it until Judith said, "Josh, don't." In that ragged light she looked so much like my first wife. Short, blonde, intense, and loco.

"Well, of course you know," I said, "information is a commodity. It is not free. You pay the piper to pipe."

"So what do you want?" she said in a razor voice.

"Well, I wouldn't mind for your friend Drucie to do some interesting things to me." It was the truest thing I'd ever said, but it earned me an icy stare. "But I'll settle for less. Maybe just somebody saying, 'Victor, you're a sweet old guy.'"

I waited. She was a tough little cookie. I swear her eyes turned from green to steel blue. She could rip off your balls if they dangled as low as mine. I knocked down my price a notch. "How about another Scotch?"

She poured. I looked around at the others. "That'll do," I said. "What's in the briefcase… Well, it has implications." I clicked the clasp, opened the lid, reached in, fiddled a bit, and held up the wizened finger.

~

It's always a comfort when the tumblers fall into place. You've picked the lock's innards or dialed a thousand combinations, and suddenly, with a click, it's open. One day, when I was a very tiny kid, my grandma announced that the skies had opened over Korea and the clouds formed Jesus' face. I never knew how she knew that or what came of it, but ever since that primeval moment I had watched for the skies to open.

Now, nothing so astronomical, but I realized with a sharp stab of *Eureka!* that my impression of Time running backward, flowing uphill, wasn't entirely a consequence of senility. It was just the Tourists' speedboat raising a wake that jostled my little kayak. Time is an anthill: stir it and the ants go nuts.

## —21—
## *Pruneface Unmasked*

From this point on, there's no promise of running up and down hallways, much less mystical joy-rays from pocket devices. Nowadays the honchos of the entertainment industry—be it comedy specials or drone strikes or genocides—just check the purchase order, tap the keys, mutter a silent *Bingo!* and spurt out a firestorm without moving their asses out of their swivel chairs. Not that much difference between amusement and death. It's a far cry from naked berserkers screaming down the hillside brandishing battle axes. Now we're civilized. We kill antiseptically.

～

In the presence of my Bolinas fugitives, I produced the finger. They stared, not quite knowing what they were looking at. They were very quiet. Finally Sweetie broke the silence. "Ick."

The finger, I explained to the baffled trio, was a souvenir. Some guys collect stamps, some collect parking tickets, some collect ears. That particular finger was off the poor schmuck who ran a celestial stop sign in Roswell, New Mexico, in 1948. The Roswell Pruneface, we called him. No resemblance to Moshe, but consider human beings: you've got pygmies and basketball players, spindle-shanks and fireplugs, though we all look alike to the worms.

Initially, Pruneface caused deep controversy, from the Army right up to the tiny prefrontal cortex of Harry S. Truman. Should they reveal his existence to the world? The bigwigs were all for going public: scaring the holy shit out of the public was a time-honored American tradition. But our allies advised against it, and the Vatican went apeshit. What would they do with entirely new humanoids who weren't mentioned in the Bible, possibly fell outside the jurisdiction for Original Sin, and might turn out to be Jewish? Since we needed the Vatican against the Italian Communist Party, we kept the little bastard on ice.

Of course I wasn't present at the crash, being only seven years old. By the time I was recruited into America's sub-basement, Pruneface was old news. Most things at the Shop, even at Level Three Clearance, were on a need-to-know basis, and nobody really needed to know about Pruneface except the guy who kept him in the fridge. But I was briefly assigned to Roswell to spy on a suspect colonel and had a drinking buddy who got me invited to join the Pruneface Club. Pretty adolescent stuff. They'd wheel out the naked corpse on his slab, with the Stars & Stripes taped to his tiny petrified penis. As an initiate you had to chug a pinf of bourbon, and on the final swig the clutch of birdbrains screamed in raucous unison, "Space monsters!" It was an honor accorded to few.

At that point of my life I wasn't much different from the other deplorables at Level Three. If a thought flicked through my mind, it'd root there like those African worms that get into little kids' eyes. I was pretty much of a chickenshit, but access to Pruneface was a no-brainer. Hack the security code, lure the guard away by means of a low-cost hooker, pull out the stiff on the slab and make my selection. I wasn't greedy: I lopped off one curled finger and took it home. James Bond would have filched the prick.

Obviously Moshe hated me calling it Pruneface. He asked how they'd preserved it. Dead aliens, apparently, tended to resorb into the atmosphere, which limited our supply of dead aliens. Simple: they pickled it. The Tourists had a variety of body types and seemed to hold fervently to that kindergarten preachment that it's not the outside but the inside that counts. Sheer nonsense, except for guys around age sixteen when you're dying to get inside any girl on the planet no matter what the outside, and so it's definitely the inside that counts. I didn't pursue that thread.

"And so what follows from this?" asked Moshe.

"Hey, listen," said Judith, "this is a little too much."

With some restraint I declared that despite her many attributes she wasn't the one to judge how much was too much. "This is Planet Earth! Open your eyes!" I said with a melodramatic gesture, like God directing traffic.

My message was time-sensitive, but sometimes I got into a two-year-old's pout. Judith relented. "I take it you're trying to make a point." That would have to pass for an apology, so I summarized the specimen's history and the fact that the early tests confirmed that it was human. Which meant that either it represented some evolutionary eddy from a far-flung galaxy or it was fake. The Shop had concluded the latter—likely a deformed anthropoid sent by the Soviets to freak us out—but I had my doubts.

So much for the small talk. There was madness in my method. I had their rapt attention. "Well now," I continued, "when DNA came into the picture, a secret study was commissioned. Dr. Corliss Philpott, an eminent evolutionary physiologist, compared the remains of our sorry friend with present-day humans and reached remarkable conclusions. Which of course sat around dead to the world, till this wizened finger tapped my head and raised a tweet of *Aha!* This briefcase holds the file of Dr. Philpott's findings, not to mention a DNA sample of Dr. Philpott."

"We are well advanced in the understanding of DNA," Moshe said abruptly, "and various theories of cosmic diffusion, the most likely being intergalactic travel over the aeons."

"Neat idea. But think, my friend: what would be the biggest surprise?"

Dead silence.

Josh spoke, too loudly: "Okay, so I read a story where the aliens were human, but from a different time dimension, and we were their ancestors, only they didn't know it. And there was another story where humans evolved on Jupiter and then moved to other planets and— Or there's one big monster planet and the humans blow it apart, so— I mean, those are stories, but— Okay, but just stop it, okay? Stop it!" He stalked into the bedroom and slammed the door.

"Sorry to upset the boy."

The others sat blank-faced. A minute later the door opened, Josh came out, went to the desk, pulled out his algebra book.

Moshe was frozen. I had a hunch he knew what I was going to say. I had absorbed enough from his badinage with Benny to gather hints of their massive delusions, but I couldn't imagine that an old coot carrying a pickled finger in his briefcase was the only one in the galaxy who'd looked at the lab results and said, "That's funny." But things fall through the cracks. Victor's Law: Any culture advanced in knowledge was equally advanced in ignorance. It required a high IQ to ignore the obvious, and Marie Antoinette couldn't imagine the guillotine till her eyes looked up from the basket. We created vast bureaucracies to analyze diplomatic memoranda, phoneme by phoneme, whereas dogs just sniffed butts. So the aliens studied us and we studied them, but nobody studied themselves.

"Please say what you need to say." This was Moshe.

"You honestly don't know?"

"I don't buy it." It was Marge. That's all she said. Nobody knew what she meant.

"How did you come to this planet?" I asked.

He gave the expected explanations: warp drive, wormholes, old sci-fi stuff. "But I am no engineer. I don't grasp the technology, nor do I need to." It was clear that he didn't have a clue. I heard Josh huffing at his algebra book, Judith restraining her demons. I leaned closer to Moshe.

"I'll give you a hint. You were already here. You're us."

He murdered me with his eyes. After a bit Josh jerked up and said, "Oh." He got it, apparently, but went back to pretending to do his schoolwork. Clearly Judith was clueless, even though women were pretty good at puzzles, crosswords, acrostics. That's why a few of them ever put up with me.

At this point, Ray suddenly burst out. "I'm in full agreement that the entire business is absurd. Which makes it totally credible." Judith gave him a dirty look—strange, considering that he was her. I could almost see the backside of her eyeballs.

"What about Santa Claus?" Sweetie asked. It was a valid question, considering.

Moshe rose. "We should speak privately."

"Glad to." I got up, went to the door, turned to Judith. "Got any eggs? Fix me some eggs? I'd really love an omelet."

"Cheese?" she asked. I loved her for that.

When he opened the door, I was startled to see it was still night. I had expected that Time would commence its Irish jig, but we were still dancing to the dull beat of cause-and-effect: open the door, go through it, feel the nippy breeze. We walked out to the beach. The surf was quiet, the moon blaring out full. He was talking, and I was trying to listen, but there was nothing like California to stick icy fingers into every elbow and crotch. I was wearing my jacket, and all the time I was chilled to the bone.

He started off with what I'd heard a dozen times. The aliens had seen a planet heading straight for the dumpster. Species were dying like flies—except for the flies, who were doing fine. The climate was in epileptic infarction, the oceans unflushed toilets. And yet, compared to the paved-over planet they came from, it was paradise. They sent emissaries—he among them—to heal the psychoses they had managed to inflict in their first expeditions, but they had to destroy the cancer: us. That old principle of bureaucracy, straight out of the Bible: Let not thy right-hand bureau know what thy left-hand bureau doeth. That much I already knew.

His speech became more hesitant. Time was precious, and I wanted to push through the traffic jam in his head, but I held back. He went on with his chronicle, which got grimmer, as chronicles tend to do. It was the predictable mainstream sci-fi: a society achieving miraculous technology, yet there was no free lunch. Their planet had gone to hell. The devastation of nature went past the tipping point. They survived by technological back-flips, creating edible proteins out of swamp gas, and when the swamps went dry, coaxing nutrition out of rocks. Water's elements were fused dribble by dribble. Their planet was a parking lot, which gave them an even greater stake in saving ours.

He sat on a log, staring up at the moon. I was starting to shiver and my ears were going numb. I could tell his head was churning. Time was pressing, but I couldn't rush it. I could hear one cranky seagull above the ruffled surf wanting to put in a word.

"This we were taught. This we believed. This we knew to be true. From my infancy I had known we were at the end of survival. All hope at an end. We would die like all the countless species we had erased—by fire or ice, plague or warfare, drowning or thirst. And then, one day, the singularity."

I waited for the punchline. He still stared at the moon. I thought he might start to howl, crow, or go nuts.

"It was the point at which technological advancement explodes beyond the laws of causation, where speed outpaces control, where the wheels leave the freeway, spinning on air. Or the point where the rage and pain and grief boil up in volcanic ejaculate. Or where lightning strikes every one of your forty billion siblings. Our world spun into mindless flux, expecting the cloudburst, the blinding, the blast, but nothing like what transpired."

Singularity is a one-time thing, like the Big Bang or the Second Coming or the Cubs winning the Series. So it was no wonder that he had some trouble finding his words to describe it. He was struggling like a man buried alive, clawing up to the light. Whereas I was freezing my ass off.

"I should have mentioned—"

"Get on with it, for chrissake!" He turned his gaze to me. For a moment I'd forgotten: he was an alien. "Sorry."

He continued at his own pace. "A chain reaction. A linkage of souls. Like an accumulated capacitor charge discharging a hurricane through us. Where we expected nuclear holocaust, we fused into communion. Oneness. Peace. A calm. A silence over the face of the deep."

I had never thought of this guy being into the Bible, but I guess we all duck under those thin black covers once in a while. "What? God?" I asked.

"Many theories. Perhaps God flashed through us for an instant, then back into nonexistence." He smiled. My mind was on my feet. "But your Bible does prophesy the advent of a Messiah. A singularity: a child from a virgin birth. It seemed that Messiah was born among us: it was ourselves. Ourselves, joined as one."

"Just basically *Shazam*?"

"The point of super-saturation, then a crystalline precipitate."

"I flunked chemistry. I was into art." The surf was louder. "Would you mind, my friend, getting back to the point?"

"Still lodged in our own souls, with all our warts and quirks, but united by— What to call it? Kindness? Simplicity? Love? But then terrible disruptions: millions of soldiers unemployed, industrial collapse, the terror in newborn eyes. And yet we evolved. We built new structures born from consensus. No competition in our diversity, only a fluidity, an urge to hear, to be heard, to serve the good of the whole. Imagine waking up to a world made whole. Imagine such a world."

The man had a poetic streak when shaken out of his comfort zone. The ocean wind cut through me, and the pickle smell of kelp.

"Age of Aquarius, like?"

"Yes, we had our mockers, comedians, but they were valued as ballast when we floated too high to the clouds. They began as dissenters but became the siblings who love to tease, and we valued their teasing."

Indeed, the impact of his so-called singularity seemed messianic, titanic, inexplicable. As he told it, all the irredeemable souls—so corrupt or diseased or rotted away with rage—they simply disappeared. They didn't go into hiding or form armies of the night: they just became *not*. As if, in separating the sheep from the goats, the goats had never been born.

"And you were there? This was like in the Sixties? This Woodstock moment?"

"No, no!" An apologetic grin flickered in his face like a lonesome firefly. "No, of course— No, many generations, it would have been millennia, seven millennia, at least— No, this we were taught, though we felt it to the core. But if—"

He grimaced. A pain in his heart. A shark attack from within. He was floundering between received wisdom from the first dawn of a toddler's mind and the insistent throb of an inconvenient truth. I considered asking to go back to the cabin and fetch something warmer to wear, but you don't interrupt an extraterrestrial in the midst of his delusional avalanche.

"And we lost history."

He said it before he knew what he meant. Their singularity, freeing them from the bloody baggage of the past, had blotted the past. They had vast libraries, layers upon layers, but fact and fantasy, truth and lies were shelved side by side, intermixed. Reality was a consensual shadow show.

No surprise. The warehouse of history was filled with toxic fumes, clogged with carcinogens from war chronicles to literary masterworks to nursery rhymes. They required a new past. Fact and fancy were interchangeable, and so by degrees a consensus emerged. The Flood, the Tower of Babel, the Fall of Troy, the Twin Towers were intermixed in chronology that included the sagas of interstellar exploration from that precious factual epic, *Star Trek*.

"And so you are telling me…"

I had no need to tell him the facts I'd gleaned from the Philpott files. But I did. He stood like a pillar of salt, looking backward at himself. I laid it out as fast as I could between chattering teeth.

The facts were these: Pruneface was *homo sap*. He was evolved, but not over millennia in a distant galaxy. The genetic tweaks, the blips in the DNA, were minuscule, suggesting that the specimen was evolved not more than a hundred years beyond us—hardly time to explore the reaches of the Universe and come home for Thanksgiving. Their technology, whatever it was, had waltzed them through Time and back to the same old planet Earth, a mere century before they'd left.

"So you are saying…" and he told me what I was telling him.

"Why it never occurred to me," I said, "carting around this souvenir pinkie for years, I guess— Since I got involved in this business, you and your lady and my own multiple realities, I've had these occurrences." I was having a hard stool with this, hearing myself sound as goofy as him. "Time. It's flopping around like my grandma's headless chicken— I keep thinking about chickens— It's like somebody wiggled the sky. It must be something from your Time juggles—"

"Impossible to—"

"I'm just—"

"Hardly—"

"But if—"

We were starting to talk in beeps and wheedles, phonetic hiccups, and yet we slowed to an understanding. Consensus, he might call it. We both stood there, chilled and stupid. Then he seemed to get his feet under him.

"The Biblical concept of Apocalypse: an uncovering, a disclosing, a revelation. Creating both utopia and monstrous delusion." I was hearing this man, at the sight of one shriveled finger, disclaim his life-long notions of reality: the culture that had nurtured him, its history, its myths, its aspirations. Those moments when truth hits like a bus from the direction you didn't look. The lightning bolt that unhorsed St. Paul on the road to Damascus. The skid on freeway ice at eighty mph, or it's 8:15 a.m. Hiroshima time, and you're late for work, then it's 8:16 and your life will never be the same.

He stumbled on through the tangle. Their great comradely *Shazam!* had meant liberation from the blood, the fire, the rapine—history's defecations. The scales fell from the eyes and a dawn shattered the darkness. "All delusion," said Moshe. "We knew it, but we didn't. We knew the truth the way we assume our feet are there, without looking downward. No looking, for fear we might walk into a tree. No one could have fooled us, we were much too smart for that, but fooling ourselves? Consensual unreality."

∼

For a time, delusion can serve you well. I knew a guy who'd been a serious drunk for years. One bright sunny afternoon, walking down the street in Charlotte, North Carolina, he met Jesus. Jesus grabbed him by the elbow, looked him in the eye, told him, "Shape up, jerk!" He did: became a moderately functional human being. Far be it from me to question his epiphany. So these people had bought into a mythos that, aside from its falsity, had served them well. Who would have risked disrupting consensus?

∼

The moon had gone under, and Moshe stared out at an ocean he couldn't see. How they lost all concept of chronology, how they mistook time travel for movement through linear space, and how this one man saw through it all in one blithering flash—I was clueless, as was he. Shit happens. Always has.

The time-travel thing was outside my realm of expertise. I didn't even wear a wristwatch. I should have read more science fiction—all sorts of schemes for flitting back and forth. However it worked, the vehicle that brought the cocooned aliens to us was in fact, by some high-tech whoop-de-doo, bringing them down just inches away from their starting point. To their own planet, back in Time. Returned to an Earth they had never left, back a hundred years to the planet trashed by their great-great-grannies-and-gramps. By us.

"I knew it," he said, "but I didn't know it. It had come clear to me in my first days among you. But not until you held up this shriveled thing, spoke the few words, could I risk seeing it. Yes: we ourselves raped our mother, paved her over, killed all life except ours. We blinded ourselves like rooting hogs. We killed Gaia and returned to destroy you for killing her."

Compelling thoughts, but our philosophic tempo was hardly appropriate when urgent issues were screaming at us. I shivered in the ocean's bite. "It's pretty chilly out here."

"I will speak again. They will hear me now."

I wasn't sure what he intended to do, but I made no objection. Probably look up at the stars and commune with the celestials standing a hundred years and fifteen inches from him. I speak to the elders, he'd say, or some such New Age babble with a big blurt of wind and temple gongs. The chill went deep in my bones, and I went back to the cabin, envisioning the omelet I hoped would be waiting indoors.

It was a beautiful omelet: three or four eggs, bits of bacon, cheese, some hot sauce on the side. I sat down to it, forked a mighty forkful and tasted the juiciness that Judith put before me. Oh dammit, I started to cry.

## —22—
## *Negotiations*

Saving the human race wasn't as exciting as it might sound. I knew I should get up from the table and move into action, even if I had no idea what to do beyond what I'd done. For a time, I was focused on my omelet. It really hit the spot. But I couldn't entirely take my mind off the prospect of multinational death. A pity, given the human capacity to produce such succulent grub.

My premise was always that our actions were based on the survival urge, inherited from the primal worm. We bulge our war budget, it wrecks us, but it's in the name of defense—not so much against the enemy as against humiliation, impotence, losing the spelling bee. We kill, kill, kill, and even carpal tunnel syndrome from landing the hammer blows won't stop us. We'll even commit suicide to save ourselves from metaphoric death. Though I sometimes wondered: what if we pursue suicidal strategies because we're suicidal? That we'd really dig annihilation? No more headlines! Nevermore!

For me, though, survival wasn't metaphoric. It meant simply what it would take to keep my ass in place. How many bucks, how many billy clubs, how many screaming eagles would it take to preserve my ass? Maybe a simple plot twist would do it. The plot is what makes the story end before all the characters shuffle off to Buffalo.

∼

As I finished my omelet, Judith was sitting on the sofa, staring into past or future. Josh was hunched over his algebra, trying to finish his homework before death caught him up without knowing it. Moshe was communing with the stars. Turk, by now, would be dead drunk.

I had one more device to switch on, so I switched it on. It was a tiny earplug, a hearing aid disguised as a hearing aid, with a gizmo that let me tune in voices at specific distances. By digging into my earwax I could hear Moshe on the beach. I picked up a heated debate: Moshe's low insistent voice and Benny's post-nasal jabber. I had never heard either of them exhibit much emotion, but Benny was heated to the point where his English was almost comprehensible.

"No, I will not. You are asking betrayal as if I throw a bomb. We open—"

"We open the door to truth—"

"Which is doubt, dissension, demons. Which we have in millennia overcome. You invite undoing."

A still small birdie told Moshe, *Control, tweet twitter, control*! "Are we so fragile that we cannot face the truth?"

Apparently he had told his cohort that their core myth—their Star Trek fantasy, their evolution over aeons—was fantasy. Not an easy truth to accept. Truth rarely comes pounding in with banners and fists. More often it's a squirmy little rodent skittering through the house, making Granny spill soup in her lap. It's the teeny fungus that brings down mighty oaks. It's an old lecher who can't keep his arthritic feelers to himself. Its behavior is very rarely appropriate.

"Please hear me, Benny. There are implications—"

"Implications. You bet, Sherlock. You are too long being there. Their gun fights, food fights, prize fights—"

I gobbled the last bite of omelet, got up, went to the window. I could see the dark time-traveler on the beach, stark against the moon. The surf was low. There was a blackness in his voice. There are things you have to say that you're never ready to say. Telling your wife the diagnosis. Telling your boss what you think of him. Telling Mommy you didn't mean to break it. Never the right words, and once you've said it you have to answer what comes. But sometimes, if you have to, you go ahead and say it.

The quiet burr of my listening device made him sound like a drunken gull, but I caught enough to get the gist. He reiterated his early suspicions, the years he'd spent with the natives absorbing the smell of the way things were. He spoke of his denials, to himself, of the evidence before him. He spoke his grief.

"We were taught lies. Out of the goodness of our hearts, we teach our children lies. We fervently believe our lies."

Project Chemo must be halted, he said. They were stepping into the old time-travel paradox: a breach in the past sending the future into a tailspin. "Killing your grandfather before you were born," he asked, "what follows?"

"What follows?" Benny asked. He liked a good riddle.

"We cycle into absurdity. Our grandfather is dead, and therefore we cannot be born. Yet if we are unborn, we cannot kill. So he engenders us, and we kill him again, but again we do not exist, and so he lives to engender us to kill him again. Is there an exit ramp from this paradox? Does Time fall into perpetual fibrillation? Or Gaia sprout its fruition, go sterile, sprout, die, unendingly? Are we set to unleash the whirlwind just to see what happens?"

Benny was silent. I tried to imagine his appearance, but the image never formed. Short and pear-shaped, maybe, but was he pacing around waving his stubby arms or sitting lotus-wise on a bed of moss, communing with his navel? Not a clue. The only certainty was that right now he was a very unhappy guy.

As was Moshe. He had no desire to throw a monkey wrench into the works. The great achievement of these people—first time I'd considered them people—was their comradeship and compassion. They acknowledged their misdeeds, sought to heal the damage they'd done, and now they were whammed by the eighteen-wheeler onrush of their ignorance.

Over the heavy breath of the surf, Benny emitted a torrent of beeps and squeaks. "English, please." As if Moshe felt Earth's reality under his feet and demanded the language of Earth.

Benny was grim. "But my buddy, my chum, from where does our language come? We beep, we boink, we crackle. No diphthongs or fricatives, no flapping of tongues in the breeze. Where comes our so different speech, if not from aeons?"

"Video games." Moshe granted that it was merely his hypothesis. "Our structure is Indo-European. But in the spasms that seize us, our phonemes are derived from video games."

It was strange to hear two characters quarrel when neither had experience in it. Benny tried to hold his own with his fractured syntax, but he had never faced vehemence, whereas Moshe had years of breathing the toxic fumes of our politics, our media, our playground taunts, our road rage and binges of slaughter. It was no equal match.

Benny, impaled on the fishhook, still gave a few weak wiggles. "Not credible. Not believable." Moshe said nothing. "Other possibilities. Countless. Many." Benny's voice broke. "You throw it away? You trash it? You blow us off for it?"

"They would say *Blow us off*. Or *Blow it off*."

"Okay."

It was nothing I heard. It was something whispered in their hearts' ventricles. A gasp, a grief. For each of them a friend was receding, fading, losing hold. I thought of Kenny, when I was eight. Kenny Burd. He lived down the block in a rattier shack than ours. Scrawny, weaker than me when we wrestled. Other kids called him Burd-turd. We played late into dusk, cowboys and Indians, and I'd get shot off my horse and he'd come to fix me, *fix fix*, and we'd ride off to kill Indians. But the last day I saw him—my mom remarried and we were moving to South Dakota—I went down to Kenny's house to say goodbye. His cousins were there, and when I came into the yard Kenny shoved me, "What's the matter?" I said, and he shoved me hard, showing off for his cousins maybe. "Burd-turd!" I yelled and ran back home and never saw him again. We'd never kill Indians together.

Benny's voice came out in dribs and drabs. His good buddy had been too long in the company of strange cousins, he said. Suddenly they were separate. You could hear love in his strangled articulation, and amazement that his comrade would throw it all over—their achievements, their brotherhood, the flood of warmth that came in their presence. He seemed on the verge of shouting "Burd-turd!"

I could hear surf, wing flutters and whispers, the whispers fading, faint beep clusters, electronic buzz. Two punch-drunk fighters, staggering, in tears.

"Okay. Fine. So I will tell it as you tell it, yes?"

"I must speak to the Elders."

"You must will settle for me." His English was failing.

"The message is urgent."

"I will tell it urgent."

"Benny—"

"Nosireebob!" A pause. "Do they still say *nosireebob*?" No response. He added, "We will see if the cookie crumbles."

Dead silence. Nothing more to be said. The surf was catching its breath. One cry from a late-carousing gull, or it may have been Benny sobbing.

"Benny…"

"So what?"

"We were kids together."

"Okay."

"We were five. You said your sister was dumb."

"She was."

"It was bad to say it, though. I loved your sister. I even gave her a name so I could think of her name. *Springtime*. We had no experience of springtime, but I'd heard it in a song. I punched you in the head."

"Bad."

"Unforgivable. They punished us. We had to sit for an hour, face to face, looking at each other. Cruel and unusual, but effective. We started to giggle."

"It was funny."

"We thought we'd outfoxed our elders. But I suspect they giggled at our giggling." A soft chuckle from Moshe. "The point had been made."

"Buddy…"

It was the first time I'd felt these men as men with stories. Up till then they were knights or pawns in a game I was kibitzing. I had viewed them the way they wanted to view themselves: souls blended into a smoothie, enlightenment skimming every lump and wrinkle, boiled as bland as my mother's Brussels sprouts. But their kinship wasn't bland; all the spurts and sputters of the reptile brain were still in operation.

I heard Benny mumble something about doing what he could, whatever, and Moshe murmuring, "Friend." Then they clicked off, and the ocean sustained the murmur.

Judith got up from the sofa, fetched my plate, took it to the sink. I stifled an impulse to tell her there was no point to wash the plate as we all might soon be dead. She set it on the counter.

"So what's up?" she asked. "Do I get a clue? Or do I just stand here making omelets?"

I nodded but didn't elucidate. A crisis demanded action, and I was just sitting around, but that's all there was to do. I owed it to her to tell all, to elucidate the prospects of disaster, but I still had that old male instinct of protecting the lady from the truth. Victor's hat gave me no clues, having been burnt to a crisp.

"You guys, you're like my voices: all the best intentions to protect me from growing up."

"Okay. Truth is, we might all die. Thanks for the omelet." I could have said it less bluntly. She made no reply, just stared at me, past me. *How?* The question mark hung in the air.

Moshe came in, said something about things being under control or under way or under water, I couldn't quite make it out. Judith offered to make a floor bed for Josh so I could sleep on the couch, but I said I'd sack out in my camper van. Better let this family have its own four walls.

In the course of my checkered career, I had spent overnights in a bathtub, a barrel, upright in a closet, under a busy bed in a Mexican brothel, in the bridal suite of a luxury hotel, on the concrete floor of a cell, so my vehicle offered relative comfort. I would reclaim Turk tomorrow if I woke up alive. Stretching out in the back of my van, I had just drifted off to half-sleep when my phone burbled. A coded text from Van Mullen:

*OH DEM WATERMELONS!*

Very bad news.

## —23—
## *Goodbyes*

One night long ago, drunk as skunks, Jared and I made a pact. On an empty fifth of cheap Scotch, we pledged eternal loyalty.

"I'll have your back, buddy—"

"Right totally—"

"I mean I swear—"

"Hold on, I gotta piss…"

We swore we would always look out for one another, keep each other covered, and if either should be threatened with torture to spill the beans, we'd send the code and both gulp down suicide pills. (You might not comprehend this vow if you'd never been in the room with a bellowing, screeching, twitching naked hunk of gristle that used to be human.) At that moment we were brothers. We were deeper than brothers. We were drunk.

Now the prearranged code had come through: a hip phrase from a Sixties film we'd both seen in college. We'd drunkenly debated the merits of that phrase as opposed to *Tough shit, Sherlock*, but opted for the watermelons as more personal, more existential, more French.

I was deeply moved. Jared Van Mullen was the guy they made jokes about, a pasty-faced milquetoast who devised euphemistic legalisms for all the shit we pulled. We were true buddies, though I couldn't resist chuckling at a colleague's joke directed at Jared. "Even more pathetic than a fairy," Lennie had cracked, "is a fairy who can't get laid." I would have wept for Jared if I hadn't already wept over my omelet.

A second text followed the first. GOODBYE, FRIEND: R.I.P. So I believed it. Jared was gone.

My hands and feet were leaden, though my pulse went into overdrive. Could the Shop be onto me? Were they sending Navy Seals to pluck me out of Bolinas, or might they just erase Bolinas with a drone? Had I made a wrong move that betrayed me to their quark-sniffers? Indeed, my primitive stumbles were surely what saved me. Using my iPhone, iPod, iPad or microwave nuke led to my punching every icon that reared its hoary head. Their techies weren't capable of tracking such incompetence. If I were in imminent danger, I'd already be hanging from a meat hook. I decided to get some sleep.

Still, one thought rankled. Jared had given his life to save me. Should I not fulfill my vow? Within easy reach I had a tiny snuff-box of suicide pills—way more than a lifetime supply. But it made no rational sense, his giving his life only for me to take my own? Not to mention my obligation to the folks I was trying to protect. I came up with countless rationalizations to save my skin, and yet the face of Jared, my one true friend, stood before me in the night. Did I not have a sufficient sense of honor, trust, nobility of soul, to pop the mega-cyanide?

No. Sorry, Jared. Enough with the fucking honor crap. I wadded my jacket into a lump for a pillow, shoved it under my head, and slept.

Slept for a while, anyway. They had given me two blankets, and my van offered plenty of room to stretch, but somehow I crunched myself between the spare tire and my duffel. The crunch was painful, so I adjusted to a newer crunch and tried to get back to a promising dream, something involving Judith. I was trying to tell her I was sorry, though unsure what I ought to be sorry for. Too many possibilities.

I lay there past dawn, squirming, refolding my legs. The day dawned, splattered with question marks. The sun glared in. On the beach the gulls were bleating their bleats. I had an urge to flee. I would unkink myself, roar off on a back road out of this nightmare and leave the poor souls to fend for themselves. It's a free country, so it's only patriotic to exercise the freedom our boys died for by copping out, flying the coop, hitting the road. I wasn't above pulling a little stunt like that.

But where? Back to Gravenstein to face the gaze of Turk or back to the city where I'd confront my own doggy eyes? I climbed out of the van, straightened the clothes I'd slept in, pissed on the left front tire, and walked up to the cabin. Again, Victor's defunct leather hat was dribbling compassion into my brain. Plus, I was lonely.

They were sitting at the table in the kitchen nook. Judith had used all the eggs for my omelet, so she'd made oatmeal with raisins. I hated the stuff, which my mother had served every day of my growing up, but this morning it felt comforting to eat what your mother had served. I joined them. We were silent, as if waiting. For what? Moshe had a clue, and so did I.

"Oatmeal. Oh, ick," Sweetie moaned. Strange to hear the complaint squeaking out of the woman who served it.

"Sir? Mister, uh—" Josh began. "What are you—"

"Don't talk with your mouth full," Judith said. My mother's precise inflection: boyhood flashbacks. Five minutes to live?

"Sir, no offense, but could I ask a question?" I turned toward Josh. "Who are you? Why are you here?"

I took a moment to chew a vagrant raisin. "I'll tell you when I know," I said. It sounded sharper than I meant. Josh looked at his mom, then at Moshe, then focused on his oatmeal as if puzzling over a quadratic equation. I wondered at the silence of Judith's alters. Except for Sweetie's complaint, they were mute. They were as puzzled as I.

I had one ear tuned to Moshe's channel with Benny, awaiting word, the other to a frequency given me by Jared—a Somali hacker monitoring the UAP (Ultimate Actions Protocol) Room of the Pentagon. I had seen this room once: no windows, walls no color, fluorescent light with a flicker, gray carpeting with dark stains. A swivel chair stood at a countertop with two rows of shiny black plastic buttons. I knew something of it through scuttlebutt. Eight or ten buttons were for nuclear missiles targeted in various tour packages. Five or six were for nerve agents, viral epidemics, biotoxins—some targeted on ourselves. Two would trigger volcanic eruptions in Hawaii, Italy, or the entirety of Iceland, which had been getting uppity lately. And one magic button to launch our version of Operation Chemo. The room was off-limits to all but the most senior officials with the deepest security clearance. I managed to see it once because I knew the cleaning lady.

Via the media, we all knew that the President was the one with his finger on the button, but the President couldn't always keep his finger primed when his thumb was up his ass. So it was assigned to a team of generals tending the room in rotation on eight-hour shifts. No music, no TV, no porn: not a highly sought-after post. "Thirty-eight years, five wars, Medal of Honor," said one, "and I'm assigned to the typing pool."

On this shift was a two-star general, Randal Jockett. Known to subordinates, inevitably, as Randy Jock Itch, the general had spent many sleepless nights. His responsibility weighed heavily, and his memory was wifty. Tending the double row of buttons, he couldn't tell which eggs would hatch which chicks, which buttons did what. They were unlabeled, for fear that foreign agents might penetrate the set-up, so he needed to recollect what he'd been drilled on, but he was having difficulty each morning to remember even to anchor his toupee. A mistake on the buttons would surely be noticed by the media.

~

"Are there plans?" Moshe asked. He appeared to be asking me. A low grunt of discontent—it sounded like Marge. I shrugged.

"Did you sleep okay?" Judith asked. I shrugged again.

"So what's next?" Josh asked.

"I guess the next thing is the future," I mumbled.

"Funny, funny," said Josh.

The boy was too young to know that most activities in life were equally on hold, and in literature as well. There was a Russian novel about a guy who never got out of bed, and a play with a woman buried up to her neck in sand. The crew on that whaling ship: they had to sail for months while the writer jotted down all the facts about blubber. Right now, all we could do was to eat our oatmeal, savor the raisins, and wish it had walnuts in it.

"There's a future." Judith spoke with determination. "You gotta believe it. Even if it's horrible. Even if there's nothing left but roaches." She scraped the rest of the oatmeal into Josh's bowl without asking if he wanted it. She didn't talk much beyond how her mother sprinkled brown sugar on the oatmeal. "It tasted kinda brownish. Like sweet cat-fur." It seemed as if she had to name things or else there might be no future. Smells and sounds, tiny pops of sweetness in the oatmeal. "There's so much to live for," she said, not really sure if she meant it.

"What, like butterflies?" Josh smirked.

She gave him a light swat. "Or smart-ass kids." Then her lips went taut. "No, just not be afraid. Not be afraid of dying, or hey, not be afraid of living." I expected comment from her voices, but the voices were silent now.

Josh picked out a few raisins and popped them into his mouth with a flourish, as if making a statement. "Is this an issue that's on the table right now?" he asked. No one responded. He seemed to be grappling for something clever to say. "No, what I'm doing, I'm practicing drawing noses. Noses, they're so weird, sticking out there, but I mean, diversity, that stuff, we oughta yell, *Hey, hurray for noses!* Only my noses are pretty pathetic." He went on as if survival depended on his sustaining a furious tap-dance, then suddenly sat there, staring at his bowl. Josh was like me in one respect: when he was totally clueless, he got silly.

Judith did an I-can-make-more gesture, but we three guys shook our heads. A burble. Moshe checked his phone. "Excuse me." He rose and went into the bedroom. Josh stared at his empty bowl. Judith looked at her son. My left-ear hearing aid picked up Moshe's signal.

Benny's familiar voice. "So we lie over the barrel. Do they still say *over the barrel?*"

"Not often. The decision?"

"The decision is, you take the cake."

"Meaning?"

"No, better like say, hit the jackpot."

"Benny, what is happening." Silence. "What is happening, Benny?"

"We stop dead."

"You mean they suspend the plan?"

"Out to lunch." His tone carried the meaning. A long sigh from Moshe or from the sea. A whimper from Benny or the gulls.

Humanity was saved. One pebble spurred an avalanche. With us, an astounding revelation might get a day's headline, spawn a blue-ribbon panel that coughed up a report three years after we'd already started the war. But with the aliens—ourselves upgraded—the collective mind made one burp and the scales fell from a billion eyes. Benny stuttered on, explaining that other evidence corroborated the testimony of the finger. Apparently others had held the opinion that black was not white and that Time and Space had been inadvertently misfiled. "So tally-ho with the human race. Which are us, we see it. We don't take the risk to kill grandpa."

"Benny, thank you."

"I am sorry." A string of twiddles and grackles, then Benny squeezed out his bitters. "You are gone. The camel through the needle that made the squeeze. You are out of us." Benny went on spewing twitters and blats. Their people had no capacity to lie, yet they'd evolved a great blue whale of a lie, subverted by one sardine. One crack in the mirror shattered the face. Moshe was to be lauded for his courage and forever shunned for his dissent.

It took Benny five minutes of babble, amidst his quacks and trills, to find words for what he couldn't conceive. "So this is bye bye, buddy." There was grief in his chirpy voice. "Carry on. Kill Mama. Damn shame. I love the trees where I saw pictures of. Scenic are trees."

"Benny…"

∽

The next event was inevitable, and there was not a damned thing I could do. The Pentagon chugged forth with Greensleeves, their own Operation Chemo, having adjusted the DNA codes. I heard the telex. They still used telex for that military feel.

"General?" He had some sort of attendant with him.

"Captain Fenstermacher?" A captain, apparently.

"All set, General. Any time."

"Codes verified?"

"Yes sir."

"Redundancy?"

"Yes sir."

"Operators are standing by?" A shuffle. "That was a joke, Captain."

"Yes sir." No laugh.

The general was taking his time. His cerebral rigor mortis was evident. He made a stab at high spirits. "I suppose we're ready then. We'll have to break out the champagne on this one. Not as flashy as your H-bomb, but hey, *Ready, Eddie*. It gets the job done, right?"

"Yes sir." A moment. "As you know, sir, this is time-sensitive."

"It is. Yes indeed." His batteries were draining. "Just to verify, the button…"

"Third from the left on the top row, sir."

"Of course. Yes, I'm aware of that, Captain. I'm perfectly aware, but these things require redundant verification, as you know. Third from…" A moment.

"From the left, sir."

"You know, Captain, it's funny, I've never…" His voice was shaking, ready to break, like a kid leaning toward the lips of his first date. "Actually never been…"

"In combat, sir?"

"Not as such."

I wanted to scream out incomprehensible malediction: *Stop! No need! Hold on!* But my state-of-the-art communications were one-way. One-way was the standard mode for communications these days.

"Captain, many men have the privilege of fighting and dying for their country, but others face equal challenges. For myself, logistics. Many elements required to fight a war: not only munitions but items of first aid, grooming, nutrition, toilet paper. Even with amazing battlefield technologies, today's soldier still needs toilet paper. Though I suppose in Imperial Rome or the Huns, what did they use? Corn husks? Papyrus? You wonder, but—"

"General Jockett, sir, with all due respect, you need to press the button."

"Third from…"

"Third from the left, top row."

"I'm not feeling terribly well right now, Captain, you know…"

"I'm sorry, sir, but with your permission, sir, my orders are that if you decline the responsibility to which you have been assigned, my orders oblige me, which I would regret, sir, to shoot you, sir."

"Oh?"

"I have a son, sir. Eight years old. How would I explain it to my son? If he asked?"

"Interesting. I have a son myself, older of course, not in the military, actually in public relations, although he writes short stories on the side, really quite— However, yes, although I would certainly—"

"So then—"

"I quite understand—"

"And so I would be grateful, sir, if you could— Third from the left, top row—"

"You're sure they've adjusted the parameters? We wouldn't want to kill ourselves just by accident?"

"No problem with the DNA read-outs, sir. Very slight adjustments. They're double-checked."

"Because it's lots of numbers, and numbers are weird."

"No problem, sir. Just a click."

They must have taken time to go over the adjusted numbers, to check the corrected variables. Then I heard the click of the button.

∽

We were sitting at the table with our coffee when the button clicked. Moshe had poured a small dribble of cream, bent toward me and formed the words with his lips: "We're safe." I gave him a wide-eyed look as if to say *Oh that's nice*. He seemed to feel a twinge.

"Excuse me," said Moshe, rising, "I need to walk for a bit." He took his jacket from a hook and walked out, closing the door softly behind him. Did he already know?

Judith's alters came spewing out in a flood. "Can I have ice cream? Can I have a candy bar? Can I ride the horsey?" "Give it to me. Give me what it feels like!" "You're fat! You're fat and ugly and you don't know how to love!" "Be calm, Judith, take a breath—"

Her eyes rolled up in a seizure, shoulders frozen, body aquiver, head in a vise, a spasm at each new voice. Her teammates played their game while she sat on the bench.

"Mom! Mom, it's okay! Mom!" Josh took her by the shoulders, shook her.

"Let me feel it, let me have it, let me—"

"If I'm a good girl? If I smile?"

"You're a beautiful loving woman. People say, 'Glad to see you, Judith, see you smiling—'"

"You take and you take and you never give and it's Mommy this, Mommy that—"

"Mom, please—" Josh held her face to make her see him.

"See this guy and you start to cream—"

"Pretend you've been abused, but you're a liar, liar, liar—"

"Run the fingers down there and curl over the itch inside—"

"Please! Please, Mom!"

"Judith, you're here, you've overcome the wreckage, you do it every day, you get out of bed and make breakfast—"

"Bite. Suck. Lick. Pinch. Poke. Dirty me!"

Josh let go his grip and rushed away, flinging himself on the bed, sobbing. It was a kind of madness he'd never seen: four cats fighting for life inside her head, her heart, her belly.

"Don't you remember, Judy—" It was Raymond. "We met in high school. In the hall you'd say, 'Hi Ray,' and I was different from the guys who sniffed around Drucie and got into Drucie and then you'd go home and vomit, but I was there. And I took you once to the prom, we had a lovely time until Drucie ran off with Steve and fucked him the rest of the night—"

"I want Mommy!"

Abrupt silence. Dead calm. Her shoulders relaxed and her eyes came into focus, and in its deep slow baritone voice her fifth soul spoke: "End it. Knife. Hot water. Dead eyes. Slit. Silence."

I was at her back, grabbed her hair and jerked. "Shut up!"

That got her attention. She began to sob like a normal human being. Josh sprang up, came to her, embraced her from behind, his forehead to her shoulder. "Mom, I love you…"

I went to the window. Moshe was at the seashore. The tide was going out. I recalled him once saying to Judith, something like, "The first I saw of the ocean, I wept. One weeps for grief, but one weeps for beauty as well. Because beauty is beyond you, it's racing past—" He stood there waiting to die.

## —24—
## *Flight*

He fell face flat in the surf. The tide was going out, trailing dangles of kelp. I knew better than rush out to help him or roust the family into panic mode. I knew the effects. They just flopped over dead, and that was it, nothing to be done. The water lapped him gently.

At the top of the hour: Homeland Security announced coordinated raids on an international ecoterrorist network. Many suspects chose suicide to avoid arrest. Groups including Greenpeace and Sierra Club have denied involvement but remain under surveillance. More news at six.

I stood at the window. Strange sense of relief to know that all had come to naught. Judith and Josh sat frozen over their oatmeal.

The stock market rebounded today with Senate passage of the Earth First Energy Bill, providing support to the fossil fuel industries. The President called global warming "welcome relief from home heating bills" and condemned solar technology as threatening to use up the sun.

I watched the shoreline. The dark figure was fading in the surf, licked away. Back through the crack in Time from whence he came? That would have been merciful, at least as much mercy as the Universe ever offered, laying out its cards with quantum imprecision in its great lonesome game of solitaire. Some brain-wiggle came to me about the river of Time. In Time, the water wears rocks away; in rocks, Time wears water away; rocks and water wear Time away. I had no glimmer of what it meant. First time I'd ever thought of Time as merciful. It felt comforting at the time.

The Vice-President described today's ominous UN global famine report as "one more reason to take down the UN's britches and paddle its little brown butt." UN officials declined comment.

∼

I don't recall what I intended to say to these two remaining souls, nor if I said it. I didn't know how to find the words. *Your boyfriend is dead, dissolved. The ocean licked him clean.* If we've been to college, we think we'll know what to say in the face of doom, but we spin our wheels. The great poets find magnificent words, but they get to do rewrites: at the moment they only manage to tell their kids, "It's okay, honey, Fido's asleep. He's happy."

I turned to the table to make the report.

∼

I had wanted to speak to that man, the one licked by the surf, but it only takes a moment's hesitation to miss the bus. My friend, I wanted to say, you had a good cause, but you blew it. Your boys canceled their plans, but my old spook buddies, they're the eighteen-wheeler that skids at you down the ice at eighty miles an hour, so you can't rely on having the right-of-way. Here, we keep elephants for pets, they have to shit, and we have to deal with it. And he would have nodded, without appreciating the humor, or made that slight sideways tilt of his head.

But I would have charged him and his fellows with never transcending the wretched tradition of anthropoid stupidity. They had bleached out a few stains in the human fabric and soothed one lady's nerves, but they might have done more. The keychain gizmo that sent those stubble-chinned thugs into bliss, that was pretty neat. Their New Agey wisdom might have eased us a few inches past our horrific dog-eat-dog. Dogs never tasted good, even to dogs.

I wish I'd said all that, but I never said it.

And he might have replied with some wise tweet that would go viral and mellow out the jackhammer blows of history: the wars, crusades, migrations, the madness of crowds, the suicide vests, the day's lobotomies, the unnerving rasp of crickets. He might have said something poetic about the curvatures of ears, or something like this: "In the brief span between your lives and ours, our science made great advances. We found no gods. The Universe had no need of a traffic cop: the law for driving beyond the speed of light was self-enforcing. We saw only a vast inventive dynamic, a counterforce to entropy, an imagining impulse, yes, an astonishing presence. But we still felt the need to take the role of a god. We would nurture life by healing our misdeeds. And by killing."

Sounded so familiar, even though he never said it.

"But $K^2=I$: knowledge squared equals ignorance. We came to your world—no, to ours, to this slice of Time—to save it. We inflicted pain, implanted fear and loathing, then plotted destruction, for the sake of the Mother, of what the Mother had borne. We believed what you yourselves believed: that none would hear the truth, that only death could cure. We might have done otherwise."

I was only daydreaming what might have got said. Daydreaming what you want to hear is standard practice. He didn't say any of that. There wasn't time.

∽

I don't recall what I said to them. I know that it took a while. Somehow the words elbowed their way into the waiting line and crept through the door. I expected an outburst from her hecklers, but she sat there dumb. Finally, she understood, more or less, that walls were made of water and mirrors were doorways and that the Mad Hatter was throwing this party. She stuttered out a question, as if asking the weather report, something about the physics of it all.

"Damned if I know," I said.

"It makes no sense," said Josh. "It's insane."

"Very true," I replied.

Judith flew up, bolted out the door, down to the beach to look for any traces. It was low tide, and she stopped to check every piece of kelp, mollusk, driftwood or beer can that caught a glint of the dying sun. Finally she stopped, petrified. Josh walked out, came to her, held her. He seemed to be practicing how to hold people who needed comfort when there was nothing to be done. It never really comes naturally. It takes experience. I never learned it.

I went into the bedroom, stuffed stuff into a suitcase, took it out to the van. I would give them ten minutes to figure out which way was up, and then we had to get gone. A lot to do and a short time to do it. The blitzing of the Tourists might create a momentary pause in the Shop's depredations, but it was no guarantee of safety for those in Judith's category. They would still be on the books as collaborators—no reason to suspect them of anything, but no reason not to. Surviving was in itself a suspicious act. The Shop could never end an operation before destroying a sizable number of innocents, at which point there'd be a leak to the *Washington Post*, headlines for a week, and a Congressional inquiry leading to firing a couple of girls from the typing pool. We had just enough breathing space before the jaws clamped down—a couple of days, maybe a week, to engineer our survival.

As I watched those distant figures on the beach, I concluded that Judith and the boy would have to flee the country. I would put them on the bus to Vancouver with Canadian passports—I knew a guy who'd do it on a while-you-wait basis—and move them in several stages to Quebec. I could only hope that on the trip Judith's alters would behave themselves.

For myself, the evidence was inconclusive. They must have seen Jared in collusion with the wizened hippie at Tommy's Joynt, but my core identity, being an utter muddle to myself, might still be a muddle to them. I could lose myself in the city or go back to sweet little Gravenstein and spend out my days in Rosella's pneumatic embrace. Or something. Even if Judith asked me to, I couldn't tag along. And she wouldn't ask.

Josh was in the passenger seat. Judith was behind, perhaps having chosen the back seat so she wouldn't reach the future so soon. If I expected agreement with my plan, it would have to start with the boy. I knew he was no fan of mine: he likely viewed me as the rascal who turned his world into bubble wrap. Both of them were stunned to the point of catatonia, so I waited till one of them broke the silence.

"So what are we doing?" Josh said. Being fifteen he couldn't stay shut up for long.

"Well, so my thought is this," and I outlined the plan. "If that works for you."

"And where are we right now?"

"Heading to Vallejo for stuff you'll need, and we should pick up food for your trip. Bus goes from San Rafael. If that makes sense to you all. If it doesn't, well…"

No one ventured dissent. I punched on a classical station, nice music, but punched it off. It was all toot-toot-tweedle-ta-tum, a bit too simplistic for the world as I knew it.

"What do I—" Josh started to speak, then his bottom dropped out. A feeling I knew well: that chemical plunge into mud. "What do I do with my schoolbooks? I've got schoolbooks along."

"I'll deal with it."

Years from now the kid would wonder why he ever asked about something so trivial. Hopefully, though, he'd know by then that it was trivial concerns that kept you sane. Myself, I was worried for Turk. I'd left him plenty of food and water, but he had this quirky trait: he never liked to shit in the same place twice. After he'd used the newspaper in the kitchen and I wasn't there to walk him, he'd face a deep crisis of conscience.

The boy said nothing more. At that age you can never tell if they're on the brink of suicide or totally bored out of their minds. He didn't give me static, even though his life was turning upside down. A guy had just dropped dead. He was heading to Vancouver. Sherry Nybold had smiled at him. If I'd told him that the law of gravity had been rescinded and that we clung to Mother Earth only by virtue of God gluing us on with epoxy, he'd have said, "Awesome." But he would not have been awed.

Was this the future? Watching our lives play out like the third year of an HBO series, when the writers could toss in any wild plot complication—Presidential impeachment, mass slaughter at the Oscars, the birth pangs of a famous giraffe, the girl shot in the face—and we'd discuss it tomorrow with the distant distracted passion of a devoted but jaded fan. For the first time I felt a kinship with this kid. I didn't really want to feel it.

We did our stuff in Vallejo, and I handed them their documents. They were now Ruth Addison, age forty-one, and her son Zachary. Ruth Addison was the name of a girlfriend in college, and Zach was the name of her cat, to whom I was allergic. It might have worked with Ruth if I'd found the right antihistamine.

On the way to San Rafael, I wanted to tell Judith that I cared, that it had been so long since I'd cared, that I'd lost my allergy to cats and wanted to spend the rest of my days in caring, caring, caring. But the boy was in the passenger seat, so the feng shui didn't allow it.

But I tried to be helpful, wise. I said to him, "The future is mutable, Josh. Carry that in your hands like the last dying embers, even if it burns."

"Okay," he said, "the future is mutable. Got it." He didn't have the foggiest idea what I meant, nor did I. But words were the only flyswatter we had: you couldn't hit the fly by waving your arms and calling it a sonofabitch. Language could make me sound prophetic though I stood there as a solid monument to bullshit.

I left them at the station in San Rafael. Judith had not spoken for the past two hours, nor any of her flock. We stopped for groceries to take along, and I gave them a wad of cash and a couple of ways to get in touch if needed. "So try to keep yourselves together if you can," I said. "They don't like people on the bus if they're snotting up."

Josh had his hand on his mother's shoulder as if to guard her from me. Soon he'd have to be Zach, but it would take a while. I wondered why they'd trust me at all, but they had no choice.

"Can you give me some sweet last words? Okay? Please?" I needed to hear her voice. She was silent. Having whiskers all over my face, I couldn't manage a benign countenance, but I tried to soften my eyes. "You okay, lady?" She was starting to frighten me. "You're gonna scare your boy."

"They're gone."

"What?"

"My people."

"Your alters? What are they telling you."

"Nothing." She shivered. "Nothing. They're gone."

"Gone?"

Raymond? Marge? Sweetie? Drucie could never be gone. The bus was loading, but it was still ten minutes before it was scheduled to leave. We stood there, and I waited for her to speak.

"They never said goodbye."

I had seen other subjects like this—men, women, folks who didn't know from minute to minute who they were. Their voices would drive them crazy, screw up their lives, drive away their family—but the real terror was normalcy: integration, it was called, the goal of treatment, And suddenly she was alone, standing there naked and cold. She began to shiver, and Josh held her. Already he was practicing to be Zach.

She straightened, hugged me a quick little hug, turned away. The boy grabbed me and held on hard. I was astonished. Then he broke the hug and walked away. They got on the bus without looking back.

∼

I had sent my pilgrims up the 101 to Eureka, where they'd make a change to go north—a less sensible route than up the I-5, therefore less predictable. Driving to San Francisco, after a long contemplative lunch at a noodle place, traffic into the city was slow, then slower. An accident: we had to creep past and pay our respects. I tuned into my fugitives through a bug I'd planted three hours ago in Judith's lipstick case.

No excuse for eavesdropping except the gut urge to hang on as long as I could. Not a word for maybe half an hour, then Josh's voice. "I've never been on a long-distance bus."

"You were. You were born in Denver when your dad was working in Midland, Texas, I got on the bus right outta the hospital. Long trip. You wouldn't remember, being like two weeks old."

"I guess I couldn't see out the window."

"Changing diapers on a bus, I didn't make a whole lotta friends."

"Sorry bout that. Just couldn't hold it." Good: he was making jokes, or trying to.

"Actually, you gave me some reason to live." She was starting to cry: that break in the voice, like trying to swallow an egg.

"Mom, hey, please. You know our old guy said you shouldn't start to cry on the bus. Or snotting up, as he called it. So maybe, okay?" Then a vehement whisper: "I feel like I'm five years old! I can't even—" Meaning, I guess, that he needed to be a superhero but wasn't.

About that time, traffic started to move. Two cars to the side, a tow truck, a half dozen cop cars, and a dark smear on the pavement. But that was another story, as improbable as this.

"I don't know if you can understand…" Judith began.

"Try me," Josh replied.

"Never mind." I heard her fiddling with something, then abruptly, "I can't see him."

"Who?"

"This guy that I love, and he's gone. He's a dream, he's—"

"Are those redwoods."

"I think."

"Hey, all this time and you never took me to see the redwoods?" He fumbled for the makings of a joke. No one wants to see their mother naked.

She held her words close to her for a time, then let them roam free, like a cat exploring a new room. "I can't see him. In my mind. He's not there. I can sort of remember he was there, and now he's not. Once he said he really liked my hair, but I can't hear him say it. It's like something I read. Like when I was little, I dreamt I was walking under the water, under … magical … but I can't remember the dream, I only remember the remembering it. And Marge, Ray, Drucie— Like playmates that moved out of the neighborhood." More shuffle, maybe the sandwiches I'd packed.

Josh's voice, a frail little boy: "Mom?"

"You want a sandwich?"

"Sure."

More shuffling: "But this silence in my head— Like some old dog that got left in the car, that's all done with barking— We've got liverwurst."

"I hate liverwurst."

"Well, Victor gave us liverwurst."

"Gimme one." Shuffle, shuffle. "What's Vancouver like?"

"I dunno. Lotta rain, I think. I knew somebody, what's her name, Janis, she liked it."

"Look at those trees."

I listened to them seeing the trees. Good thing I sent them up the 101. They needed trees.

"Yeh… So… Well…" Judith tried to chug up to talking, like an old starter trying to catch when it's cold and wet. Finally she spoke. "My people just went out the door. But my other one, the one that never said his name, he was still there. He stuck. He wouldn't talk out loud, it wasn't like me saying the stuff, but I knew he was there and I heard what he said. *You've lost it all*, he said. *You lost Ronnie, you lost Ralph, you lost Moshe, they vanished without a trace.* And I knew what was coming then. *This is my final offer*, he was saying. Saying, like, *Take my hand.*"

Noise from the bus. Munch of liverwurst. Sniffles, and she went on. "And right at that moment you said— What's your name now? Zach? That's so weird, that's— No, it's not bad, it's— Right at that moment, that's when you said something to the old guy, old Victor, the old— Something about the future, or he said, or I heard the sound of your voice, and Mister Death was gone." She took a bite. "Sweetie would have said, *He's scary.* I miss her."

"Those trees are incredible."

## —25—
## *The Deeper Meaning*

As Operation Greensleeves, whatever, wiped out the aliens, it wiped out all their traces. A couple of hundred dead, I ascertained from various sources, but more than that: it wiped out their past existence: the traumas, the memories, the entirety of ERP's Tourist files, old news of flying saucer sightings, old *National Enquirer* archives, all the nutty Web chat regarding the Roswell incident. I had perfect recall. There may have been some quanto-relativistic principle in play, or it may have been a perk of membership in the Pruneface Club.

Judith could barely summon the memory of Moshe, except in fragments, like the old TV midnight movie with breaks for ads and the weather. At times, she remembered remembering, and then the tears would come. Her alters—the effects of her alien encounters—had vanished like the gold of leprechauns.

In a sense it was comforting to know that no creatures were left to heal us or to kill us. Whatever they might have taught us, in their goodhearted bumbling way, we would have to learn on our own. I wondered: had we wiped out only their emissaries or had we erased the future? Did our death ray stop at the hands of the clock on the wall, or did it penetrate the next minute, next century, seeking out the target genes in every corner of Time? They brought us pain and possibility. Had we scrubbed both?

When was it I had the thought? Maybe next day on the can at a McDonald's around San Rafael. I was driving back and had the urge. McDonald's is always easy to spot and has clean restrooms. I did my job and then it hit me.

What loomed ahead for Planet Earth? No way to know. At least I sensed no more squirmings in the fabric of Time. The calendar and the seasons remained in conventional alignment, and disgruntled Effect flowed from ambivalent Cause like clockwork.

∽

The last I heard of the migrants was an email from Josh, signed Zach, a few years later. He was finishing high school, going into pre-med. That felt right: he had that sardonic smart-ass quality I associated with doctors, and he'd make a decent living. I'd advise him not to go into psychiatry. Maybe a podiatrist: stay as far away from the head as he can.

Judith had a job grooming dogs, and she'd met a guy. Wendall works for the phone company, and he's from Indianapolis, which is more Past than Future. It's probably better for her that he's not very interesting.

And she doesn't hear the voices any more. Sometimes I've heard her crying when she's alone, but then sometimes I hear me crying, so I guess it's no big deal. *But hey, we never got a chance to say thanks. Kind of stunned at the time.* Josh wrote—Zach wrote. *So thanks. I'll keep you posted.*

Meaning he'd try but he wouldn't. Still, I appreciated the thought.

∽

Writing this now in a noisy Mission District bar. Two TVs on different channels, a jukebox cranking out tinka-tonka, and a guy trying to order a drink in high school Spanish, with the Mexican bartender yelling back at him to speak English. It's late Friday, but nothing promises murder tonight. In a certain mood, you feel good to find a loud bar and crawl deep inside the noise. It's very quiet in there.

Earlier, over a mocha at Cafe Trieste, where they do them really well, I considered my long-range security. I had spent forty-one years thinking the way they thought, and my review of options didn't bode well. I'd pissed on too many fireplugs to assume that my pisser was secure. I wanted to stay alive: it had become a habit. Time to make a change, so I compromised. I'd have been safer moving to Phoenix, but my heart was in this little fragment of the planet. I decided to stay in San Francisco but to trade in my soul once again. I am now Stanley Dick.

Stanley Dick is two inches shorter than me, on account of his slouch. He has a neat little chin beard, which he dyes a grayish red, and a Prince Valiant hairdo, same color. To foil retinal scans, his lenses are embedded with nano-glitter that creates a nice firefly effect on foggy days. He wears—I wear—a tweed sport jacket with blue jeans and a sweatshirt that says *Why Not?*—a sentiment Victor would have shared, whatever it means. My hope was that Stanley Dick might remember Victor as someone he'd like to be.

True, I'd rather be Victor. He had grown on me or seeped into my scalp. I had burst the cocoon of Eddie Funston and had my brief flight on the wings of Victor Otis, and it caught me upside the head how much I missed that. I had wept real tears over an omelet. I had fallen in love. I had funded nights of boozy bliss for a smelly dog and a rat-faced drunk—two creatures of Earth who, whatever their failings, did no one any harm. I had helped save the world, though for that I might be forgiven.

So I felt a need to acknowledge my host persona's push toward moving me a few inches past a lifelong zombiehood. An idea percolated: I'd take Muni to the seashore and cast Victor's drooping leather hat to the ebbing surf. My second wife Trish was into stuff like that and had such beautiful eyes, had I ever dared to look into them. But I couldn't find the hat. I recalled that I'd baked it in the oven but then found it with pristine droop. Its absence was final evidence that Time had recommenced its mulish plod.

∼

At times the loneliness gets to me. My room has developed a sixty-cycle hum—from the ceiling lamp or the roaches, I can't tell—but it reminds me of Miss Ketter's World History class in high school, so my deep reptilian brain feels young again. I think about my days in Gravenstein, where I'd sit in the square with Turk, and these scroungy young guys would come up and ask if I was dealing meth. When I said no they were nice about it, and they'd get around to asking about my wild hippie past. I'd make up stories I'd gleaned from the *East Village Other* a thousand years ago, and I'd enjoy telling these lies as much as the guys would enjoy hearing them. About every month I still have flashes of the old times with Rosella, and I miss them, but that's life—or the scraggle-tail decline of it. Once I tromped drunk down the hall to talk with Roscoe, knocked, and it took me a couple minutes to realize that the ratty little guy I was talking to wasn't Roscoe. Apparently there's a ratty little guy at the end of every hallway. My former disguise worked its way inward, and at times I still feel I'm that amiable codger in the leather hat who lets his nose hairs grow.

Turk: the one loss that hurts. I can't say I ever liked him. He was just a part of the deal, like Judith's voices: she cursed their presence, but the absence hit hard. I had just come back from sending off mom and kid to their future whateverness, expecting that Turk had found some new way of revenging himself on my absence, but he wasn't there. Inside the door lay the collar with tiny bells, plastic flowers, and a purple knit sleeve for his torso to intensify his canine stink. No sign of the huffing bratwurst himself.

I sat down to figure it out. Had some famished derelict stolen him and, behind a dumpster, was turning him on a spit? Or an abduction to a black site in Chad? Perhaps he was smarter than he looked and had finally heard the call of the wild and made his break? Or what if—most bizarre—he had followed Moshe? Suppose some vagrant humanoid gene lurked in his DNA, from aliens or from us, a gene that picked up the transmission of death, and he discorporated, slipping off to reassemble where Moshe would feed him, love him, and persuade him gently to bathe? He was getting too fat to live, but I grieved to see him go. I hung up his collar and body sock on a hook by the stove.

I missed Rosella. In my head, yes, I made fun of her, pudgy nympho, all that, but among all the souls who weren't who they were, I had no doubts of Rosella. She was purely, simply Rosella. I'd experienced a falling-off in the potency gig, but there are at least a dozen different ways that lovers can make love, and we ran through nine or ten. After, I gazed into her eyes and saw millennia there. She was who we all were, if we could see it.

The original Victor I still hear from at Christmas. He sends me an unsigned birthday card from some place off the map in Idaho. The card has nothing more on it than a paw print. He must have another dog, or maybe it's Turk.

At sunset you do expect the light to fade. Nowadays I have to take a midday nap, and my eye for passing female buttocks is blurry. At a certain point the old rooster starts to think *So many hens, so little time.* You feel a gray juice seeping into your veins. You feel like an old greasy dishtowel. You feel you're gradually, in various locations, getting dead. At my age, you either start to lose folks to dying or they lose you, and no one can quite decide which is better.

Today it's chilly but sunny. I took the bus down Haight to Stanyan, walked in the park to the lake and watched the coots for a while. Then I had the crazy urge, again, to walk the length of the park to the windmill and the grazing bison. Now, I roam the park's abundance—its curvatures, plantings, eddies and flows—almost forgetting that we're well on our way to the caustic asphalt world we'll leave to Moshe, Benny, our heirs, if we do. We're well under way with the die-off, spewing out the carbons, the GMOs, the insecticide. Great patches of Earth sprawl their baldness, a necrotic whore awaiting the CEOs to grunt their grunts and excrete their dry seed. We'll plow the forests for the sake of a stylish polyester double knit on sale at Walmart, and we'll methodically update all our definitions of evil.

But I shouldn't say evil. Consider a cancer, if you've got one handy: some vagrant cell in your lung or your brain or your butt forgets its ABCs or falls for a scheme to get rich quick. No nasty intent, just doing its job, following its biological imperative to grow. At some point, of course, it kills you. If it attained a princely status it'd qualify for a golden parachute, but being only a foul little lump of meat, it dies in the process of killing. Let's just call it stupid.

I walk through a magical park, sculpted atop sand, a thousand acres of dunes made to raise green fingers in blossom. Is our species truly lethal? Will anything last but the snapshots? Will the sea, after licking away its space invader, start to lick itself clean of us? Or, given that this park sprang from human hands, might we ask those cherubim with the flaming swords to let us sneak back into the Garden if we promise not to litter? The wind comes up, and I see fog blowing in from the coast. This is the beauty part of the day, and all the rest is waiting.

www.ingramcontent.com/pod-product-compliance
Lightning Source LLC
LaVergne TN
LVHW021235080526
838199LV00088B/4533